Smoke and Mirrors

Also by Elly Griffiths

The Stephens and Mephisto series

The Zig Zag Girl

The Ruth Galloway series

The Crossing Places

The Janus Stone

The House at Seas End

A Room Full of Bones

Dying Fall

The Outcast Dead

The Ghost Fields

The Woman in Blue

ELLY
Griffiths

Smoke and Mirrors

Quercus

First published in Great Britain in 2015 by Quercus
This paperback edition published in 2016 by

Quercus Publishing Ltd
Carmelite House
50 Victoria Embankment
London EC4Y 0DZ

An Hachette UK company

A CIP catalogue record for this book is available from the British Library

PB ISBN 978 1 78429 028 3
EBOOK ISBN 978 1 78429 055 9

14

Typeset by Jouve (UK), Milton Keynes

Printed and bound in Great Britain by Clays Ltd, Elcograf S.p.A.

For Carol

Aladdin

A BERT BILLINGTON PRODUCTION

CAST IN ORDER OF APPEARANCE

THE EMPEROR OF PEKING	THE GREAT DIABLO
PRINCESS JASMINE	HILDA THOMPSON
ALADDIN	ANNETTE ANTHONY
CHIEF OF THE PEKING POLICE	RON HUNTER-WHITE
WIDOW TWANKEE	DENTON MCGREW
WISHY WASHY	KENNETH NEIL
ABANAZAR	MAX MEPHISTO
GENIE OF THE LAMP	PEREGRINE PELLOW
GENIE OF THE RING	RITA SANTORINI

DANCERS: THE BOYS AND GIRLS OF PEKING

Choreography: Daniel Barnes
Directed by Roger Dunkley
Script by Nigel Castle, based on a traditional tale from

The Arabian Nights

PROLOGUE

Hastings, 1912

Stan entered stage left. Of course he did; he was the villain. Villains always enter from the left, the Good Fairy from the right. It's the first law of pantomime. But, in this case, Stan Parks (the Wicked Baron) came running onto the stage in answer to a scream from Alice Dean (Robin Hood). He came quickly because Alice was not normally given to screaming. Even when Stan had tried to kiss her behind the flat depicting Sherwood Forest she hadn't screamed; instead she had simply delivered an efficient uppercut that had left him winded for hours. So he responded to the sound, in his haste falling over two giant toadstools and a stuffed fox.

The stage was in semi-darkness, some of the scenery still covered in dustsheets. At first Stan could only make out shapes, bulky and somehow ominous, and then he saw Alice, kneeling centre stage, wearing a dressing gown over her green Principal Boy tights. She was still screaming, a sound that seemed to get louder and louder until it reached right up to the gods and the empty boxes. Opposite her something swung to and fro, casting a monstrous shadow on the painted forest. Stan stopped, suddenly afraid to go any further. Alice stopped screaming and Stan heard her say something that sounded like 'please' and 'no'. He stepped forward. The swinging object was a bower, a kind of basket chair, where the Babes in the Wood were meant to shelter before being covered with leaves by mechanical robins (a striking theatrical effect). The bower should have been empty because the Babes didn't rehearse in the afternoon. But, as Stan got closer, he saw that it was full of something heavy, something that tilted it over to one side. Stan touched the basket, suddenly afraid of its awful, sagging weight. And he saw Betsy Bunning, the fifteen-year-old girl who was playing the female Babe. She lay half in, half out of the swinging chair. Her throat had been cut and the blood had soaked through her white dress and was dripping heavily onto the boards.

It was odd. Later, Stan would go through two world wars, see sights guaranteed to turn any man's blood to ice, but nothing ever disturbed him quite so much as the child in the wicker bower, the blood on the stage and the screams of the Principal Boy.

CHAPTER 1

Brighton, 1951

It was snowing when Edgar Stephens woke up. The view from his window, the tottering Regency terraces leading down to the sea, was frosted and magical. But the sight gave him no pleasure at all. He hated snow. He still had nightmares about the Norway campaign, the endless march over the ice, his companions falling into the drifts to freeze where they lay, the moments when the bright white landscape seemed to rearrange itself into fantastical shapes and colours, the soft voices speaking from the frozen lakes: 'Lie down and I'll give you rest for ever.' They hadn't had the proper gear then either, reflected Edgar, pulling on a second pair of socks. The Norwegian troops had skis and fur jackets; the British had shivered in greatcoats and leaking boots. Well, he still didn't have a pair of snow boots. It wasn't something that you needed as a policeman in Brighton, generally speaking. But today was different.

Today was the second day of searching for two lost children. A search made a hundred times grimmer and more desperate by the soft white flakes falling outside.

Edgar squeezed his multi-socked feet into his thickest shoes. Then he put on a fisherman's jumper under his heaviest coat. As a final touch he added a Russian hat, given to him years ago by Diablo. He knew that he looked ridiculous (he must remember to take it off before he got to the station) but the hat made a surprising amount of difference. As he slipped and staggered down Albion Hill, holding on to parked cars and garden fences, his head at least remained warm. The Pavilion was a fairy-tale wonder of snowy domes and minarets. The Steine Gardens were smooth with snow but as Edgar tried to cross the road he slipped twice on hard-packed ice. As he limped down the alleyway by the YMCA building (once the home of Maria Fitzherbert, the secret wife of the Prince Regent, and said to be linked to the Pavilion by a secret tunnel), he wondered if they would be able to get any cars out at all. He'd have to get on to the army barracks in Dyke Road. Perhaps they would be able to lend him a jeep or two. They really needed to search on the downs and in the parks but the snow might make that impossible. The children had now been missing for forty hours.

When he reached Bartholomew Square, he was exhausted and his feet were soaking. In the lobby he met his sergeant, Bob Willis, apparently disguised as a deep-sea fisherman in waders and oilskins.

'Nice hat, sir.'

Damn, he'd forgotten to take off the Russian hat. Edgar snatched it from his head, its wet fur feeling unpleasantly like a living animal.

'Is anyone else in?' he asked.

'One or two,' said Bob, sitting down and starting to pull off his waders. 'The super's snowed in in Rottingdean.'

'Let's hope he's the only one. We need every man we can get.'

'Charming.' Turning round, Edgar saw Sergeant Emma Holmes, the latest recruit to CID and recipient of a lot of teasing about her name, her sex and just about everything else, really. Not that this seemed to bother her. She was unfailingly calm and professional. This, combined with her white-blonde hair and blue eyes, gave her an almost Nordic aspect although, as far as Edgar knew, she had been born and brought up in Brighton.

'Man as in person,' said Edgar, wondering if he was making things worse.

'Why not just say person then?' said Emma mildly, taking off her duffle coat.

Edgar was about to answer when Bob's waders came off with a hideous squelching sound.

'Let's get ready for the morning meeting,' he said.

At least he knew not to ask Emma to put the kettle on.

Edgar addressed the team promptly at nine. A few people had been delayed by the weather but most had struggled in, some of them walking long distances through the snow. Edgar knew that this was indicative of the strength of feeling about this case. As he summarised the investigation so far, he was aware that every eye was on him. These people cared, not just because they were police officers and it was their job to care. They cared because there were children involved and even the most unimaginative plod could put themselves in the position of parents waiting for news, watching the snow outside and knowing that it was covering up precious clues. Knowing, too, that their children were outside in the cold, alive or dead.

Mark Webster and Annie Francis had gone missing some time on Monday afternoon. Mark was twelve and Annie thirteen. They had come home from school and had spent some time playing with other local children in Freshfield Road, a long residential street that led all the way up to the racecourse. It was thought that Annie and Mark had then gone to the corner shop to buy sweets. The parents weren't worried at first; the children were old enough to look after themselves after all. It wasn't until night had fallen (early in these dark days of November) that Sandra Francis knocked on Edna Webster's door and suggested searching for the truants. 'I wanted to give Annie a good hiding for worrying us so much,' Mrs Francis admitted to Edgar. 'It wasn't until later that I . . .' Here she had broken down in tears, mopping them on the apron that was still tied around her waist.

The parents searched the surrounding streets and nearby Queen's Park. It was nearly nine o'clock when they made their way to the home of Larry McGuire, a neighbour who was also a policeman. Sergeant McGuire had telephoned the station, who had contacted Edgar. He had met them at Bartholomew Square, given the usual assurances ('Children go missing all the time . . . They'll probably come home when they're tired . . . Try not to worry too much') and organised a search party. They had scoured the streets until midnight and again at first light. All Tuesday they had knocked on doors, from the seafront to the racecourse, even dredged the duck pond in Queen's Park. Then, on Tuesday night, the snow had come.

The children's ages had led some people to speculate that they might have run away together. 'A kind of Romeo and Juliet thing,' Superintendent Frank Hodges had suggested. But Edgar wasn't buying that. He knew that Shakespeare's Juliet was only thirteen (and he had actually read the play, which he betted Hodges hadn't) but he didn't think it fitted the picture of the two children playing in the street. 'Annie isn't like that,' said Mrs Francis. 'She's a tomboy, if anything.' Edgar tried not to register the use of the present tense. Annie had to be alive. He had never dealt with a case involving a dead child and he didn't want to start now. Mark and Annie were friends, like brother and sister, everyone said; they had been friends from primary school. Edgar, who had been to an all-boys grammar school, thought how nice it would have been to have a friend who was a girl. It might have helped him understand women for a start.

No suspicious characters had been spotted in the area, he continued briskly. Anyone with a conviction involving minors had been checked and double-checked. It had been a winter afternoon, no one had paid much attention to the children playing in the twilight. 'Annie always made up the games for the little ones,' someone said. 'She had ever such a good imagination.' Her teachers had agreed. Annie Francis was clever, she was going somewhere. Mark Webster too, though quiet and shy for his age, was highly intelligent. Where were they now, those intelligent, innocent children?

'Bob, you and Emma go back to Freshfield Road and talk to the neighbours again. Someone must have seen something.'

Bob would usually have complained about being sent door-to-door but today nobody was complaining, even if it meant tramping a mile in the snow.

'And talk to the children again,' said Edgar. 'The ones that were playing with Mark and Annie on Monday afternoon. They may have been too nervous to talk yesterday, especially with their parents in the room. Try and get them on their own. Children always notice more than adults.'

'Sergeant Holmes can do that,' said Bob. 'Children trust women more than men.'

Emma gave him an icy blue glare but said nothing.

'No, you both go,' said Edgar. 'I'm sure you're great with kids, Bob.' In Edgar's mind Bob was hardly more than a child himself. That was the trouble with the war: it had placed a great gulf between people like Edgar, who had served and, despite being only thirty-one, felt that he had aged several lifetimes, and people like Bob, who had just missed out on it.

'I've managed to get hold of a couple of army jeeps from the barracks,' he said. 'You can take one up to Freshfield Road if it can manage the hill. We've got a few squaddies too and they can go up to the racecourse and start searching the wasteland there. I'm going to Hove to talk to the grandparents.'

'Someone must have seen something,' he told the team. 'Someone always has. People don't just disappear.' As he said this, he thought of a magician leaning over a girl lying on a table. A swirl of his cloak and the girl has . . . disappeared. But that was magic; this was real life.

'I saw the grandparents yesterday,' said Bob.

The grandparents had been first on the list (children often run to their grandparents) but Edgar wondered whether Bob had got the best from the interview. Maybe it was a job for someone older. Right now he felt a hundred.

'I want to talk to them again,' he said. 'We've got to keep asking questions until we get some answers.'

As the jeep began its slow process along the coast road, Edgar thought about the disappeared children. What had happened to them after they had set out to buy sweets? Had they been spirited away by some malignant power, some infernal deus ex machina? Or was the truth more prosaic? Had they wandered into the park and frozen to death under the bushes? The seafront was deserted, the snow swirling like a stage effect. The Christmas lights were on, casting eerie blue, green and red shadows. As they passed between the piers, Edgar saw the same poster again and again. A saturnine-looking man in a green robe holding aloft a glowing lamp. 'Max Mephisto in *Aladdin*.' 'Fun for all the family.' 'Give me the lamp, boy!' Wasn't Abanazar a child-snatcher too?

And, all the way, the snow continued to fall.

CHAPTER 2

Max Mephisto hated snow. But then he liked to say that he hated all weather. He was happiest indoors, in a bar or a club or, best of all, in a theatre. When he dreamt of leaving the business (which was quite often these days), he knew that what he would miss most would not be the applause or the satisfaction of a neatly executed trick but that particular backstage smell – greasepaint and Calor gas and musty costumes – the same the world over. In a theatre the outside world didn't matter. Rain or shine, it was always night-time in a theatre. But this winter it was hard to ignore the weather, and cold was what Max hated most. He wondered if this was a legacy from his long-dead Italian mother. Surely he was made for sun and fast cars and drinking Campari in roadside cafes, not for slogging through grey slush in his best shoes, sleeping with his overcoat on and, when he woke in the night, seeing his breath vaporising around him like the ectoplasm in Mamie Gordon's fake medium act.

Max had chosen his lodgings in Upper Rock Gardens solely because they were the only theatrical digs available that boasted central heating. When he got to the thin, melancholy house with its shallow bay windows and aura of having seen better days, he discovered that the much-vaunted heating consisted of a single radiator in his attic bedroom. It was only on during the day, so when Max was rehearsing on the pier presumably the place was positively toasty but by the time he returned the radiator and the room were both icy cold.

On Wednesday morning Max looked out of his bedroom window and saw that the snow was still falling. The houses opposite – gracious Regency edifices like this one, now mostly flats and B&Bs – were barely visible and, at the bottom of the hill, the sea had merged into the grey sky. He surveyed the scene dourly, smoking his first cigarette of the day. Walking to the pier would be no fun in this weather but it was the technical rehearsal so he'd have to get there. The technical was important because he was performing several magic tricks in the show. It was the only thing that had resigned him to the role of Abanazar.

Max had always sworn that he would never do pantomime. It was the final straw, the end of the line, the graveyard of hopes. Ingénues past their prime, comedians who were no longer funny, acrobats getting a bit stiff in the knees – they were all to be found in the cast lists of *Cinderella*, *Jack and the Beanstalk* and *Aladdin*. Every summer the requests started coming in and every year Max refused them. He tried to take a break over Christmas, maybe even go abroad. Anything to get away from the men in drag, the baying children, the shouts of 'Behind you!' It was like some existential nightmare. Where's the grim reaper? Behind you.

So why, this year, was Brighton's Palace Pier Theatre advertising 'for the first time ever' Max Mephisto in *Aladdin*? Why were there posters all over the town showing him in a ghastly green robe waving a lamp that looked more like a gravy boat? Well, partly it was because the show was being produced by Bert Billington, a hugely influential show-business impresario. An invitation from Bert Billington was not to be turned down lightly, even if it involved wearing false whiskers and pushing an ageing Principal Boy into a papier mâché cave (crash of cymbals, green lightning, evil laugh). If Bert liked his performance, then he might book him for a tour of provincial Number Two theatres, maybe even a Number One. Then there was the appeal of Brighton itself. Max had always liked the town and now it was the home of his daughter, Ruby. Not to mention his old friend Edgar. But Ruby and Edgar presented an altogether different problem, one that he didn't like to confront too often. Even so, a season in Brighton was not the same as Blackpool or somewhere in the frozen north. There were quite a few decent restaurants in Brighton.

Finally, the bitter truth was that work was thin on the

ground these days, even for the great Max Mephisto. The new comedians were taking over and their baleful influence was everywhere. Magicians like Tommy Cooper were going on stage, getting the tricks deliberately wrong and – even worse – *showing the audience how they were done.* There was no mystique any more, no glamour. Then there was television. Apparently most families in America owned a set and, if TV's popularity ever spread to Britain, variety would die quicker than you could say 'abracadabra'. So, all in all, well-paid work from November to January was not to be sneezed at. And it was not as if he was playing Wishy Washy or Buttons. He was Abanazar, the Demon King, and the villain always had the best lines.

So Max dressed in his warmest clothes and prepared himself for the walk to the pier. He still had his beloved Bentley but that was locked in a garage in Kemp Town. Besides, cars would be no good today. In the hall he met his landlady, Joyce Markham, a dyed blonde with a head for business and a good line in sardonic banter.

'Morning, Mr M. Lovely day.'

'Indeed it is, Mrs M. Just going out for a stroll along the promenade.'

'Mind you don't get too chilled. I've known many a pro die from the cold in Brighton.'

'That's a jolly story, Mrs M. I'll look forward to hearing it one evening.'

'Are you not having breakfast? Can I press you to a kipper?'

'Charming as that sounds . . .' Max reached for his hat.

Joyce eyed him with amusement. 'Not exactly dressed for it, are you?'

Max looked down at his cashmere coat and brogues. 'This is my arctic attire, Mrs M.'

'I've got some gumboots that belonged to my late husband. Not that it did him any good, poor fool.'

Joyce always talked about her husband as if his death were some frivolous indulgence designed solely to inconvenience her. Max was horrified at the thought of the gumboots but there was no doubt that the snow wouldn't do his shoes much good.

'That would be very kind. Thank you.'

'Don't thank me, thank Arthur. If he can hear you where he is.'

'Max Mephisto in gumboots. Never thought I'd live to see the day.'

'Well, now you can die happy.'

Lou Abrahams, the stage manager, didn't seem in a hurry to die. Chortling to himself, he put down his paper and retreated into his cubbyhole. Max hoped that he was making him a cup of coffee. He sat down and pulled off the boots. In their ugly, rural practicality they reminded him of his father, who liked nothing better than striding over fields looking for wildlife to kill. Still, there was no denying that they'd kept his feet dry. He took his brogues out of the paper bag given to him by Mrs M and put them on. He was feeling better. The smell of coffee was emanating from the cubbyhole and it was pleasantly warm in Lou's office. He pulled the paper towards him. It was the local rag, the *Evening Argus*.

'Desperate search for lost children' screamed the headline. Max read on: 'Police are continuing to search for Mark Webster and Annie Francis, who vanished yesterday whilst playing outside their homes in Freshfield Road, Kemp Town. The children were last seen walking to Sam Gee's corner shop to buy sweets. Mr Gee says that the children never arrived. Detective Inspector Edgar Stephens, who is leading the hunt, says that the police will leave no stone unturned in their search for the missing youngsters. "We know how much the parents must be suffering," said DI Stephens, "and we ask everyone to be on the lookout for Mark and Annie." '

The paper was yesterday's. Max thought of the snow covering Upper Rock Gardens. If the children were still outside, surely they'd be dead by now. He thought of Edgar continuing to search, marshalling his men, knowing that he would have to face the grieving parents at the end of the day. He would take it hard, Max knew. He didn't think that Edgar would have used the cliché about 'no stone unturned' either.

Lou placed a cup of black coffee in front of him. 'Terrible thing about those kiddies, isn't it?'

'Yes,' said Max. 'Terrible.'

'They'll be dead now, mark my words.'

'Maybe not,' said Max. He felt curiously reluctant to accept Lou's gloomy prognosis, though it was what he'd been thinking a few moments ago. 'They could just have run away. They could be with grandparents or friends. I ran away from school a few times.' Once he'd run to an old nanny who'd been good to him, once he had caught the train to Portsmouth and tried to join the navy. Both times he'd been sent straight back to school. He'd never thought of running to his father.

'No, they'll be dead,' said Lou. 'There are a lot of bad people out there.'

Max could hardly argue with this. He looked out of the tiny porthole window. The sea ran grey and silver all around them. The garish colours of the pier had been softened by the snow, the helter-skelter a spectral white tower. Brighton itself had disappeared.

'My money's on the shopkeeper,' said Lou.

Other people also suspected Sam Gee. He was a married man with children but, as Frank Hodges had pointed out that first day, that didn't stop him from being a murderer. Edgar had interviewed Mr Gee himself and had found him believable, if slightly nervous (and that too was only to be expected). Sam Gee had known the children by sight but had been certain that neither Mark nor Annie had visited his shop on Monday afternoon. 'I would have remembered,' he said. 'They were quiet kids. Polite kids. Not like some of the others. But I would have remembered them. The girl had red hair and the boy had glasses. Nice kids.' There had been nothing odd in the way that Gee had recalled Annie's red hair and Mark's glasses. He'd just been anxious to help and concerned for the children. Even so, Edgar had told Bob to go back to the shop today. It wouldn't be the first time that a member of the public had faked concern to hide their own part in a crime.

That was Annie's grandfather's first question when he opened the door of his Brunswick Square flat. 'Have you arrested the shopkeeper? He was the last person to see them.'

'But he didn't see them, Mr Warrington,' said Edgar. 'Can I come in?'

The flat in Brunswick Square told him what he had suspected before: that Sandra Francis had married beneath her. The house in Freshfield Road was a basic two-up two-down, housing parents and four children. Annie's father, Jim, was a labourer. But this flat boasted antimacassars and side tables, even an upright piano. There was a coloured photograph of all four Francis children on the piano, their bright hair rendered almost orange by the colourist. Annie, the eldest, was in the middle, seated with her youngest brother, still a baby, on her knee. The other two – twins, Edgar seemed to remember, a boy and a girl – squatted awkwardly on either side.

The red hair obviously came from their grandmother. Mrs Warrington's hair, pulled into a neat bun, was a faded version of this colour, liberally streaked with white. She saw him looking at the picture. 'Annie was a little mother to her sister and brothers,' she said. 'Such a lovely girl.' Edgar rather doubted this. There was something stiff in the way that Annie was holding her little brother, something in the way that her head was tilted. She didn't look like a girl who saw motherhood as her vocation. Annie was clever, everyone agreed that. Edgar wondered what dreams she had for her future. He hoped to God that she still had a future. He noticed that her grandmother, unlike her mother, used the past tense.

'Does Annie come here often?' he asked.

'Yes,' said Mrs Warrington. 'She comes most weekends, sometimes in the week too. Gets the bus here by herself. She likes to look at the books.' She gestured proudly to a small glass-fronted bookcase beside the door. 'She's a lovely little reader.'

Edgar wandered over to look at the books. He sometimes found it easier to ask questions without eye contact.

'Does she sometimes find it a bit much at home?' he asked. 'All those siblings.'

'Sometimes,' Mrs Warrington admitted. 'She shares a room with the others, shares a bed with Betty. She doesn't get much time to read or do her homework. She likes the peace and quiet here.'

'Does she take after her mother?' asked Edgar, examining the spine of *The Golden Bough*. 'Did she like to read?'

'Oh, our Sandra was ever so clever. She could have been a teacher if she hadn't married that Jim Francis. Michael was a teacher. He's retired now.' She pointed to her husband in the same way that she had gestured towards the bookcase. Michael Warrington frowned.

'This isn't getting us anywhere. Why haven't you arrested that shopkeeper?'

'I've got no reason to arrest him, Mr Warrington,' said Edgar. 'But I promise you I have interviewed him and I'll do so again. I've got officers going door-to-door in Kemp Town at this very moment. But it's possible that Annie might have gone missing of her own accord. As you say, she's a bright girl. She might have planned this. So I wanted to ask you, please, to rack your brains. Apart from her parents, you're the people who know her best. Is there anywhere you think she might have gone? Anyone she might have run to?'

The grandparents sat side by side on the chintz sofa. They looked at each other for a long moment, during which Edgar heard the cuckoo clock in the hall strike eleven.

'There's Uncle Brian,' said Mrs Warrington at last. 'He's friendly with all the children.'

CHAPTER 3

Bob, who liked order, had made a list of the children involved.

Kevin O'Dowd – aged 10
Agnes O'Dowd – aged 8
Betty Francis – aged 10
Richard Francis – aged 10
Lionel Roberts – aged 9
Louise Roberts – aged 7

The children sat in a circle on the wood-blocked floor of the school hall. Bob sat awkwardly on a chair apparently designed for midgets but Emma immediately squatted down on the floor next to the children. They were in the primary school attended by all the children and once attended by Annie and Mark, who were now at separate grammar schools in Hove. Outside it was break-time and they could hear the joyous cries of the pupils playing in the snow. Occasionally there would be a soft thump as a snowball hit one of the high, reinforced windows. From the kitchens came a smell of cabbage and boiled meat. It reminded Bob so forcibly of his own schooldays that he felt a wave of nausea rising in his throat. He had hated school. He didn't share this feeling with Emma because she was obviously the type to have been teacher's pet (white socks, neatly plaited hair, hand constantly in the air).

He did think it was odd that all the children were younger than Mark and Annie. There might only be two years between Mark at twelve and Kevin, Betty and Richard at ten but Bob knew that the gulf between primary and secondary school was a vast, unimaginable distance. Besides, Annie and Mark had passed the eleven-plus. They had entered the new, cloistered world of grammar school, the first step in the process of moving away from their childhood playmates. Bob had failed the eleven-plus. Another reason not to mention schools to Emma. He was sure that she had passed with flying colours.

Betty and Richard were Annie's siblings. Maybe she had been asked to keep an eye on them. Mark was an only child. Maybe he was nervous of children his own age (he had been described as shy and quiet) and preferred the company of these youngsters. Bob looked at Betty Francis and was surprised to find her staring at him. She was very like the photograph they had of Annie (a picture now imprinted on Bob's brain): pointed face, red hair in long plaits, freckles, greeny-blue eyes. Richard was thicker-set and his hair inclined more to chestnut. He stared up at the high window as if wishing he was elsewhere. There was a febrile atmosphere of fear and excitement in the room.

Emma tried to diffuse the tension by chatting about the snow and elicited the information that Lionel and Louise had travelled to school on a sledge pulled by their big brother Lennie (someone in that family enjoyed alliteration). Betty and Richard had slid down the hill on coal sacks. 'Mum thought we should go to school like it was an ordinary day,' said Richard. Bob looked at the twins, sitting very close together on the floor, and wondered if they'd ever see an ordinary day again. Kevin didn't offer any information about his trip to school and Agnes looked near to tears.

'We wanted to talk to you about Monday afternoon, when you were playing with Annie and Mark,' said Emma. 'I know we've already asked you some questions but there might be something you'd forgotten or thought it wasn't important. There might even be something you didn't want to say in front of Mum and Dad. You can say anything to us. You won't get into trouble, I promise.'

The children stared at her, round-eyed.

'So, you came home from school and you played in the road. Is that right?'

The children were silent and then Betty said, slightly defensively, 'We're allowed to play in the road until it gets dark.'

School ended at three, Bob knew, but it got dark around five in November. Those two hours could be vital.

'Who was playing?' asked Emma. 'Just you lot?'

'Yes,' said Richard, 'until Annie and Mark got home.'

'And they joined in, did they?'

Another silence and then Betty said, 'Yes. Annie wanted . . .'

'What did Annie want?'

The children said nothing. Emma looked at Bob. He said, 'What game were you playing?'

'I'm trying to remember what I liked to play at your age,' said Emma. 'Hopscotch? Skipping?'

'Tag?' suggested Bob. 'British Bulldog? Kiss chase?' This last got a giggle from Agnes at least.

Eventually Betty said, 'We were doing a play.'

Emma and Bob looked at each other. 'A play?'

Betty looked around the circle before continuing. 'Annie writes these plays and we act them out. We're her acting troupe.'

Her acting troupe. This explained why Annie sought out the company of younger children. Presumably they were easier to control and direct. Annie, Bob was beginning to realise, was quite a girl. Is quite a girl.

'What was the play about?' asked Emma.

'It was called *The Stolen Children*,' said Betty. 'Richard and I were the parents.'

'I was one of the children,' said Agnes suddenly. 'I

was called Star. Louise was my long-lost brother.' The younger children started to giggle. 'And Lionel was the policeman.' Lionel smiled shyly at Emma and Bob as if to acknowledge their kinship.

'What part did you play, Kevin?' asked Bob. He had already identified Kevin as the potential leader of the group. He was a large boy with a definite presence, cropped-haired and fiercely freckled, saying little but frowning when it seemed that the others were getting too voluble. Bob noticed that Betty had glanced at Kevin before telling them about the play.

Kevin fixed Bob with a steady pale gaze before answering, 'I was the Witch Man.'

'The Witch Man?'

'The Witch Man who steals children and eats them,' explained Agnes, who seemed to have recovered her spirits. She leant forward now, eyes sparkling. 'He steals children and keeps them in a cage until they get fat enough to eat. All the villagers are scared of him. At night they say to their children, "Children, children say your prayers . . ."'

To Bob's surprise the other children – except Kevin – joined in.

'Children, children, say your prayers.
Children, children, stay upstairs.
Children dear, don't stay out late,
or the Wicked Witch Man will be your fate.'

Emma didn't look at Bob but he could see the shock in her shoulders and spine.

'Did Annie make that up?' she asked.

'Oh yes,' said Agnes. 'She's good at making up songs and rhymes.'

'What about Mark?' asked Bob. 'What did he do?'

'He was her assistant,' said Betty, sucking on the end of her plait.

I bet he was, thought Bob. He betted Mark had played second fiddle to Annie from the day that they met. It probably suited him just fine.

'So, in this play,' said Emma, shifting position on the floor, 'the Wicked Witch Man steals the children and eats them?'

'No,' said Betty proudly. 'That's what you're meant to think but in our play it's the parents who're going to kill the children and blame the Witch Man. It's a twist, you see. Annie likes twists.'

Brian Baxter (the 'uncle' was purely courtesy) lived at the top of Freshfield Road, near the racecourse. His house was bigger than the terraces where the children lived and boasted a large, overgrown garden.

'Can you wait for me?' Edgar asked the driver. 'I might need you.'

The man saluted silently. On the way there they had passed the first jeep and a group of soldiers searching the undergrowth opposite the racetrack. Edgar had a sudden awful presentiment that the hunt for the children would end here, under the snowy piles of rubbish in this suburban garden. Don't jump to conclusions, he told himself as he negotiated the icy front path. Brian Baxter is probably a perfectly harmless man who just enjoys the company of young children. He was already imagining the arrest. It was why he'd asked the jeep to wait.

The path was icy but it showed signs of having been cleared recently. This must mean that Brian had been out of the house today. To go where? It was a long walk to any shops and there was a bitter wind on the race hill sending whirlwinds of snow eddying into the air and falling in drifts on either side of the road. Even the jeep had had trouble at the brow of the hill. Why had Mr Baxter felt the need to leave the house?

Edgar knocked and the door was opened almost immediately. The man who answered was not the seedy monster who had begun to grow in Edgar's imagination but an eminently respectable-looking man in a blazer and tie. He was grey-haired, slightly below average height, wearing owlish glasses and a belligerent expression. He looked like a retired bank manager.

Edgar introduced himself. 'I'm Detective Inspector Stephens from the Brighton police. We're speaking to everyone in the area about the disappearance of two children. Can I come in?'

'You'd better,' said Brian. 'It's freezing out there.' He said it accusingly, as if the weather was Edgar's fault.

The house was unexpected too. Neat sitting room, hardback books standing to attention, large gramophone, small table with *The Times* spread out on it. Was that why Brian had ventured out in the snow, to buy his daily paper? Maybe he, like Edgar, was a fan of the cryptic crossword. Try as he might, Edgar couldn't imagine a child in this room.

'We're investigating the disappearance of Annie Francis and Mark Webster,' he said, taking a seat on a hard-looking sofa. 'I believe you know them.'

Brian didn't attempt to deny it. 'I know all the children,' he said.

Edgar waited. Brian took off his glasses and polished them. 'I suppose it looks odd to you,' he said at last.

'Why don't you explain?' said Edgar, trying to keep his voice neutral.

Brian stood up. 'Let me show you.' Edgar followed, his skin crawling. What was he about to see? A gruesome collection of teddies, puppies and other child-bait? Was he about to encounter the dark side of this strange, neat little man? He wished that he had called for backup before knocking on the door.

Brian led him through a large, chilly kitchen with yellow linoleum and blue Formica doors. Then he opened a door at the back of the room.

'Converted the garage,' he said laconically. 'Through here.'

Edgar took a look around the kitchen. He should be

able to overpower Baxter if it came to a struggle. Maybe he should just grab one of those saucepans as he went past.

He stepped through the door. Brain switched on the lights and Edgar blinked from the stalls of an exquisite mini theatre. Red curtains framed a small stage, which showed a backdrop of woodland. An actual chandelier swung overhead.

Edgar turned to look at Brian, who was smiling proudly.

'Did it all myself,' he said. 'Took me over a year.'

'Why?' asked Edgar.

'I've always loved the theatre,' was the unexpected answer. 'My wife was an actress and, when she died, I hit on the idea of doing this as a tribute to her. One of the teachers from the school heard about it and she asked if she could bring some of the children round to have a look. Part of a project she was doing. One of them was Annie. Bright little thing, is Annie. Turned out she loved writing plays and she asked if she could put them on here, in my garage. That's when it started.'

'When what started?'

'Annie's acting troupe. She'd write the plays and they'd put them on here. It's a really good little outfit. The younger children act and Annie directs. Mark's her assistant. Nice boy but a bit shy.'

Edgar looked around the room. Apart from the garage door at the end there was nothing that betrayed the space's original purpose. There was carpet on the floor and flocked wallpaper on the walls. The seats were laid out in two rows.

'Who comes to see the plays?' he asked.

'Friends, family, teachers,' said Brian. 'I give the proceeds to the church organ fund.'

Dear God, thought Edgar, they even sell tickets. Why hadn't anyone mentioned the theatre group before? He turned to face Brian, who was fiddling with the curtains. They were tied back with gold tassels.

'Mr Baxter, Annie and Mark have been missing for nearly two days. Do you know anything about their disappearance?'

'No,' said Brian. 'I only heard about it when I went to the shop this morning.'

'When did you last see the children?'

'I saw Annie at the weekend. She came up to tell me about the new play she was writing. Sometimes she comes to do her homework. She likes it here because it's so neat and tidy.'

Just like her grandparents' place, thought Edgar. Annie, the eldest child, the perennial big sister, had obviously craved a calm, adult environment. But, all the same, was it really that innocent? There was undoubtedly something odd about the garage theatre, so shiny and glittery, hidden away inside this dull, utilitarian house. Was it really an elaborate trap to lure away lonely, stage-struck girls like Annie? But the parents and teachers had obviously known all about it and no one had even mentioned Brian. Even Annie's grandparents had only referred to him as someone who knew all the children, not as a possible murderer. It was Edgar's nasty policeman's mind that had made that connection.

'Mr Baxter,' he said carefully. 'You obviously know all the children. Is there anything you could tell me about their disappearance? Did Annie say anything to you? Do you have any idea where they could be?'

Brian looked at him and, suddenly, his face seemed to collapse. He took off his glasses and wiped them. Tears ran down his cheeks.

'They wouldn't have run away,' he said. 'I was going to take them to the pantomime next week. They were looking forward to it.'

'The pantomime? The one on the pier? *Aladdin*?'

'Yes, it's got that magician chappie in it. Max Mephisto. Have you heard of him?'

'Yes,' said Edgar. 'I've heard of him.'

'They say he can make a person disappear into thin air.'

And he's not the only one, thought Edgar.

CHAPTER 4

Edgar arrived back at the station just as Bob and Emma appeared around the corner, heads down against the wind. It had actually stopped snowing but the wind was still whirling the flakes around as if it couldn't decide on the correct place for them. Edgar watched his officers approach. Both had their hoods up, Bob in his absurd fisherman's gear walking slightly ahead, Emma in her duffle coat following behind. There was something ecclesiastical about her hooded figure emerging through the snow. Appropriate really, considering that Bartholomew Square used to be the site of a monastery.

'Did you leave the jeep on the race hill?' Edgar asked Bob.

'Yes, they're still looking through the undergrowth there.'

'Good.' Edgar had sent his jeep to the park, to look again in the playground, shrubbery and formal garden. Usually they'd get the public to help with a search like this but the weather was making that impossible. The children's parents and their friends were still combing the streets though, looking through gardens and outhouses, continuing to hope that somewhere the runaways would be found, cold and frightened but still alive. For Edgar, though he wouldn't have admitted it even to himself, that hope had faded hours ago.

'Let's get inside,' he said. 'You look frozen.'

'We're OK,' said Emma, whose nose was bright pink. 'It's quite bracing really.'

'Speak for yourself,' muttered Bob. Edgar wondered whether he'd done the right thing in sending them off together.

The subterranean CID offices, unbearable in summer, felt like an oasis of warmth. Someone made tea and they sat drinking it, clothes steaming, condensation forming on the walls. Bob munched slowly through his sandwiches. It was two o'clock.

'Right,' said Edgar. 'What have we got?'

Emma told him about the acting troupe.

'It's interesting that Annie wrote the plays even if they never actually put them on.'

'Oh, they put them on all right.' As succinctly as he could, he described the garage theatre.

'That is perverted,' said Bob, 'building a place like that just to entice little kids in. He sounds like our man to me.'

'There's no "our man",' said Edgar irritably. 'This isn't a murder investigation.' The 'yet' floated in the air. 'And

I didn't think Brian Baxter was perverted. A little strange, certainly, a little obsessive. But he spoke about the children with real fondness.'

'All the more reason to suspect him,' said Bob, whose mind could be a dark place sometimes.

'What about the shopkeeper, Sam Gee?' said Edgar. 'Did you talk to him again?'

'Yes,' said Emma. 'He said that he didn't see Annie and Mark on Monday. We managed to trace some other children who were in the shop and they hadn't seen them either. Last sighting was on the corner of St Luke's Terrace. They're all a bit hazy about time but we think it was about five o'clock because they said the number 12 bus went past a few minutes later. I checked the timetable.'

Once again, Edgar was impressed by Emma's thoroughness. 'Good work. What were the children doing in St Luke's Terrace?'

'Talking, somebody said. But someone else said that they may have been arguing.'

'That's interesting. Who said that?'

Emma took out her notebook and flipped through the pages. 'Arthur Bates, aged ten. He was coming back from the park with his younger sister, Karen. Arthur said that they were standing on the street corner and he heard Annie say that Mark should "go back to primary school".'

'That's a big insult when you're twelve,' said Bob.

'Did this Arthur hear anything else?' asked Edgar.

'No. He said that they stayed on the corner, talking. Well, he said that he only heard Annie's voice.'

This fitted so well with the picture that Edgar had built up of Mark Webster that he almost felt tears coming to his eyes.

'Were there any sightings after five o'clock?' he asked.

'No,' said Emma. 'We spoke to a few people who'd been walking dogs in the park but it was dark and cold. No one saw the children but maybe no one was looking.'

'I've got people searching the park again,' said Edgar. Had the children gone back to the park? As Emma said, it was dark and cold, but they might have had their reasons for wanting to be on their own. Maybe Frank Hodges was right and they were in the throes of a pre-teen romance. But Edgar still didn't think this was likely. Everything he had heard cast Annie in the role of leader and Mark as follower. Nothing about their relationship suggested Romeo and Juliet. It was more Don Quixote and Sancho Panza.

'Did you get anything more from the children at the school?' he asked.

'Not really,' said Bob. 'But they all seemed a bit wary, especially the older ones. They opened up a bit when they told us about the play-acting but I got the impression that they were holding something back.'

'Didn't you try to get it out of them?' asked Edgar.

Emma coloured. 'I did try . . .'

'Sergeant Holmes was very good with them,' said Bob

unexpectedly. 'She got right down to their level. They trusted her.'

Emma shot him a grateful look. Edgar felt a bit ashamed of his question but he was frustrated by the feeling that they were missing something, something momentous just out of their line of sight, like a great cloven hoof in the doorway.

'Tell me again about the play Annie wrote,' he said.

Emma looked at her notes again. 'It was called *The Stolen Children*. Louise and Agnes were the children, Richard and Betty were the parents. Lionel was the policeman. Kevin, one of the older children, was the villain, the Witch Man. Everyone thinks that the Witch Man has stolen the children but really the parents have killed them.'

'Good God,' said Edgar.

'There was this really chilling little rhyme,' said Emma. 'I wrote it down. *Children, children, say your prayers. Children, children, stay upstairs. Children dear, don't stay out late, or the Wicked Witch Man will be your fate.*'

'Good God,' said Edgar again.

'Betty said that Annie loved a story with a twist,' said Bob.

'Betty is Annie's little sister?'

'Yes, Betty and Richard. They're twins. There's a baby brother too.'

Edgar thought of the photograph in Annie's grandparents' house. The four red-haired children posing together in perfect harmony.

'Well,' he said, 'do you suspect the parents?' He raised his hand to stop their protests. 'In cases like this it is often the parents, you know. It's horrible but there it is.'

'I know the figures,' said Emma, 'but I can't believe it in this case. The parents all seem so distraught.'

'And why would they kill them?' asked Bob. 'It just doesn't make sense.'

'No,' Edgar agreed. 'It doesn't make sense.' He looked at the clock. Two-thirty. Soon it would be forty-eight hours since the last sighting of the children. 'I think I'll talk to the parents again.'

He walked up to Freshfield Road. It was hard going. Although the snow had stopped, it was still several inches deep with drifts as high as Edgar's waist in some places. The main roads had been cleared but, as Edgar climbed the hill leading to the racecourse, cars were marooned in mounds of snow and only criss-crossing lines of footprints broke the whiteness. As he approached Mark's parents' house, a sledge shot past him containing two yelling children. Edgar watched them sourly, envying them their carefree enjoyment of the snow. Did they know that two children were missing, possibly buried under this magical winter wonderland? Did they care? He plodded on, Russian hat pulled down over his ears.

Mark's mother took a step backwards when she saw the fur hat on her doorstep.

'Mrs Webster?' Edgar hurried to remove it. 'Detective

Inspector Edgar Stephens. We met yesterday. There's no more news,' he said hastily, seeing her face, 'but I just wondered if I could ask you a few questions. Is your husband in?'

'He's gone up to the race hill to join in the search,' said Mrs Webster. 'The army are up there, you know.'

'Yes, I know.'

'And it's stopped snowing. That should make things easier.'

'Yes, it should.' Edgar offered to take off his wet shoes. At least if he was stooping to undo the laces, he could avoid seeing the desperate hope in Edna Webster's eyes.

'Don't bother, honestly. Reg and his mates have been tramping in and out all day.' Reg was her husband, a bus driver.

Edgar sat opposite Edna in the tiny front room. A large photograph of Mark smiled at them from the mantelpiece. He was an only child.

'We tried for such a long time to have a baby,' Edna told him. 'And we just weren't blessed. But then Mark came along.'

Edgar tried not to think about what it would mean to this woman if her precious, miracle child had been killed. He wondered about the word 'blessed'. Were the Websters religious? There were no crucifixes or signs of Catholic regalia around but maybe they belonged to one of those dour Nonconformist sects.

'I just wanted to talk to you about Mark,' said Edgar.

'We're building up a picture of the children and any little thing you can tell us might be helpful. I understand Mark is quite a shy boy.'

'Yes.' Edna's hands twisted a cushion as she spoke. She looked like a woman who never sat with her hands still. Edgar's mother was the same.

'Reg used to get impatient sometimes because he wasn't one for the rough and tumble. He didn't like football and boxing and what have you. He liked reading.'

She said it like it was something shameful. Edgar smiled encouragingly. 'I liked reading as a boy too, Mrs Webster.' Although he might have liked some rough and tumble if the chance had come his way.

'When did Mark and Annie become friends?' he asked.

'Oh, they were friends since kindergarten,' said Edna proudly. 'Annie took him under her wing from the start.'

'Under her wing?'

'Some of the bigger boys used to bully Mark because he wore glasses but Annie always stuck up for him. She's a feisty little thing. And so clever.'

'Mark must be clever too,' said Edgar. 'He got into the grammar school.'

'Oh, that was Annie,' said Edna. 'She carried him through the eleven-plus. She was so determined that he wouldn't be left behind.'

He wasn't left behind, thought Edgar. Annie had always taken Mark with her, even on that fateful day. Maybe it would have been better for him if Annie hadn't carried him along in her slipstream. Maybe even now he'd be sitting safely at home with his mother.

'I understand they like to put on plays,' he said.

'Oh yes,' said Edna. 'They do them at Uncle Brian's house. He's got a proper little theatre in his garage. You ought to see it.'

'I have,' said Edgar. He paused. Edna obviously didn't see anything sinister in the connection with 'Uncle' Brian and he didn't want to put the thought in her head. All the same, there were questions he had to ask.

'Do you know Brian Baxter well?' he said at last.

'Not very well,' said Edna. 'I went to his house last summer to see a play Annie was putting on. It was called *Red as a Rose*. Sweetly pretty, it was. All the little ones played different flowers. Brian seemed a very nice man. Educated. He worked in an office, you know.'

She said this in a tone of hushed awe. The lustre of a white-collar job was obviously enough to put Brian Baxter above suspicion.

'Have you heard anything about the play they're working on at the moment?'

'No,' said Edna. 'They're always quite secretive. No one must see it "in rehearsal", that's what Annie says. She's a caution.'

Bob and Emma had said that the children had seemed reluctant to talk about the play. Was this just loyalty to their leader? Or was something else troubling the cast?

'How well do you know Annie's parents?' he asked.

'Not very well. We keep ourselves to ourselves really.'

Is that possible, thought Edgar, on a street like this? On the other hand, his own mother had made every effort to avoid her neighbours whenever possible. Maybe the Websters, a quiet couple with an only child, were the same.

'Did you ever chat with Sandra Francis, about the children maybe?'

'Sometimes. She seems a nice woman. Her father was a teacher, you know.'

'And Jim?'

'I don't really know Jim at all. I mean, he's a labourer . . .'

Her voice died away, leaving Edgar to guess at the layers of class distinction involved. Clearly Reg Webster, as a bus driver, rated above Jim Francis, a manual labourer, even if his wife was the daughter of a teacher.

'Must be difficult for the Francises,' he said casually, 'with all those children.'

Edna said nothing, twisting the cushion round and round.

'Annie must like coming here.'

Edna smiled. 'Yes. Sometimes she says she doesn't want to go home.'

'Does she? Why?'

'I don't know. I think her parents can be strict.'

'Jim? Her dad?'

'More her mother, I think. She expects a lot from Annie. She's the eldest, of course.'

'Has Annie ever said anything to Mark about her parents? Anything to show she's scared of them?'

Edna smiled sadly. 'Even if she had, Mark would never tell me. He knows how to keep a secret, does Mark.'

That seemed an odd thing to say about a child. Edgar was about to ask more when a sound outside made Edna cock her head, listening.

'It's Reg,' she said.

Edgar knew that Edna was hoping that her husband would come in with some news, a sighting or a witness or even just a report that the weather was lifting. Even Edgar was half hoping, although he knew that if there had been news Reg Webster would have shouted it out, rather than clumping about in the hall taking his boots off.

Reg entered the room in his stockinged feet, a thin wiry man who looked some years older than his wife.

'Anything?' asked Edna, still with that unbearable tinge of hope in her voice.

'Nothing,' said Reg. 'We went right to the top of the race hill, all along the number 2 route. Searched the scrubland by the stables, everything.'

'The army will keep looking,' said Edgar, trying to inject some confidence into his voice. 'They're experts at this kind of thing.'

'We'll all keep looking,' said Reg. 'It's what we might find that scares me.'

There was no answer to this. Edgar said goodbye and

made his way seven doors up the road to the Francis house.

Bob and Emma were looking back through yesterday's witness statements. It was Emma's idea. Bob had wanted to go back out, to search the park, to join the army team on the race hill, but Emma insisted. 'This is more useful. Anyone can dig through the snow. This is using our brains.'

'I suppose you'd know all about that.'

'What's that supposed to mean?'

'Nothing.'

Bob looked back at the papers on the desk, some in Emma's neat hand, some in his sprawling capitals. He didn't know why Emma made him feel stupid but she just did. Maybe it was her voice, quiet but somehow confident, or maybe it was just the way that her hair was never untidy, her nose never ran, her shoes were always polished. Not that she was smartly dressed. Bob liked girls to look like girls; he particularly liked the skirts that were coming into fashion now with the nipped-in waists and stiff petticoats. Emma wore tweed and grey flannel and she often wore slacks. Today, he supposed, that was allowable but as a rule he didn't like women wearing trousers (he would be horrified to realise that he had inherited this prejudice from his Methodist minister father).

Emma was writing notes, her hair falling forwards over her face. Even her hair was slightly too short, although he supposed it was a nice colour. He thought of her at the school, sitting on the floor with the children and chatting to them about the snow. She'd certainly got a lot out of them.

Her thoughts must have been running along the same lines because she said, 'Thank you for saying that to the DI. About me being good with the children.'

'Well, you were.'

He wanted to ask if she had younger brothers and sisters but it seemed too intrusive somehow. There was something about Emma, something guarded and cool, that prevented you getting too close, like Snow White in her glass coffin (he had been to see the film with his mother during the war and it had had a great effect on him; he had had nightmares about the huntsman for weeks). He knew Emma lived in Brighton but that was all. Did she share a flat with other glossy, confident girls, the way they did nowadays, or was she living on her own? Bob had a room at the top of a tall, gloomy house on Third Avenue. He never asked himself if he was lonely because he was afraid of the answer.

'Are you writing up today's interviews?' he asked.

'Yes. I'm sure the plays and the acting are important somehow.'

'Weird about the bloke with the theatre in his garage.'

'Yes.' She had her prim look on. 'We've got no reason to suspect him though.'

'Except he knew both children and he's a weirdo.'

Emma said nothing and for a few moments the only sounds in the room were the pipes gurgling and Emma's pen scratching. Bob was looking through the witness statements.

'The boy who saw the children arguing . . .'

'Arthur Bates?'

'Yes. Do we have an address for him?'

Emma checked her notebook. 'Queen's Park Road.'

'Where's that?'

'The other side of the park. It's posher than Freshfield Road.'

Bob made a note. 'Have you always lived in Brighton?' he asked.

'Yes, I was born here.'

'What was it like here in the war?'

'Not much fun. There was barbed wire along the beach. Lots of soldiers and sailors everywhere. I didn't see too much of it. I was evacuated to the Lake District.'

'Were you? Did Brighton get bombed then?'

'No, but they always thought it would be.'

'They got Maidstone a few times. I remember Mill Street being bombed and going with my brother to look in the rubble.'

'Have you got lots of brothers and sisters?'

'Two older brothers. Archie was in the RAF, hell of a fellow. Colin's only a year older than me. He's a draughtsman. What about you?'

'I'm an only child.'

She said it in her closing-down-the-conversation voice. Bob took the hint. 'Might be worth going to see young Arthur again,' he said. 'What do you think?'

Sandra Francis opened the door immediately. She too was hoping for news. Her husband, Jim, was also out searching.

'He won't stop until the light fades,' said Sandra. 'That's the sort of man he is.'

She didn't say this admiringly, more with a sort of weary knowledge of her spouse. What sort of a man was Jim Francis? thought Edgar. When he first met him, on the day of the children's disappearance, he'd thought him an unlikely partner for the careworn yet obviously genteel Sandra Francis. Jim was a big man, handsome in a rock-like way. Maybe this was what had originally attracted Sandra. Jim hadn't spoken much, then or since, but there was no doubt that he was an indefatigable searcher; he'd been out all night on Monday and Tuesday, despite the snow that fell in the early hours of Tuesday. He had more stamina than thin Reg Webster – he would probably search all Wednesday night too. Was he also violent, this strong untiring man? But Edna Webster had intimated that Sandra was the strict one. Edgar remembered her saying, that first night, 'I wanted to give Annie a good hiding.' He'd dismissed it then but maybe he was wrong to do so.

Sandra was definitely not forthcoming today. She had

the baby on her hip and responded to Edgar's questions mechanically. Annie was a good girl and always helped in the house. She was good with the little ones, always telling them stories and suchlike. No, not really motherly, more . . . well, more like a little teacher really. Yes, she was good at school. Passed her eleven-plus, always kept up with her homework. She was close to her grandma and granddad. She liked going to their house. Granddad had been a teacher so they got on really well, talking about books and that. She did think of being a teacher herself once but she met Jim and well, that was that. Uncle Brian? She'd met him a couple of times but she didn't think that Annie was especially close to him. All the children knew him. He was just that sort of man. What sort of man was that? Oh, you know, didn't have children himself but liked to see them around. Kind, that's what he was.

Edgar left the house feeling that he had learnt nothing new. Annie was a clever girl, obviously more at home in the neat Hove flat than in the crowded terraced house in Freshfield Road. But she helped with her little brothers and sister, did her homework and generally got on with things. She gravitated towards people like her grandfather and Brian Baxter, adults who had time for her. If she had any worries, she probably told them to Mark, who, as his mother put it, knew how to keep a secret.

At the bottom of the hill he met the jeep and was happy to hitch a lift. It was only four o'clock but already growing dark. The driver, a bald man with sergeant stripes, greeted him with, 'What do you reckon then? We've looked all round the park and up by the racecourse. They're not anywhere round here. You think someone's kidnapped them?'

'Why do you say that?'

The big man shrugged. 'It's what people are saying, isn't it?'

'Is it?' Edgar made a mental note to talk to the PCs who'd been in the search party. It was the first time that he'd heard anyone mention kidnapping.

'Who'd do something like that to a kiddie?' said the sergeant. 'They must be sick in their heads.'

Edgar said nothing. He felt chilled to the bone and not just from the cold. Either the children were dead from exposure or they were in the hands of someone 'sick in their head'. In a few hours' time, maybe tomorrow, maybe the next day, he was sure he'd have to go into Edna Webster's house with Mark grinning gap-toothed from the mantelpiece and tell her that her son was dead.

The roads around the hospital were clear but Kemp Town was a no-go zone, the narrow streets clogged with snow and stationary vehicles. The jeep bumped its way down to the coast road.

'I can walk from here,' said Edgar. 'You get back to the barracks. You've been really helpful. Thank you.'

The sergeant gave him a salute that was only half ironical. Edgar forgot to salute back. The army seemed a lifetime away.

He set off, keeping the railings on his left. He couldn't see the sea but he knew it was there, whispering against the shingle. In Norway, the sea itself had frozen, fossilised into great stone waves. At least it wasn't that cold. One day he might even feel his feet again.

The coast road was deserted, the Christmas lights between the lampposts casting little pools of coloured light, blue, green and red. What sort of a Christmas would the Webster and Francis families have? Come to that, what sort of Christmas would he have?

He was nearly at the pier when a figure appeared suddenly out of the gloom. A tall shape in a trilby hat and voluminous overcoat. There was something incredibly familiar about it.

'Max?' said Edgar.

'Bloody hell. Is that you, Ed?' Max approached the streetlight. As ever, he looked as if he'd just stepped out from a London club, elegant and debonair, hat at an angle. Edgar looked downwards.

'You're wearing gumboots.'

'A present from my landlady. Apparently they belonged to her dead husband. What are you doing, tramping along in the snow?'

'I've been searching for some missing children.'

'I know,' said Max. 'I read about it.'

Edgar was surprised. He never thought of Max as reading anything beyond his own notices. It touched him somehow.

'Any news?' Max asked.

'No. I'm on my way back to the station.'

'I've got digs at Upper Rock Gardens.'

There was a tiny, awkward pause. Edgar wanted to ask Max to walk back with him, wanted to enjoy a few moments talking to someone who wasn't involved with the case. But it was a filthy night, he ought to let Max get back to his digs. Besides, he didn't want to get onto the subject of Ruby.

He realised that Max was holding out a silver flask. 'Brandy,' he said. 'All the St Bernards carry it.'

'I can't,' said Edgar. 'I'm on duty. I'll probably be on duty all night.'

'Oh, go on.'

Edgar took a sip and felt the warmth flooding through his body. Those dogs knew a thing or two.

'Have you been rehearsing?' he asked.

'Yes,' said Max. 'We open at the weekend.'

Edgar thought of Brian telling him that he'd planned to take Annie and Mark to the pantomime. She would have enjoyed that, the stage-struck Annie. He imagined her sitting wide-eyed in the front row, watching Max conjuring genies from thin air.

'I've got a free morning tomorrow,' said Max. 'Why don't we meet for a drink?'

'I'll be working,' said Edgar.

'Coffee then. Midday. I'll come to the station.'

This was a definite concession. Max hated the police and, indeed, authority of all kinds.

'That would be great. See you then.'

'Bye, Ed.'

He looked back once and saw Max still standing under the lamppost, the cigarette in his mouth glowing like a burning ember.

CHAPTER 5

Edgar stayed at his desk all night. The search was called off when the light faded but Edgar knew that the parents would not sleep while their children were still lost, and neither would he. He sat in the CID room in his little circle of light reading through all the notes on the case. Somewhere, he knew, there would be a clue that led him to Annie and Mark.

Who'd do something like that to a kiddie?

Sometimes she says she doesn't want to go home.

Children, children, say your prayers. Children, children, stay upstairs.

He heard Annie say that Mark should 'go back to primary school'.

It was called The Stolen Children.

I was going to take them to the pantomime next week.

The room was deathly cold in the early hours of the morning. Edgar was wearing his coat and fur hat but he was still freezing. He remembered seeing a two-bar electric fire somewhere. Was it in the reception area? He decided to go and look. It would do him good to get some circulation going in his legs.

The police station at Bartholomew Square was over a hundred years old, but the solid Victorian edifice squatted on top of something much older. There had once been a monastery on the site and, on rainy nights, you could still hear the water rushing into the well below the cellars. There were ghosts too – the usual monks and bricked-up nuns but also the spectre of Henry Solomon, a former chief constable, killed as he interrogated a suspect in one of the upper rooms. Edgar, hurrying along the dark corridors, thought of these former inhabitants with something almost approaching affection. They were company, at least. Please, he prayed to Chief Constable Solomon and the unnamed monks, please help me find the children. But the low ceilings and heavy brick walls gave nothing away. Everything was silent, waiting. Even the rodents that usually scuttered along the skirting boards appeared to be asleep.

He found the electric fire in the reception area and decided to stay there for a while. At least there was some light here, even though it was rather eerie and blue, the lamp above the porch reflecting the snowy street. He switched on the fire and pulled it as close to the desk as he could.

What would his mother think, if she could see him? It would probably confirm her belief that he should never have joined the police, that he should have gone into some comfortable white-collar job with luncheon vouchers and the possibility of a pension. It was for this that she had made him stay inside and do his homework rather than playing in the street with the other children, not so that he could go to Oxford. 'People like us don't get degrees,' she said when he got the letter with the Balliol crest. Well, Oxford had only lasted two terms because of the war, and afterwards he had just felt too old to go back to university, though many people did. He had argued with Max about it, he remembered, in the bar at Victoria Station, Edgar saying pompously that he wanted to do a job where he could help other people. Max had retorted that he, for one, was going back to his old life and was never going to think of anyone else again.

Maybe it was the cold that was making him think of his childhood. One of his earliest memories was of lying in bed in the house in Willesden watching his breath billow around him and wondering if he was on fire. Jonathan was in bed next to him but he had been very little, probably only a toddler, and so too young to be any comfort. The downstairs of that house had been fairly warm, with open fires in the kitchen and front room, but upstairs was arctic. Just getting out of bed was a trauma, your feet freezing as they touched the floorboards. Lucy was always suffering from chilblains. They had moved from Willesden to the bungalow in Esher when Edgar was ten, Lucy eight and Jonathan five. For Edgar's mother, Rose, the move meant she'd arrived: central heating, fitted carpets, tiled bathroom. But it had seemed a flimsy, shoddy place to Edgar, not substantial enough to be a home somehow. The terraced house in Willesden had been home, solid, unmoving, comfortable in a stern, parental way. But all the years that Edgar had lived in Esher he had never felt that he really belonged there. Perhaps that was why he visited so seldom now, even though Rose was alone in the house; her husband dead, Jonathan dead, Lucy married, Edgar selfishly pursuing his own life.

He could feel his head drooping forwards. He mustn't go to sleep. Memory shifts and he's at Oxford, coming home after an all-night party. That heightened sense of reality, the honey-coloured buildings and soft ochre river more beautiful than ever. He could be there now, fast asleep in his rooms facing the quad, or even in a little house in Jericho with a wife asleep beside him. He had gone into the police because he wanted to do some good, because life had become very serious and the thought of going back to academic research while his brother and the woman he had loved lay dead seemed self-indulgent and pointless. But was he doing any good now, sitting at a desk waiting for bad news to come, powerless to prevent it?

He must have fallen asleep. He dreamt of ice floes, of Jonathan lying asleep, of faces looking up from frozen water, of a puppet theatre, of a child with an adult's face, of hands reaching up and voices calling. *Children, children, say your prayers. Children, children, stay upstairs.*

He woke with a start. The phone was ringing and sparks

were coming from the fire. It was still dark outside but the clock on the wall said six-thirty. Edgar unplugged the fire and picked up the receiver. It was a police officer from the station in Hove. An early-morning dog-walker had found two bodies on Devil's Dyke. He thought they were children.

Edgar leant back in his chair and let out a long sigh.

Edgar went to the lock-up garage where the police cars were kept. The street outside had been cleared and there had been no more snow in the night but everything was covered in a fine layer of ice. When he finally got a car out, it skidded almost the length of the road and came to rest by a milk float. The milkman, a hardy figure in an immense sheepskin coat, helped him get the car pointing the right way and Edgar set off, slower this time, keeping to the main roads. It was seven o'clock and the sun was just coming up over the downs.

He'd rung Bob and Emma and told them the news. 'Go to the station,' he'd said. 'There's no point in us all trekking up to the Dyke.' He wondered if he was trying to save them the sight that awaited him.

Devil's Dyke was a beauty spot on the outskirts of Hove, a soaring stretch of downland that must have been used as a beacon and gathering place from the days when the first prehistoric farmers started to clear the land. Archaeologists had found remains of an Iron Age hill fort and a Bronze Age cemetery. In Victorian times there had been a funfair and funicular railway. But the Dyke was also a lonely and ill-starred location. The funfair was disused and a grand hotel, built to cater to visitors, had burnt down in 1945. But on this November morning none of these landmarks were visible. The funfair and the hill fort were all buried under the same smooth white counterpane. Only the ruined hotel remained, a glowering presence to the east.

Two policemen were waiting in the car park and Edgar also recognised the flashy Lagonda owned by Solomon Carter, the police surgeon. He'd called Carter before he'd left but he wondered how he'd got there so quickly.

One of the policeman saluted sharply, though he looked frozen to death.

'Inspector Stephens? I'm Sergeant Ron Harris. This way.'

Harris led the way along a track leading to a stile. The path had clearly been used, even in the snow, because it was rutted with footprints, both animal and human. Carter got out of his car and followed. Despite everything, Edgar was still irritated to see that he was wearing a fur coat.

The bodies were not far away. They were lying in a shallow ditch just off the main track. Edgar could see marks where the dog must have scrabbled in the piled-up snow.

'We sent the dog-walker home,' said Harris. 'He was frozen and so was his dog. I got a statement though.'

'Is he local?'

'Yes, he lives up Preston Park way.'

All this was delaying the inevitable. Edgar knelt and gently pushed away the snow. Harris helped him and, within a few minutes, the bodies lay uncovered. Two children lying as if asleep. Annie's red hair, shocking against its white pillow. Mark turned towards her as if seeking her protection, his glasses held together with sticking plaster. Edgar heard Carter's intake of breath and the other policeman blew his noise loudly. Beside him, Harris crossed himself.

'It's them then?' he said.

'Yes,' said Edgar. 'It's them.' He didn't feel close to tears himself. Right at that moment he felt nothing but rage, no less murderous for being calm. He would find the killer and see them hanged. He would do that or die in the attempt.

'Cause of death?' he turned to Carter.

The doctor leant forward. 'I'd say strangulation. It's hard to tell because the bodies are so cold but look at the marks around her neck.'

Edgar looked and, as he did so, he saw something else. Something as bright as Annie's hair, lying just under her curled-up legs. Edgar bent down to look closer.

'What is it?' asked Harris.

'It's a stick of Brighton rock,' said Edgar.

Max knew something was up as soon as he reached the station. Uniformed policemen were standing around in the reception area and there was the air of suppressed excitement that he associated with first nights. He asked for Edgar and was not surprised to hear that he was unavailable. Standing under the portico lighting a cigarette, he noticed a dogged-looking group of people sheltering in the doorway of the pub opposite. Strolling over, he recognised a reporter from the *Evening Argus*.

'Hallo, Don. What's up?'

'Max Mephisto. What are you doing here?'

'I asked first.'

'There's a rumour that the children's bodies have been found.'

'Jesus. Where?'

'Devil's Dyke. That's what I heard.'

'Dead?'

Don nodded solemnly but his eyes were bright. 'Looks like we might have a murder on our hands.'

'Yes, let's look on the bright side,' said Max.

He walked back to the station. He'd spotted Bob, Edgar's gormless-looking sergeant, standing in the doorway talking to a blonde policewoman, the sort who denies their good looks by scraping their hair into a ponytail and not wearing lipstick.

'Hallo.' Max raised his hat. 'I'd arranged to meet Inspector Stephens but I understand that's impossible now.'

Bob stared at him. He had a round face and a boyish-looking mouth but there was something determined about him all the same. Max could see why Edgar said he'd make a good policeman one day.

'You're the magician, aren't you?'

'Yes, I am.'

'He's the guv'nur's friend,' Bob said to the woman. 'They were in the army together.'

The girl looked at him but said nothing. She was harder to read. A cool, arctic face with pale-blue eyes.

'I hear that the children's bodies have been found,' he said.

'Who told you that?' Bob looked angrily towards the knot of reporters.

'We can't comment,' the woman cut in quickly.

'They're saying they were found in Queen's Park.'

'They're wrong. It was Devil's Dyke.'

'I won't detain you.' Max raised his hat again in farewell. Really, young people were depressingly stupid sometimes.

Max had a trying afternoon at the theatre. Aladdin still didn't know her lines and Widow Twankey's face looked suspiciously flushed. Wishy Washy fluffed the business with the ironing board and the Emperor of Peking seemed to have disappeared altogether. The director, Roger Dunkley, was literally tearing at his hair by the end. The author, a nervous-looking young man called Nigel Castle, sat in the front row with his head in his hands.

'Don't take it too hard.' Max strolled downstage during a hiatus involving the Peking police. 'It'll be all right on the night.'

Nigel raised a haggard face. 'Is that really true or is it just what people say?'

'Well . . .' Max felt for his cigarettes. 'It is what people say but there's a certain truth in it. Most performers are better with an audience.'

'But my lines.' The writer seemed almost tearful. 'I wrote these lines. I wanted it to be different from other pantomimes. You know, really witty, not just old jokes and wordplay, and Denton McGrew just says the lines that he always says every time he plays Widow Twankey.'

Max felt sorry for him. It was true that Nigel's lines were quite good, a step up from most pantomimes at any rate, and Denton McGrew, a famous Dame but a rather tiresome human being, was enough to try anyone's patience.

'The script is excellent,' he said. 'You even managed to avoid the one about the Brighton Belle.'

Nigel managed a wan smile. 'McGrew says it anyway. Everything's innuendo with him.'

Max remembered hearing a rather good joke about innuendo being an Italian suppository. He decided that now wasn't the time. He wasn't really in a joking mood, one way or another. He took out his lighter.

'Max!' Roger Dunkley called up from the orchestra pit. 'No smoking in here. New fire regulations on the pier.'

'Good God.' Max replaced the packet. 'Is nothing sacred?'

Roger came closer. He was a solid man in his late forties

but today he looked about a hundred. 'Do you have any idea what's happened to Dick Felsing?'

'Who?'

'The Emperor of Peking.'

'No. Sorry. Maybe he's just forgotten the rehearsal.' The Emperor, an aged character actor, was notoriously absent-minded.

Roger groaned. 'That's all I need.'

'Old age. Forgetfulness. It comes to us all.'

'Oh yes?' Roger nodded sourly towards Annette Anthony, the actress playing Aladdin. 'Then what's her excuse? She forgot her name a moment ago. Thought she was Red Bloody Riding Hood.'

It was dark by the time Max left the pier. The snow had stopped but the pavements were icy and treacherous. He walked in the road for most of the way. There still weren't many cars about. One double-decker bus did brave the coast road, swaying like an ocean-going liner, its illuminated interior strangely comforting in the darkness. Max wondered what it would be like to hail the bus and be driven away, somewhere, anywhere. He imagined that was what Edgar felt like at the moment. But no, Edgar would be doggedly setting about the task of finding the killer. Escape wouldn't be an option for him. He was tough, Edgar, tougher than he looked. Just as well really.

He had planned to avoid supper with the other pros. They were a mixed bag at Mrs M's this year. Thank God there was no one else from the pantomime but the line-up included Wee Bobbie McPherson, who played the accordion, Walter Von Krum, a German ex-POW who had a strong-man act, a singer called Eloise Hanley ('The Croydon Nightingale') and a double act called Tommy and Thomas, two elderly men who shared a double room. They were all involved in a variety show at the Hippodrome. Nothing Max had seen or heard so far had made him keen to see the show.

As he walked up Upper Rock Gardens, he prayed that the dining room would be empty and his prayers were answered. The room was empty and the table clear. From upstairs came the plaintive strains of Wee Bobbie practising his accordion.

Mrs M came out of the kitchen. She wasn't wearing her usual apron and, in fact, looked rather smart in a black dress and glittery earrings.

'You're late, Mr M. Don't worry, I've kept something warm for you.'

'That's very kind, Mrs M. Are you going out?'

Was it the light or did she blush?

'No. I just got dressed up for a Townswomen's Guild lunch today.'

'Sounds a wild occasion.'

'You wouldn't believe it if I told you. Sit down and make yourself comfortable.'

And it was comfortable in the dining room. The curtains were drawn across the bay window and the only light came from the standard lamp and a flickering gas fire. Mrs M brought him a sherry and he sat in front of the fire listening to the gas popping and thinking about Edgar and Ruby and whether Annette would ever do the disappearing trick properly. Mrs M brought his supper on a tray and sat opposite him while he ate, regaling him with stories about the townswomen and the idiocies of her past husband. It was very pleasant, even if Mrs M was blowing smoke over his food.

When he'd finished eating, Joyce produced a bottle of brandy.

'I keep it locked away. You know what pros are like.'

'Only too well.'

She leant forward to fill his glass. 'So, how's the panto going, Mr M?'

'Well, it's going, Mrs M, that's all that can be said for it.'

'I'm coming on the first night. I can't wait to see your tricks.'

Was it his imagination or was there a speculative gleam in her eye? It was hard to tell through all the cigarette smoke.

'It's a family show, Mrs M.' He risked a raised eyebrow.

'What a pity.' There was no doubt about it now. She blew smoke into the air and eyed him coolly. She wasn't bad-looking. A bit brassy and overly made-up but her figure was good and he liked the way that she seemed to be calling the shots. She was older than his usual girls – probably his own age, in fact – but he liked that too. It might mean that there wouldn't be any tears or demands or declarations of love. On the other hand, 'never sleep with the landlady' is one of the first rules of the touring life. Upstairs, Wee Bobbie embarked on 'The Rose of Tralee'.

Joyce was still looking at him. Slightly amused now, red lips parted. 'Should I be scared?' she asked.

'Of what?'

'Of you. They say you can make women disappear.'

He raised an eyebrow. 'You shouldn't believe everything that you hear about me.'

'Well, that's a relief, I must say.'

He was just on the verge of making a move (a kiss on the hand would probably do it) when there was a sound outside. Footsteps. They looked at each other, more alarmed than they should have been. The house opened straight onto the road and callers weren't unexpected at a guest house, after all. But something about the snow and the firelight had made them feel isolated, as if they were alone in the world. Max reached for his cigarettes and Joyce stood up, smoothing down her skirt. She was at the door almost before they heard the knock.

Max heard voices in the hall and then Joyce saying, 'Someone for you, Mr M.'

It was Edgar or, at least, Edgar's ghost. A tall figure in a long dark coat, black eyes in a white face, mouth twisted in a parody of a smile.

'Thought I'd just drop in.'

'Sit down, you look like hell.'

They sat at the table. Mrs M tactfully withdrew, saying that she was putting the kettle on. Max thought that the situation probably called for more than tea.

'Have some brandy. I'll get her another bottle tomorrow.'

'Thanks.'

Edgar drained the glass in one gulp. Max poured some more. Edgar held the glass up to the light, squinting slightly.

'Good stuff.'

'Yes. She normally keeps it locked away.'

Edgar looked at Max as if seeing him for the first time. 'Have you heard? About the children?'

'Yes. I was at the station at lunchtime.' He didn't remind Edgar about their missed appointment.

'I saw them, Max. I saw them lying in the snow.'

Max said nothing. He didn't think that he could say anything that would help. He'd seen death in the war – they both had – but those had been soldiers, men who had marched out knowing that they might die. Nothing like this.

'I had to tell their parents,' said Edgar.

'God. Don't they have special people to do that sort of thing?'

'I thought it was my duty.' Edgar gave a hollow laugh. 'After all, I hadn't done anything else for them.'

'Jesus, Ed. It wasn't your fault. You tried your best to find them.'

'But my best wasn't good enough, was it? Mrs Webster, the boy's mother, she just fell to the floor screaming. She really thought that we'd find them alive.'

'But you didn't.'

Edgar rubbed his eyes. His hands were shaking but Max thought that it was tiredness rather than alcohol. 'No,' he said. 'As soon as they went missing, I knew. I knew that we were dealing with a murderer.'

Again, thought Max. But he didn't think it would be a good idea to mention the last time that they'd hunted a killer together.

But it seemed that Edgar's thoughts were moving in a similar direction. 'I want your help, Max.'

'*My* help?'

'Yes. The way the bodies were found, there was something theatrical . . .' He took another gulp of brandy. 'When we cleared the ground, there were sweets . . .'

'Sweets?'

'Yes, a trail of sweets leading to the bodies. And the bodies were meant to be found. They were just in a shallow ditch. If it hadn't been for the snow, they would have been found almost immediately.'

'You say there was a trail of sweets?'

'Yes. Brighton rock. Humbugs. That sort of thing. A whole line of them leading to the ditch where the bodies were.'

'What the hell did that mean?'

'I don't know,' said Edgar. 'But it's a clue.' He looked

owlishly at Max. 'And you're good with clues. Smoke and mirrors. Sleight of hand. Mis . . . misdirection. Isn't that what you're best at?'

He had started to sound slightly belligerent.

'Of course I'll help you,' said Max. 'But I think you should try to sleep now. You can stay the night here. Mrs M will make you up a bed.'

'Sleep!' Edgar almost shouted the word. 'I'll never sleep again.'

But by the time that Joyce came back in with the tea, Edgar's head was on the table, his brandy dripping gently onto the carpet.

CHAPTER 6

Max woke with a headache and the feeling of impending gloom that he associated with first nights in difficult venues. He looked around the room, gradually noting his surroundings: sloping ceiling, sash windows, Brighton, *Aladdin*, Joyce Markham, Edgar, dead children. He groaned and sat up. He hadn't pulled the curtains and the light was blue and cold, which meant that the snow was still there. Max pulled on his dressing gown and went to the window. The gardens and pavements were still white but he could see cars moving along the coast road. There would be no reason for the show not to open tomorrow. He sighed and set off on the arctic expedition to the bathroom.

Coming downstairs half an hour later, he found Edgar sitting at the dining-room table staring into a cup of coffee.

'How do you feel?'

'As bad as I look.'

'I've got some Fernet Branca upstairs.'

'I don't think I could keep it down. I woke up on a sofa. Couldn't remember how I got there.'

'You passed out at the table. I got you onto the sofa with some help from Mrs M.'

'She's been very kind. She's making me some breakfast. Says it will help.'

'Well, she's had a lot of experience in this sort of thing.'

Edgar flushed. 'I wasn't that drunk. It was just not sleeping for twenty-four hours and . . . well, everything else.'

'I promise you, what you saw was enough to make anyone pass out.'

'Well, today the real work begins.'

Max noted that this last statement seemed to energise Edgar. He sat up straighter and took a thoughtful sip of coffee. He wondered again at his friend's resilience. Last night he had seemed broken, traumatised by the horror and sadness of the case. But now, with the task of finding the killer before him, he seemed to be gaining strength by the second. Even the appearance of a huge fried breakfast didn't unduly disturb him.

'Got to keep your strength up,' said Joyce.

'Thanks very much,' said Edgar. 'You're very kind.'

Joyce placed black coffee in front of Max. 'You ought to have some breakfast too, Mr M.'

'Thank you, Mrs M, but you know I never eat in the mornings.'

When the landlady had left, Edgar set to with a will.

Max averted his eyes. 'Are you working today?' Edgar asked, cutting into black pudding.

Max winced slightly at the word. Edgar would be tracking a murderer; he would be dressing up in a green gown and shooting firecrackers from his sleeves.

'Yes,' he said. 'It's the dress rehearsal. We open tomorrow. Saturday.'

'Is it Friday today? I've lost count.'

'I'm not surprised. You're welcome to a comp but I'm sure it's the last thing you feel like.'

'Is Ruby coming to see it?'

It was the first time that Edgar had mentioned her and he managed it well enough, thought Max. Just a slight hesitation before the name and the suggestion of a blush. Tells, they were called in the business.

'I sent her a ticket,' he said. 'She's only in Worthing. She's in the panto there. If you can call it that. Back row of the chorus in *Cinderella*.'

'I know. I'm going to see her show next week.'

This time there was a definite hesitation. Edgar was clearly worried about Max's reaction. Max tried to keep his face completely blank. 'I hope you enjoy it,' he said.

'I'm not sure I can enjoy anything any more,' said Edgar.

'This is now a murder investigation,' Edgar told the team. 'We've got to put aside all feelings of sadness and regret and concentrate on finding the person who killed Annie and Mark. We owe it to their parents and we owe it to the community. Because, if I'm sure of one thing, it's that this person will strike again. They'll be feeling clever, they'll be thinking that they've outwitted us, they'll want to try again. Well, we've got to stop them.'

He looked at the faces in front of him. Emma had cried yesterday when she'd seen the photographs of the dead children but now she was utterly calm, notepad open on her lap. Bob, who had turned away and punched the wall, was now registering only professionalism and determination, his boyish face a picture of concentration. Edgar felt proud of them all.

'The crime scene has been thoroughly searched,' he said. 'Carter thinks that the children were strangled and then laid in the ditch. It's probable that they weren't killed at the site so we're looking for anyone seen with a car near Devil's Dyke on Monday evening or Tuesday. The cold has made it difficult to ascertain time of death but we're pretty sure that the bodies were put in the ditch before the snow started to fall on Tuesday night. The positioning of the bodies, almost in the open near the footpath, makes it seem as if the killer wanted them to be found quickly. It was the snow that scuppered that plan. And these were found at the scene.' He upended a plastic bag onto the table. Chairs scraped back as people leant forward. Emma was scribbling furiously.

'It's a selection of sweets,' said Edgar. 'They were placed along the path as if they were leading to the children.

Some sweets, like this stick of Brighton rock, were actually thrown into the grave with them.'

Bob was the first to say it. 'Does this point to the sweet-shop owner, Sam Gee?'

'We'll compare the sweets to the selection sold in Mr Gee's shop,' said Edgar, 'but we have to be careful about concentrating on any one suspect at this early stage. We have to keep an open mind.'

'If anyone bought that lot,' said Bob, 'it would be a year's worth of rations.' Bob had a sweet tooth – Edgar had noticed this before – and often talked about the halcyon day when sugar rationing would be over.

Emma pushed the hair back from her face. 'It's a bit like "Hansel and Gretel", isn't it? Didn't they lay a trail through the forest? And they were imprisoned in a house made from sweets.'

There was a murmur in the room. Edgar said quickly, 'Excellent observation, Sergeant Holmes, but let's keep it to ourselves. The last thing we want is for the press to call this the "Hansel and Gretel murder".'

'I was just wondering about Annie's play,' said Emma. '*The Stolen Children*. There was something in it that reminded me of "Hansel and Gretel".'

'The bit about the Witch Man keeping them until they were fat enough to eat,' said Bob. 'I remember that too.'

'It's worth checking,' said Edgar. 'Let's speak to her parents and her teachers. Emma, you go to Annie and Mark's schools. Bob, you come with me to talk to Mr Gee.'

Frank Hodges had been standing in the background, watching Edgar critically. Now he came forward to examine the photographs. 'Hansel and Gretel,' he said. 'More like Babes in the Wood. Poor little sods.'

Max was met at his dressing-room door by Roger Dunkley.

'Bad news,' said the director.

Max opened the door. 'Surprise me.'

'We've found Dick Felsing pissed out of his head on a park bench. He's hit the bottle in a big way. There's no way he can go on tomorrow.'

'Has he got an understudy?'

'For the Emperor of Peking? Do me a favour. The management doesn't run to understudies. But I've had an idea.'

This struck Max as even worse news. He shrugged off his coat and took out his cigarette case.

'Want one?'

'Thanks.'

'What about the fire regulations?'

'Bugger the fire regulations.'

Max inhaled deeply. 'Well, what's your idea?'

'Stan Parks. Isn't he a friend of yours? I heard he was living in Hastings. Anyway, I tracked him down. He's staying with a theatrical landlady called Queenie. I rang him last night and offered him the part. He jumped at it. Said he couldn't wait to see you again.'

Stan Parks. The Great Diablo. Max didn't know whether to laugh or cry.

Annie and Mark attended adjoining grammar schools in Hove. Today both schools flew the Union flag at half mast but, as Emma entered the girls' school, she was comforted by the unmistakable signs of life going on: girls giggling in the corridors, posters advertising the Christmas carol concert, lists of hockey and netball teams. She was sure that some of the people in the building would be mourning Annie but it also felt right that most of them were carrying on as usual. Maybe there would be a memorial to Annie, a cup named in her honour, but then she would be forgotten. In some brutal way it made sense.

The hallway – polished oak, scuffed skirting boards, imposing staircase with notices saying 'Keep Right' – reminded Emma of her own school. She had been to Roedean, something she kept very quiet from her colleagues. She remembered Bob making some comment once about the school, which towered above the cliffs at Black Rock, saying that it was 'a prison for posh girls'. Emma was a posh girl ('Nothing but the best for my princess,' her father had said whilst signing the cheques) but she didn't see that it was her fault exactly. Besides, when she thought about school, she didn't think about the fortress on the cliffs but of the wonderful few years when the school had been evacuated to Keswick and she had experienced the country childhood that she had previously only read about in books. At Keswick, she had ridden, rowed and skated on frozen lakes. She had a furtive romance with a village boy called Ernie. Recently she had read an interview with Nancy Mitford in which the author had described the war years as 'heaven'. Miss Mitford had received a lot of criticism for this but Emma thought that she knew the feeling. Certainly going back to Roedean for her last few years of schooling had been dull and depressing. Maybe that was why, despite achieving excellent academic results, she had been determined not to go to university, which she saw as a bigger, grimmer Roedean, but to go out in the Real World. Well, this was the Real World, if you like, a place where children could be murdered and their bodies left out in the snow. Emma squared her shoulders and set out in search of the headmistress's office.

The headmistress, a surprisingly young woman called Patricia Paxton, shook Emma's hand and agreed that it was a very sad day.

'She was an extraordinary girl, Sergeant Holmes. Exceptionally bright, especially considering that she came from a home where . . . well, maybe academic achievement wasn't automatically expected.'

Emma thought of Annie's home, of the bedroom shared with her siblings, of her attempts to find somewhere 'tidy' to do her homework. She said, 'Annie was in the second year, wasn't she?'

'Yes, she was one of the oldest in the year, thirteen in

October. That was one reason why she was made form captain.'

'Had she settled in well here? Made friends?'

Emma had half expected to hear that clever, working-class Annie had struggled to fit in at the grammar school but Mrs Paxton smiled warmly. 'She was very popular. A natural leader. Always surrounded by friends.' She took a lace handkerchief from her sleeve and dabbed her eyes. 'There are going to be a lot of very sad girls here today and for many days afterwards. The teachers too. She was a pleasure to teach.'

'She was good at English, wasn't she? We know about the plays she wrote.'

Mrs Paxton gave Emma a sharp look, as if suspecting her of asking a trick question. 'Plays? I've never heard of any plays. Annie was an all-rounder but she excelled at maths and science. She talked about becoming a doctor . . .' She brought out the handkerchief again.

'Do you do any drama here?'

Miss Paxton drew herself up. 'Indeed we do. We put on *Twelfth Night* last year.'

Emma's mind boggled slightly at the thought of *Twelfth Night* with an all-girl cast. Her school had put on *The Tempest* and that was bad enough (Emma had played Gonzalo).

'And we had some drama workshops only a few weeks ago,' Miss Paxton went on. 'I didn't notice Annie being particularly interested, though she took part, of course.'

'What did you know about Mark Webster?' asked Emma. 'Did you ever see them together?'

Now Mrs Paxton looked properly horrified. 'We never have anything to do with the *boys*. It's a completely separate school. And I certainly never saw Annie with a boy. It's strictly forbidden by the school rules. Girls must not fraternise in any way.'

Emma's school had had a similar rule but she seemed to remember that fraternisation had gone on anyway. She smiled placatingly. 'Thank you very much, Mrs Paxton. I won't take up any more of your time. I know this must be a very difficult day for you.'

'It's a terrible day,' agreed the headmistress. 'But life must go on.'

Yes, life must go on, thought Emma, as she followed Mrs Paxton's upright figure through the panelled corridors and somehow, seeing the red-blazered schoolgirls scuttling past, casting awed looks at their headmistress, Mrs Paxton's cliché began to sound like an exhortation. These girls could be in danger from Annie's killer. It was up to Emma to make sure that life went on.

The girls' and the boys' schools had adjoining playing fields. There were signs saying 'Girls must NOT walk across the field' but it was quicker than going back round by the road so Emma took the path around the edge of the pitch, noting the point at which hockey turned into rugby. There was still snow on the ground but both schools had teams running about, being yelled at by teachers in sheepskin coats. The hockey players and rugby players studiously ignored each other but Emma wondered if it was always like this. It would have been easy enough for Mark and Annie to meet at the Rubicon, maybe even to pass notes. She must remember to ask Annie's friends when she interviewed them.

Mark's headmaster, Dr Martin Hammond, was an older, drier character than Mrs Paxton but he, too, had nothing but praise for his pupil.

'A model student. Well behaved, diligent, full of promise. Dear me . . .' He took off his glasses and wiped them. 'To say that now . . .'

Dr Hammond didn't need to say what he meant. Mark's promise would never be realised. He would never leave this school with academic honours, just as Annie would never become a doctor. The headmaster stared bleakly ahead of him while Emma asked about Mark's school career.

'A solid citizen. A little quiet in lessons, some of the masters said, but always hard-working and well prepared. And, as I say, his written work was of an excellent standard. He was shaping up to be quite a decent little batsman too.'

Emma looked at the framed cricket bat above Dr Hammond's head and realised that this was quite an accolade.

'What about drama?' she asked. 'I'd heard that he was interested in acting.'

Dr Hammond looked quite as affronted as Mrs Paxton

before him. 'Acting? I've never heard of anything like that. We do a Gilbert and Sullivan every year and, as far as I know, he never took part.'

Perhaps he was a music lover then, thought Emma. She asked about Mark's friends.

'Simkins Minor, I think, and Warburton. A small group of the quieter sort. I can make enquiries if you'd like to talk to them.'

'I would, but perhaps we should leave it a day or two.'

'I think that would be wise. We're all quite cut up at the moment.'

'Dr Hammond, I know this sounds a bit strange, but did you ever hear of Mark being involved with writing plays? We know that he and Annie Francis, the girl who died, that they enjoyed writing and producing plays for younger children.'

Dr Hammond shook his head. 'Not as far as I know. In my opinion, he wasn't the sort.'

What sort is that? wondered Emma. She thanked the headmaster for his time and made her way out of the school. The rugby players were still dashing about in the sludge. Emma had never been able to work out the rules of the game. She tried to imagine quiet, sensitive Mark, his glasses mended with sticking plaster, in the middle of these confident, yelling boys. She couldn't do it. To her, Mark still belonged in the primary-coloured safety of junior school, putting on plays with Annie's acting troupe. Emma went through the gates and started to walk down the Old Shoreham Road. She suddenly stopped in the middle of the road, remembering. What had Annie said to Mark on the night that they had disappeared? That he should go back to primary school. Bob had said that it was an insult but what if it was, after all, just a suggestion? That the two of them should go back to their old school, perhaps to see someone. But who? Emma quickened her pace, looking for a bus to take her to Kemp Town.

CHAPTER 7

Sam Gee stared at the array of sweets spread out on his counter-top: Taveners Pontefract cakes, pear drops, Mighty Imps, liquorice sticks, Sherbet Fountains, Parma violets, fizzers and dolly mixtures. In their red, yellow and orange wrappers they looked innocent and festive, recalling the pre-war days when sweets could appear in this sort of profusion, the products of a visit from a favourite relative or a particularly fruitful Christmas stocking. Edgar saw Bob staring hungrily at the hoard, and at the glass jars behind Sam Gee's head. Only a few mud-stained wrappers ruined the effect. That and the fact that this confectioner's treasure trove had been found in the grave of two murdered children.

'Do you sell these sweets here?' asked Edgar.

Sam Gee rubbed his eyes. He was a small man, probably nervous at the best of times, but now, after three visits from the police in as many days, he was almost quivering with terror.

'Some of them we do,' he said at last. 'Haven't had the Imps for a few months now, and I don't think I've ever stocked Pontefract cakes, but the others, yes.'

'What about Brighton rock?' The stick of rock found under Annie's body had been liberally stained with her blood. Edgar hadn't been able to bring himself to touch it.

'There's no rock these days. Not with the sugar rationing. That must be pre-war.'

That was interesting. Edgar and Bob exchanged glances.

'Mr Gee.' Edgar deliberately assumed a more official manner. Bob got out his notebook. 'Can you tell us again what you did on the night of Monday the twenty-sixth of November?'

The voice, or perhaps the notebook, did the trick. Sam actually backed away from them until he was standing behind the counter with his back to the wall.

'What's all this about? And why are you asking me about sweets?'

The detail about the sweets had not been released to the press. Edgar didn't want to give fuel to any 'Hansel and Gretel' fantasists, nor did he want a gang of vigilantes at Mr Gee's door. Even so, the morning papers had been full of the discovery of the bodies. He was dreading the appearance of the *Evening Argus*.

'We're investigating the murders of Annie Francis and Mark Webster,' he said. 'And we're speaking to anyone who might be connected with the case.'

'But I'm not connected,' protested Sam. 'I've got nothing to do with it. Those poor children. I hope they hang the bastard who did it.'

So do I, thought Edgar. This despite being against the death penalty. 'The children disappeared on their way to your shop,' he said again. 'We're going over every second of that day.'

'They never came here,' said Sam. 'I told you, I knew them by sight and they never came here. I closed up the shop at five-thirty, had my tea and stayed in with the missus all evening, listening to the wireless. She can vouch for me.'

'We'll certainly be speaking to Mrs Gee,' said Edgar. 'What about Tuesday the twenty-seventh?'

'I opened the shop at seven and worked here until five-thirty. There's precious little time to be committing crimes in my line of work, I can tell you.'

'And you didn't have a break all day?'

'I had a lunch break at one. The missus covered for me.'

'And you've got no other help in the shop? It's just you and your wife?'

'There's a boy who helps on Saturdays. Hinders more than he helps, most days.'

'What about your children? Do they ever help in the shop?'

'No, they're too young. The oldest is only eight.'

'Do your children go to the local school, Bristol Road Juniors?'

'No. They go to St Alban's in Rottingdean. I want better for them. That's why I work all hours.'

From what Edgar had seen of prep schools, he doubted that the education was better, though it would certainly be different. He had won a scholarship to the local grammar school (the product of his mother's relentless drive for self-improvement) and his schooling had been excellent, if cheerless, but Max had left his public school without a single qualification (albeit with an impressive collection of card tricks).

'Thank you, Mr Gee,' he said. 'That'll be all for now.' He nodded at Bob to gather up the sweets. He half expected Sam Gee to complain about the 'for now' but the shopkeeper seemed lost in thought. As they reached the door, he called after them, 'Make sure you find the bastard.'

'We will,' Edgar promised him. 'We will.'

Edgar used the police box at the end of the road to telephone the station. He heard that Emma was on her way to Bristol Street Juniors, the school considered not good enough for the young Gees.

'What's she doing there?' he asked Bob. 'I thought she was seeing the grammar schools.'

'She must have had an idea,' said Bob, who was red-faced from the cold. 'A Holmes special.'

Edgar considered this. Initiative was all well and good but now was not the time to be chasing false trails. 'We'll meet her there,' he said. 'It's only round the corner.'

Bob grunted his assent and they set off through the

dirty snow, sometimes in single file, like a modern-day King Wenceslas and his page.

Bristol Road Juniors didn't have a flag to fly at half mast but there was, nevertheless, a palpable sense of sadness about the school. It was an ugly Victorian building, opening straight onto the street, with doors marked 'Boys' and 'Girls'. Emma was surprised, and not entirely pleased, to see Bob and DI Stephens loitering by the gate.

'We're going in that way.' She pointed at the word 'Girls'.

'Perhaps we should go in by the front door,' said DI Stephens mildly. He rarely rose to her challenges. Now he was asking, again without heat, what she was doing at the school.

Emma explained her hunch about the exchange between Annie and Mark. 'I mean, we never knew what the context was. Perhaps Annie was suggesting that they went to see someone at the school.'

'The witness said they quarrelled,' said Bob. Emma could see that he was not in the mood to accept any ideas that didn't appear on his to-do list.

'The witness was a ten-year-old boy.'

'He saw Annie push Mark.' That was the trouble with Bob, he had a memory like an elephant. Unfortunately he had an elephant's power of reasoning to go with it.

'Well, maybe they did argue. Maybe Mark didn't want to go to the school.'

DI Stephens cut in. 'It's an interesting idea, Emma. Have you any ideas why they would want to visit their old school? I mean, it was a winter's night, well past school hours, getting dark.'

Emma tried not to look at Bob's sceptical elephant's face. 'I think someone was influencing Annie. Someone who was behind her play-writing, her imaginative ideas. I've just been to the grammar school and I'm pretty sure it wasn't anyone there. The headmistress had her down as the scientific type, said she wanted to be a doctor. I think it's likely that she was influenced by someone here, maybe someone who taught her when she was younger.'

DI Stephens looked at her. He didn't ask whether she thought that this childhood mentor was also a killer. Instead he gestured towards the main entrance, flanked by two sooty pillars. 'Let's go in.'

The headmaster, Duncan Pettigrew, was a man whose face had already fallen into dispirited lines. Emma couldn't guess at his age: forty? fifty? sixty? Probably more than forty and less than sixty. Today, he looked as much like a bloodhound as was possible for a man in football kit.

'Can't get a male PT teacher,' he explained. 'Lost all the male teachers in the war, except those too ancient to run, and we haven't got them back. Lots of keen young women teachers but you can't expect ladies to go training with the First Eleven.'

'Where do you train?' asked Emma. As far as she could

see, the only playground was a small square of concrete flanked by dustbins.

'Queen's Park,' said Pettigrew. 'It's not far and I think we could all do with some fresh air. It's been a very difficult day.'

'Do you remember Annie and Mark well?' asked DI Stephens.

'Of course.' The lines around Pettigrew's mouth turned down even further. 'Annie was just about the brightest pupil we've ever had at the school. Mark, too, was a solid scholar. I thought they'd both go far, have great futures . . .' He looked at them mournfully.

'I'm sorry,' said DI Stephens, sounding it. 'It must be very hard for everyone at the school. Annie's siblings are here, aren't they?'

'Yes, Betty and Richard. They're not in today, of course. Betty's very like her sister, actually. Same quick mind.'

'We're looking again at the events of Monday afternoon,' said DI Stephens. 'Is there any chance that Annie and Mark could have visited the school, after school hours?'

'Visited the school?' The bloodhound lines turned upwards in surprise. 'This school?'

'We're just discounting possibilities.' DI Stephens was using his reassuring voice. 'Would the school have been open, say at five or half past?'

'I think so,' said Pettigrew. 'I left earlyish on Monday, about half past four, but there were still some staff members here. The caretaker usually locks up at six, unless we've got a concert or something of that sort. He lives next door.'

'Mr Pettigrew,' said Emma. 'When Annie was here, was there a particular teacher she was close to? We've heard that she wrote plays. Was there anyone who could have helped her? Inspired her?'

Pettigrew seemed to register Emma's presence for the first time. To her surprise, he attempted a sort of smile.

'There's Miss Young. She teaches top juniors and she has quite a way with the youngsters. Annie was close to her. I had heard that they were writing a play together.'

'Is Miss Young here today?'

'Yes. She insisted on coming in even though she was devastated by the news. She's a true professional.'

'Could I speak to her?' asked Emma.

Miss Young met them in her classroom. Her pupils were doing PT, the boys trudging up to Queen's Park with Mr Pettigrew, the girls in the gym. Miss Young was indeed young, about Emma's own age, in fact. She was also a beauty, with Pre-Raphaelite hair drawn back from a perfect oval face. Her classroom, too, in contrast to the rest of the school, was jewel-like, decorated with colourful paintings and hangings. Wind chimes glittered and the winter sun glowed through windows covered with coloured paper to give a stained-glass effect. Emma saw Bob blinking in a dazzled way. For some reason, the room and its occupant had the opposite effect on her; they made her feel brisk and coldly competent.

Outside she had asked DI Stephens if she could lead the interview and he had agreed. She had also suggested, as tactfully as could, that the presence of three police officers would be rather intimidating, so maybe Bob could . . . But Bob had flatly refused to go and the boss had backed him up. They'd stay in the background, he promised Emma, but maybe it wasn't a bad idea to show people how seriously they were taking the case.

Miss Young (Daphne) didn't seem intimidated at all events. She nodded sombrely when Emma introduced herself and turned limpid green eyes in the direction of the male officers.

'This must be so hard for you too.'

'It's our job,' said Emma. 'Miss Young, I believe that you were especially close to Annie Francis.'

She had half expected the teacher to deny this, to say that she treated all her pupils equally and had no favourites. Instead Daphne Young smiled sadly and sweetly. 'I was. She had great talent, Annie. Such imagination. I try to draw my pupils out, to find out what inspires them. Especially when they're maybe not getting that encouragement at home.'

Another disparaging comment about Annie's home environment. Emma was storing them up. She said, 'Annie's talent was for writing plays, I believe?'

Miss Young did not protest that Annie preferred the

sciences. Instead, to Emma's surprise, she drew out a folder from a pile on her desk.

'She wrote plays and stories too. I was just looking at these before you came. Morbid really. But reading them brought Annie back for moment.'

Emma looked at the first sheet of lined paper. The border was intricately decorated with pictures of unicorns and princesses in conical headgear. The writing was perfect primary-school script: 'The Wicked Stepdaughter'.

Emma started reading: 'It's the stepmother who's meant to be wicked but mine's just stupid, a fool who doesn't know what's coming to her. No, I'm the wicked one . . .'

Miss Young was saying, 'So imaginative. A retelling of the "Snow White" story with Snow White as the villain, planning to kill her stepmother. A really clever twist.'

Emma remembered Betty saying, 'Annie likes a twist.' She tried to keep the shock out of her voice. 'Wasn't that rather dark for a . . . How old was Annie when she wrote this?'

'She'd just come into my class. Ten. Maybe eleven. She was one of the oldest in the cohort.'

'So, at eleven, she wrote about a daughter killing her stepmother?'

Miss Young faced her serenely. 'Children's imaginations are dark, Sergeant Holmes. That's why they like fairy stories. Parents killing their children. The jealous stepmother. The princess dancing until she drops down dead. The Little Mermaid dying slowly for love. The wicked Queen demanding Snow White's heart. The stone falling on the bad mother and crushing her. The parents who want a baby and get a hedgehog instead. Life, death, birth, pain, happiness. It's all there.'

'Did you talk to Annie about these stories?'

'Of course. We talked about everything. She used to come here in the evenings sometimes and we'd talk. We were trying to write a play together. She was a better writer than me.'

Emma didn't look at her colleagues but she could feel their concentrated stares burning into her back.

'We're investigating Annie's movements on Monday night. We believe she may have come here.'

Miss Young met her gaze squarely, her huge eyes wide and guileless.

'I didn't see Annie on Monday night. I thought she might have come to see me, to work on the play, but she didn't.' Her voice faltered for the first time. 'I wish she had.'

'What did you do on Monday night?'

A faint suggestion of a raised chin but Daphne Young's voice was calm and pleasant when she replied, 'I worked here until six, when Mr James, the caretaker, locked up. I tidied the classroom, marked some books. I prefer to work here than at home.'

'Did anyone see you here?'

'Mr James. I think Mr Carew, the Class Five teacher, popped in at some point.'

Was Mr Carew one of those teachers too ancient to fight in the war? wondered Emma. She made a note to check. 'When Annie used to come to see you,' she said, 'did she bring Mark with her?'

'Sometimes. He was a nice boy. He didn't have Annie's originality but he was a sweet child.' A definite quaver now.

'Could I keep these?' Emma gestured towards the folder. 'And could I see the play that you were writing with Annie?'

Just for a second Miss Young hesitated. Then she rose and went to a filing cabinet, took a key from a fob in her pocket and opened it. She placed a yellow exercise book in front of Emma.

'I'd like it back, if possible. It's very precious to me.'

'You'll have it back in due course,' said Emma. Just one glance at the title had been enough.

The True Story of Hansel and Gretel.

CHAPTER 8

'Max. Dear boy. How wonderful to see you.'

The Great Diablo, resplendent in a moth-eaten fur coat, steamed through the empty auditorium, arms outstretched. The cast of *Aladdin*, halfway through a frustrating and protracted dress rehearsal, turned to stare at the apparition.

Max, who had been watching in costume from the front row, came to greet him.

'Careful, Diablo, you'll get greasepaint on you.'

'What's a bit of greasepaint between friends? Give me a cuddle, dear boy.'

Grinning, Max gave the old boy a hug. Despite everything, it was good to see him.

'Goodness me, is that Denton McGrew I see up there?' Diablo peered up at the stage. 'How are you, you old tart?'

'Bloody hell. The Great Diablo.' The Dame came forward, terrifying in striped stockings and a massive bustle. 'I thought you were dead.'

'No, I was in Hastings, dear boy. Easily mistaken. I'm going to be joining this merry band.'

'You're kidding.' McGrew closed his heavily mascaraed eyes in horror.

Roger Dunkley appeared from the wings. 'Boys and girls, meet the new Emperor of Peking.'

Diablo swept a magnificent bow. Max helped him get upright again.

Annette Anthony also came tripping forward. From this angle, thought Max, the famous Principal Boy legs had definitely seen better days.

'I think it's simply marvellous of you to help out. Will you be able to learn the lines in time?'

'Oh, don't worry about that, my dear.' Diablo beamed upwards. 'I'll just make 'em up as I go along.'

Max didn't dare look at Nigel Castle, staring open-mouthed from the stalls.

'You're not seriously saying you suspect her?'

They were back at the station. Emma and Bob were huddled around the two-bar fire, arguing; Edgar, still in his overcoat, was poring over the exercise book given to them by Miss Young.

'Why not?' Edgar could hear the irritation in Emma's voice. 'The crime scene was rigged to look like "Hansel and Gretel". The woman was writing a play with Annie based on "Hansel and Gretel". You heard her talking about the fairy stories. It was really creepy.'

'I didn't think so.' Bob, in turn, was sounding aggrieved. 'She was just being a good teacher, interested in her pupils and all that. Besides, she's got an alibi.'

'Until six o'clock. She may have planned to meet them somewhere else, strangled them and taken their bodies up to the Dyke later that night.'

'Can you really see her doing that?' Bob's voice was rising.

'Yes. You may have been taken in by that lovely-teacher act but I thought she was a very strange woman.'

'What do you mean, I may have been taken in?'

Edgar cut in. 'This isn't getting us anywhere. Emma, we have to be careful about saying things like "the scene was rigged to look like 'Hansel and Gretel'". That's your hunch, and a good one it is too, but it's not the only possible explanation for the sweets on the ground. But I agree with you. There was something odd about her manner. And this play . . .'

'What's it about?' Bob came to look over Edgar's shoulder and, after a few seconds, Emma joined him.

'Hansel and Gretel and they're both pretty unpleasant. Gretel is vain and self-obsessed. Hansel is just stupid. Anyway, both of them are planning to kill the other and blame it on the Witch Woman.'

'Like the Witch Man in the play,' said Bob.

'There are some really nasty bits. Listen to this. It's Gretel talking about her brother. "I just can't stand seeing that stupid face for a minute longer. He's always asking

'What shall we do, Gretel?' 'What's going on, Gretel?' One day I'm going to hold a pillow over his mouth until he never asks a question again." '

There was a silence. Edgar could hear the fire hissing and the sound of police-issue boots going up and down the stone stairs. Eventually Bob said, almost timorously, 'Do you think that's what Annie felt about Mark? I mean, everyone says she was the clever one . . .'

'I don't believe it,' said Emma. 'They were devoted friends.'

'Devoted friends fall out,' said Edgar. 'We've got to find out what happened after the quarrel in the street. Where did they go? Who did they see? We need to talk to the witnesses again, walk the streets, put ourselves in their shoes. Emma, you go to the library and get a book on fairy tales. I didn't recognise all of the stories Miss Young mentioned – the one about the hedgehog, for example. It's a long shot but there might be something there. Bob, we'll go to Queen's Park tomorrow. It's Saturday and the snow's clearing, there'll be lots of people about. Maybe someone saw something.'

Bob didn't protest that Saturday was his day off. He simply nodded and turned back to the exercise book. Edgar was grateful for his commitment – and Emma's too – but he must remember to give them some time off soon. No one can work effectively for days without a break. For his part, he felt as if his eyes were slowly turning inside out. The night on Mrs M's sofa had given him backache and his head was throbbing. Maybe he should eat something. It felt like years since the fried breakfast.

'Let's go to the Lyons',' he said. 'Have some food. Nobody can think straight on an empty stomach.'

Bob agreed immediately and went to get his coat. But Emma stayed staring at the book, at the clear round writing and the intricate drawings in the margin.

I just can't stand seeing that stupid face for a minute longer.

Max always knew that the day would end in a drinking session with Diablo. As they left the pier, the older man began to steer him, by imperceptible degrees, towards a 'cosy little pub' he knew. 'Just one for the road, dear boy.' Which road is that? thought Max. The road to ruin? But he followed Diablo through the Lanes towards a snug-looking corner building.

'The Bath Arms.' Diablo took Max's arm. 'They serve spirits.'

Of course they did.

But, as Max pushed his way through the crowd of after-work drinkers, he was surprised to see a tall, familiar figure at the bar.

'Ed! What's this? Hair of the dog?'

Edgar turned, blushing slightly. 'Hallo, Max. I'm not turning to drink. It's just . . . it's been a long day . . .'

'Never mind that,' said Max. 'I've got a surprise for you.'

But before he could say more, a rapturous cry of 'Edgar!

My dear chap!' filled the air. Edgar hardly had time to gasp before he was enveloped in the fur coat.

'Diablo!' Edgar emerged, spluttering. 'What are you doing here?'

'I'm in panto, my dear. The Emperor of Peking at your service.'

'The Emperor . . .' Edgar looked at Max. 'Isn't that . . . ?'

Max sighed. 'Yes, we're in *Aladdin* together. The previous Emperor disappeared on a drunken binge and Diablo stepped in.'

'Pros aren't as reliable as they used to be,' said Diablo. 'And they can't take their drink.' He downed his whisky and held out the glass for a refill.

'I thought you'd retired,' said Edgar, as Max turned back to the bar. 'You said that you were quite happy staying at Queenie's, helping out with the boarding house. Wild horses wouldn't tempt you back on stage, you said.'

'Old pros never really retire. You know that.'

'You said you couldn't remember the lines any more.'

'That's not a problem with panto,' said Diablo airily. 'You can say what you like. It's all nonsense anyway.'

Max returned with more drinks and they found themselves a corner table.

'This is jolly,' said Diablo. 'A Magic Men reunion.'

Edgar didn't know how he could refer so cheerfully to the unit to which all three had been seconded during the war. The Magic Men had been brought together by MI5 to use stagecraft against the enemy. Edgar had been the straight man, the regular soldier, but the others were all stage magicians. Max, of course, was a big star before the war. When he was in the army in Egypt, he had reputedly used misdirection and sleight-of-hand to great effect: dummy tanks, disappearing armies, the Suez Canal vanishing through clever use of arc lights. This was the story that had been sold to Edgar by the recruiting officer from MI5, that a camouflage group was needed to convince the Nazis that Scotland (so close to occupied Norway) was heavily defended. The other members of the group had been Tony Mulholland, a mesmerist with a battery of mind-control techniques, and The Great Diablo, who was already many years past his prime. The group had their successes – a full-size battleship constructed from an old pleasure cruiser – but their mission had ended in failure all the same. And none of it, in Edgar's opinion, had been exactly jolly.

'Ed's not having much fun,' said Max. 'He's involved in the case of the missing children. You may have read about it. Their bodies were found yesterday.'

Diablo's eyes filled with tears. 'Oh, my dear boy. How awful for you.'

'Worse for them,' said Edgar. But, maybe because Diablo's sympathy was so genuine, he ended up telling them slightly more than he should about the discovery on Devil's Dyke.

'You told me this last night,' said Max, when he got to the sweets. 'At Mrs M's.'

'Did I?' Edgar had completely forgotten. 'Well, what do you think?'

'Misdirection,' said Max. 'Smoke and mirrors. Classic magician's technique. Leads the eye away from the important place. The sweets are a false trail, mark my words.'

'This isn't a conjuring trick,' said Edgar, rather irritated by Max's airy tone. 'But it's true that the sweets have made people's imagination run riot. My sergeant thinks it's some sort of gruesome re-enactment of "Hansel and Gretel".'

'Do you really think that someone would kill two children just to illustrate a fairy tale?' asked Max.

'I don't know,' said Edgar. 'But it's a line of enquiry at present.' He suddenly noticed that Diablo had gone very pale.

'Are you all right, Diablo?'

'A fairy tale . . .' Diablo was distinctly blue about the lips.

Max hurried to get some water. 'Drink this, old boy.' Diablo reached out a shaking hand for the glass.

'I'm sorry,' said Edgar. 'It's a particularly ghastly case.'

'No.' Diablo shook his head violently. 'It's not that. It's just that it's happened before.'

'It was when I was a young pro. Before the war. The First World War. I was doing *The Babes in the Wood* in Hastings. I was the Demon King. Top of the bill. I was only in my thirties and I fancied myself in my cloak, twirling my moustache. Those were the days. The theatre packed every house, no nonsense about not drinking in the wings. There was a lovely little thing called Alice Dean playing Robin Hood. Oh, those legs in green tights! She wouldn't have anything to do with me at first but I think I would have won her over in the end if this hadn't happened . . . Anyway, there were two children in the pantomime, playing the Babes, you know. And one of them was this moppet called Betsy Bunning. You know the sort. She was fifteen, looked ten and acted like a thirty-five-year-old. Anyway, one day – I'll never forget it – it was the dress rehearsal. I came on stage ready to twirl my moustache and there she was, lying in her bower with her throat cut.'

'Good God,' said Max. 'Was she dead?'

Diablo took a gulp of whisky. 'Oh, she was dead all right. Her blood was running down the stage. It's a scene I'll never forget – Alice screaming, the child swinging to and fro, her dress soaked in blood.'

He stared into space, as if the crowded pub had become the bloodstained stage. Edgar asked, 'Did they find out who did it?'

Diablo came back to the present with a slight jump. 'Oh yes. It was a man called Ezra Nightingale. He was a writer, obsessed with fairy tales, the proper gruesome Grimm ones. Anyway, he befriended Betsy – the prosecution claimed it was a sexual thing but he swore he was just being kind – and then he killed her. He wanted to re-enact the original story, where the children are murdered and there are bloody footprints in the snow. He didn't approve of the pantomime version because it had a happy ending. Not a happy ending for poor Betsy, of course.'

'What happened to this man? Nightingale?' asked Edgar. He could be alive now, about Diablo's age, an old man but still obsessed, still dangerous. He'd have changed his name though . . .

'Oh, he was found guilty and went to the gallows,' said Diablo. 'He was hanged in 1913.'

CHAPTER 9

Aladdin: I don't want to go in there. It's all dark and creepy.

Abanazar: That's no way to talk about your uncle.

Aladdin: You're not my real uncle.

Abanazar: Of course I'm your uncle. Just look how alike we are. Both handsome, manly [*pause for laugh*], brave . . .

Aladdin: If you're so brave, why don't you go in the cave?

Abanazar: Two reasons. One, because the secret door can only be opened by an innocent boy called Aladdin.

Aladdin: That's a good reason. What's the second reason?

Abanazar: Because I'll kill you if you don't.

Stage darkens. Abanazar explodes firecrackers from sleeves.

It was the first night of *Aladdin*. The auditorium was full and there was an excited buzz that seemed to carry all the way through the wings and into the labyrinth of backstage corridors. It carried all the way into the Number One Dressing Room, where Max sat drinking black coffee and reading through the script. He knew his lines, of course; it was just a superstition of his to glance through the words before going on for the first time.

The script was quite funny – he had to give Nigel Castle that – even if Annette always ruined the snappy dialogue by simpering too much on 'manly' and wiggling her hips at 'innocent boy'. He could hear the opening number, 'Boys and Girls of Peking', booming through the loudspeaker. There was definitely a good audience out there tonight. Even the rather leaden dancers were getting applause, with shouts of 'Ooh' and 'Aah' for the more gymnastic stuff. Diablo was due on in a minute, walking in procession with his daughter, the Princess, being fanned by minions. The original Emperor had been carried in a sedan chair but one look at Diablo had forced Roger Dunkley to change this piece of business. 'Don't want my stagehands coming down with lumbago.'

Suddenly Max felt curious about Diablo's entrance. He was pretty sure that the old devil had something hidden up his voluminous sleeves. As far as Max could tell, he had made no effort to learn his lines, although Nigel Castle kept offering to go over them with him. 'Want to keep it fresh for the night,' Diablo told the scriptwriter airily. 'There's such a thing as over-rehearsing, y'know.'

Max put down the script and opened his door. He could hear the first number coming to an end. Twirl, spin, thump, turn, crescendo, eyes and teeth. He made his way up the wooden steps to the wings. 'Boys and girls of Peking. Come in!' Thunderous applause.

The assistant stage manager, sweating with ropes and pulleys, saw Max and looked anxious. It was rare for Max to come out of his dressing room early. Max gestured reassuringly. He could see Diablo, resplendent in purple robes, waiting stage right.

'Bow down for the Emperor of Peking and his daughter, Princess Jasmine.'

The actress playing Jasmine, a rather sweet girl called Hilda Thompson, gave Diablo an encouraging smile as they stepped onto the stage. There was no need for her to feel anxious. As soon as the old rascal had his feet on the boards he was transformed.

'Hallo, boys and girls. It's your old Emperor here!'

Max grinned in the darkness of the wings. He was pretty sure that this line wasn't in Nigel Castle's script, where the Emperor featured as a taciturn and tyrannical father.

'Welcome to Peking. And anyone caught peeking will be shot on sight. Especially if they're peeking at my lovely daughter. Isn't she beautiful?'

He leered into the stalls and the audience rewarded

him warmly, confident that they were in the hands of an expert. Aladdin's first words, 'Who is that girl?', were lost in the laughter, which served Annette right for not waiting long enough.

Still grinning, Max made his way back to his dressing room. Just time for a game of patience before his first entrance.

Edgar saw the lights from the pier as he made his way along the seafront. He was planning to take some flowers to Mrs M on his way home. The Christmas roses, bought by Emma at lunchtime, were already looking sad and wilted. It had been a frustrating day all round. In the morning he and Bob had trudged around Queen's Park asking tobogganing families if they had seen Annie and Mark on Monday evening. A few people knew the children, at least by sight ('Isn't it terrible? I don't feel safe letting the kids out of my sight') but no one remembered seeing them in the park that night. They spoke to several dog-walkers: a large man with a tiny poodle, a family with an ancient spaniel and a Great Dane that took up most of a house on the south side of the park. Although all of them had been out on Monday night, none of them had seen the children.

'Dog people only notice other dogs,' said Bob. 'My mum's the same. She only talks to people with Jack Russells.'

Edgar's mother had never owned a dog though

he'd longed for one as a boy. Sometimes, walking home from school, he'd imagined that he was accompanied by a large Alsatian called Rex. He wished that Annie and Max had owned a dog like that, one that would have ripped the throat out of anyone who had dared approach them.

Emma had spent the day researching. She hadn't complained but Edgar knew that she'd rather be there on the streets with them. Was he being patronising, trying to spare her the slog and the frustration, treating her as fragile because she was a woman? Or was it just because she was so good at the background stuff, so meticulous and thorough? In his experience, it was almost impossible to get this sort of thing right.

In any case, Emma had done her work well and, in addition to the roses, Edgar was now weighed down by a carrier bag containing several large books plus an archive copy of the *Argus* from December 1912. Diablo's killer might have gone to the gallows but Edgar still thought it might be worth reading about the case. The parallels were tenuous but nevertheless slightly too close for comfort: a dead child, a fairy tale, a seaside town in pantomime season. Even the weather. A phrase from Diablo's account had come back to haunt Edgar in the night. *Bloody footprints in the snow.* Could it be the combination of children and snow had triggered a murderous reaction in someone somewhere? He decided to add 'The Babes in the Wood' to his reading list.

He'd sent Bob and Emma home after lunch but he had stayed on, going over evidence, trying to fit the pieces together. Annie wrote plays in which children killed or were killed. Then she was murdered and a supposed clue left in her grave. Were the sweets meant to point the way to Sam Gee or to something altogether more complex and sinister? What was the role of the teacher who had befriended her or of the middle-aged man who staged her dramas? Who was writing the script here? Was it Annie, the clever girl who had trained a troupe of children to act out her fantasies, not to mention the loyal assistant who was killed at her side? Or was there another hand behind the scenes, another player yet to make their entrance?

The boarding house was quiet. Presumably all the lodgers were either in the pantomime or in other Christmas shows at the Hippodrome or Theatre Royal. But there was a light on in the front room and, before long, Edgar could hear footsteps coming towards him. He composed his face into an ingratiating smile. He was sure that the landlady would invite him in, perhaps for a drink.

So, all in all, he was disappointed when the door opened and a sullen-faced girl in a maid's outfit stared out at him.

'Good evening. Is Mrs . . .' He suddenly realised that he didn't know what the M stood for. 'Is the landlady in?'

'No. She's gone to the pantomime. On the pier.'

Of course. Mrs M would not want to miss Max's first night. He suddenly felt stupid, standing on the doorstep with his bunch of flowers like an old-fashioned stage-door Johnny.

'These are for her.' He offered the flowers. 'Can you tell her that they're from the man who stayed here on Thursday night, to say thank you?'

The maid looked at him blankly. There was no sign that she'd understood – or even heard – his message.

'Well, goodnight then.' The door was slammed shut before he got to the bottom of the steps. Edgar turned his collar up against the wind and began the long walk home.

The girl lay cringing upon the slab. Max waved his green cloak, letting the stage lights chase the shimmering garment, leading the audience's eyes up into the gods where he wanted them.

'If you won't go into the cave, then I'll send you there myself.'

'Oh, please don't, Uncle.'

Max threw the cloak over Annette's huddled figure. Grinning maniacally up into the royal box, he masked her just long enough for her to find the hidden catch in the papier mâché boulder. Goodness knows they'd rehearsed it often enough but Annette was a clumsy performer and frequently mistimed her disappearance, leaving him to twirl and ad-lib until the box closed and he was able to remove his cloak with a triumphant villain's 'Ha ha'. He thought of Ruby and how well she would have performed this trick. But Ruby was not going to have a career as a magician's assistant. Not if he could help it.

But tonight Annette found the handle quickly. The rock didn't even shake as she settled down inside it. Max stepped away as the cymbals crashed and the audience exhaled in a single, delirious 'Oooh.'

CHAPTER 10

The pipes had frozen again, so Edgar's flat was as cold as the streets outside. He picked up the post in the communal hall, noting with a lurch of the heart that there was a letter from Ruby. He let himself into his flat, keeping his coat on. There was a gas heater somewhere; he'd find it and then he'd sit and read Ruby's letter. The heater was the old-fashioned kind with a Calor gas cylinder. When he lit it, there was a blue flame and a pungent smell of gas, adding to the permanent aroma that hung around the flat however often he opened the windows. The actual temperature didn't seem to change that much. Edgar found a heel of bread and some cheese, fetched the eiderdown from his bed and settled down on the sofa.

Ruby's writing was flowing and bold; sometimes there were only two or three words a line, at other times the words ran into each other and bunched up at the edge of the page.

'Darling Edgar,' he read. Well, that was something,

unless Ruby had become the kind of show-business girl who called everyone 'darling'.

Darling Edgar,

Well, this show is just about the pits. Cinderella is forty-five if she's a day and Buttons is an awful lech. I'm a village girl dancing round the maypole in the first scene, a rat in the transformation scene and a wedding guest for the reveal. We're at the end of the pier – the theatre's been blown up, burnt down, swept away by a hurricane but it's still there. My digs are OK, the landlady's very kind, but Worthing is SO BORING. Honestly, there's nothing to do once you've seen all the shows at the flicks and walked up and down the promenade a hundred times.

How are you? When are you coming to see me? I often think about how much fun we had that day at the ice rink. I feel a long way away from everyone sometimes. Mummy and Daddy came to see me last week and that was nice. I got a postcard from Max too. Well, hey ho, back to rehearsals. The show must go on even if you're just a dancing rat.

With love from

Ruby

Edgar leant back against the sofa cushions. He couldn't decide whether he felt better or worse after reading Ruby's letter. It was dated Thursday 29th, so Ruby wouldn't have known about the children's bodies being found. But she would have known about them being missing if she ever looked at a paper, which he doubted. Even so, he felt that she should have known and asked about his work first rather than plunging straight into how awful the show was and what a lech Buttons was. (How old was Buttons exactly? Was he the sort of lech who could safely be ignored?) Some things about the letter just sounded like the outpourings of a spoilt schoolgirl. Worthing is boring but Mummy and Daddy have been down and taken her out for the day. But even this is misdirection. Ruby's father is not the man she calls Daddy but Max, who deigned to send her a postcard. This makes everything more difficult for Edgar, of course. Can he really have a relationship with his best friend's daughter? Were he and Ruby having a relationship? She had called him 'darling' and asked when she was going to see him. And she had mentioned the day at the ice rink. On the whole, he thought he felt better.

He had met Ruby when she was Max's assistant for a season. He hadn't know then that she was Max's daughter (and nor had Max) but, even then, she had seemed part of Max's world, under his protection. That summer season had ended in tragedy but, from the wreckage, Edgar managed to maintain some contact with Ruby. They had been out together twice. The first time was to the cinema, when they had both spent much of the evening avoiding talking about murder. The second time had been magic. They had gone to the SS Brighton ice rink and it had been like being in heaven for a day. Ruby clinging to his arm, her cheeks pink, her hair flying. The music playing, the ice gleaming, the moments when he could actually put his arm round Ruby's waist. He could skate quite well (he'd been taught by a Swedish sailor in Norway) and he'd enjoyed being the teacher, the one who stopped Ruby from falling, who encouraged her to glide out on her own. 'The strong arm of the law,' she'd laughed as he had scooped her up just in time, swinging her into a waltzing turn that made her breathless. Afterwards they had gone for chips and hot chocolate. And then he'd kissed her.

Did this make Ruby his girlfriend? He isn't sure. Apart from the inconveniences of her parentage, she is ten years younger than him, childish in some ways, frighteningly adult in others. And, anyhow, he is no position to be asking himself questions like 'Is she my girlfriend?' as if he's a character in one of those 'real life' magazines Lucy used to read. He is a policeman and he has to catch a murderer. Real life is serious.

He put the letter aside and turned to the books he had brought home. There were *Grimms' Fairy Tales*, a newer book called *The Secret Life of Children's Stories* and a rather sickly-looking tome called *Bedtime Stories for Little Ones*. If he was going to understand this case, he had a shrewd feeling that he would need to understand these narratives. He opened *Grimms' Fairy Tales* and searched for 'Hansel and Gretel'.

Although he had a vague memory of the story (children, forest, gingerbread, witch), he'd forgotten a lot of it.

Hansel and Gretel have a wicked stepmother. She tells their father to take them into the wood and lose them. He does so (why?) but Hansel fools him by laying a trail of white pebbles that leads them back home. The stepmother forces the father to abandon them a second time; again they come home, and find the doors locked. They wander into the forest until they come to a house made of gingerbread. They are starving and so start to eat the roof. The owner of the cottage, a witch, comes out and captures them. She intends to keep them in a cage until they become fat enough to eat. Again, Hansel saves them by putting a bone through the bars of the cage. The short-sighted witch, thinking that the bone is Hansel's finger and that the children are still too thin to make a good meal, keeps feeding them. Eventually, though, she loses patience and takes Hansel out of the cage, intending to eat him. Hansel says the oven isn't working and persuades the witch to look inside. When she does so, he pushes her in and she is burnt to death. They children then go home and find the wicked stepmother dead. They and their father live happily ever after.

Edgar thought of the snowy ground on the top of Devil's Dyke, the brightness of sweet wrappers leading their way to the dead children. The sweet trail didn't save this Hansel and Gretel. The wicked witch had done her worst and little bodies lay in the snow, curiously peaceful as they lay there turned towards each other. In Annie's play the siblings had hated each other. Edgar hoped that wasn't true in real life. He hoped that they'd been able to get some comfort from each other's presence, even in death.

He flicked through the other stories and a shape caught his eye, an illuminated 'A' made to look like a flowering tree, its roots snaking down through the page. It reminded him of Annie's margin drawings. The title of the story was 'The Juniper Tree'. 'A woman,' he read, 'wished for a child as red as blood and as white as snow.' For a moment he sat staring at the page, as the words 'blood' and 'snow' seemed to twist and mutate before his eyes.

It was a horrible story. The woman has a son but dies shortly afterwards and is buried underneath a juniper tree. Her husband grieves for a long time, then gets married again. His second wife gives birth to a daughter, Marlinchen, but she hates her stepson and plots to kill him. To this end she offers him an apple from a box and, when he reaches in to get it, slams the heavy lid on him, beheading him. She then takes a bandage and ties his head back on. She tells Marlinchen to ask her brother for the apple, and if he doesn't give it to her, to give him a good box on the ear. Marlinchen asks for the apple, and getting no reply, boxes him on the ear. The head falls off and Marlinchen is horrified, believing that she has killed her brother. Her mother comforts her and says that they will tell the father that the boy has gone to stay with his uncle. The stepmother then turns the boy's body into a stew, which the father eats, pronouncing it delicious.

Marlinchen, however, keeps the bones left over from the meal and buries them beneath the juniper tree. Immediately a beautiful bird flies out of the tree. The bird goes and sings a song to a goldsmith about its cruel death at the hands of its mother. The goldsmith gives the bird a golden chain because the song is so beautiful. The bird then sings the same song to a shoemaker, who gives it a pair of red shoes, and to a miller, who gives it a millstone. It then flies back home and sings its song in the tree. The father goes out to see who is singing such a beautiful song and the golden chain falls about his neck. The bird sings again and Marlinchen goes out and the red shoes fall to her. All this time the stepmother is complaining of heat, claiming she has hellfire burning in her veins. The bird sings for a third time and the stepmother goes out, whereupon the millstone drops on her, crushing her to death. When Marlinchen and her father come out of the house, they find that the tree has disappeared in a puff of smoke. When the smoke clears, they see the son standing there. Then they all go inside and live happily ever afterwards.

Edgar sat back and let the book fall to the floor. Despite the cold, it felt as if his veins too were pulsing with hellfire. Who on earth would let a child read this stuff? He remembered Miss Young recounting the plots of various fairy tales. *Parents killing their children. The jealous stepmother. The princess dancing until she drops down dead. The Little Mermaid dying slowly for love. The wicked Queen demanding Snow*

White's heart. The stone falling on the bad mother and crushing her. All horror is here: the longing for a child, the untimely death, the unnatural mother, murder, cannibalism, cruel retribution. Even the wicked touch about the mother making the daughter think that she was the one who killed the boy. It's all misdirection, sleight of hand, smoke and mirrors. But, when the smoke clears away, the dead walk again.

Leafing through *The Secret Life of Children's Stories*, he found a section on 'The Juniper Tree'. Marlinchen, he read, might be a corruption of Mary Magdalene and the boy coming to life could be seen to mirror the Resurrection. The millstone too has biblical echoes ('better a millstone round the neck than to cause a child to sin') and the tree could represent the Garden of Eden with the stepmother in the age-old role of Eve, the first temptress. This struck Edgar as a rather far-fetched explanation. Wasn't the story just about plain old evil, dressed up with fantastical birds and just punishments falling from the sky?

He couldn't face reading any more stories so he just flicked through the rest of the pages looking at the illustrations. Princesses on golden thrones, ghostly ships rising out of the sea, creatures in thorny forests, blood, snow, poison, apples. Hearts, clubs, diamonds, spades. A wave of nausea swept over him and he closed his eyes. Blood on the snow. The bird singing in the tree. The golden apple. The poisoned shoes.

The heavy scent in the room was lulling him to sleep. *Lie down and I'll give you rest for ever.* He sat up with a jolt and switched off the gas heater. Then he opened the window, gulping down the freezing night air. That was a close thing. Detective found gassed in his room. He could imagine the headlines. Would Ruby come to his funeral? Would they think he had done it on purpose, tormented by his failure to find the Hansel and Gretel killer? Well, he wasn't ready to give up yet. Edgar pushed the heater through the kitchen and out into the yard. It sat there, like a misshapen troll crouching in the shadows. If there had been a juniper tree handy, Edgar would have buried it underneath.

'Fantastic show, old boy.'

Diablo stood in the doorway, wearing a red dressing gown over his Emperor's robes and a triumphant smile on his face.

'The audience loved it.'

Of course they loved it, Max wanted to say. It's a pantomime. They'd love it even if the actors just stood on stage endlessly repeating 'Behind you' and 'Oh no you don't'. But there was something endearing about Diablo's delight. He might be a veteran of countless shows but he wasn't immune to first-night excitement.

'You were the star, of course,' Diablo was saying. 'The way they cheered you at the end.'

'They booed me.'

'Of course they booed you. You're the villain! But they loved you all the same.'

Actually, the boos and hisses had come as rather a surprise. He understood that they were in the tradition but he was so used to coming on to applause, even to a whoop or two, that the audience's delighted hatred had slightly taken him aback. They had cheered at the end but during the show his every entrance – from the villain's stage left – had been greeted with a bovine chorus of booing. Max had wanted to whip off the green cape and say, 'It's me. You love me. Remember?' Just goes to show how the business makes a fool of you in the end. It was never him they loved anyway, just the idea of Max Mephisto, the great magician. And Diablo was right, the boos were a tribute of sorts.

'I thought the Emperor was a bit of a favourite too.'

Diablo looked modest. 'Well, the old jokes always go down well with this sort of crowd.'

'What was Nigel Castle saying to you after the curtain call?'

'Nigel who?'

'The scriptwriter.'

'Oh, just something about my lines. I told him not to worry, I'd improved them if anything.'

Max would have given much to listen to this exchange. Diablo's next line, though, was not a surprise.

'Fancy coming for a snifter? There's a crowd of us going to the Pavilion Tavern.'

Max was impressed at the speed with which Diablo had acquired drinking companions. All the same, a solitary scotch in his room was looking more appealing by the second.

'I think I'll just head straight back to my digs,' he said. 'I don't really feel like company.'

The expression on Diablo's make-up-streaked face was surprisingly kind. 'Don't take this case of Edgar's to heart, old boy. Terrible things do happen in the world.'

'I know they do.'

'And, when they do, the only answer is to get drunk.'

It was an answer, thought Max, as he walked back along the seafront, but not a wholly satisfying one. There was something tempting about the idea of the Pavilion Tavern, the warm fug of congratulation and strong spirits. But, in the end, he'd still have to go back to his room with the cold radiator and the knowledge that the morning was only a few hours away. He thought of Ruby. Her first night was next week. What would she do after the show? He was sure that there would be a crowd of dancing page-boys who'd be only too happy to take her out for a celebratory drink. He imagined Edgar hovering nervously on the edge of the group. On the one hand, he wanted to say to Ruby that Edgar was worth a million of the stage-school types she'd come across in the business. On the other, he wanted to tell Edgar that if he laid a finger on his daughter he'd cut him into two without the help of magic. It was hell being a father. The trouble was, he hadn't had much practice. He had only become aware of Ruby's existence a year ago.

At Upper Rock Gardens he headed straight for the stairs but a voice called from the back of the house, 'Mr M? Is that you?'

'Just going up to bed, Mrs M.'

The landlady appeared in the doorway of what she called 'the snug'. She was wearing a midnight-blue dress that enhanced the impressive contours of her figure. Her hair was piled on top of her head and he could see the glitter of earrings. Her theatre-going outfit, he realised.

'Care for a drink to celebrate the success of the first night?'

'Did you enjoy it?'

'You were the best Abanazar I've ever seen.'

'Have you seen many?'

She laughed, a full-throated guffaw that sent the chandelier twinkling. It was a long time since Max had heard a woman laugh like that.

'To tell you the truth, darling, you were the first.'

He moved towards her. 'Perhaps just a quick drink then.'

He had always enjoyed being the first.

CHAPTER 11

Edgar shared his weekend reading with the team at the Monday meeting. He also told them about the murder of Betsy Bunning in 1912. Ever literal, Bob couldn't see the connection.

'I mean, they found out who did it. This Nightingale character. And he was hanged. That's the end of it.'

Emma was poring over the archive edition of the *Argus*.

'Ezra Nightingale had a son, aged ten. He would be nearly fifty now, if he's still alive.'

'And he decided to take up where his dad left off?' Bob's voice was incredulous but he was overdoing it. Emma was irritated. Edgar could tell by the flush on the back of her neck.

'We shouldn't make too much of this,' he said. 'But there are similarities. The theatrical setting. The whole fairy-tale thing. I think it's worth considering.'

'What about the man with the theatre in his garage?'

said Emma. 'Could he be the right age? To be Nightingale's son, I mean.'

Edgar thought of Brian Baxter, the neat little man in collar and tie. 'I took him for a bit older. He said he was retired. But he could have taken early retirement, I suppose. I think it's worth going to see him again in any case.'

'I think we're making too much of these stories.' Bob gestured towards the books on Edgar's desk. 'I mean, all children like fairy tales. They don't *mean* anything.'

Edgar thought of his ghastly hour with 'The Juniper Tree', the innocent deadly words seeping into his skull as the gas leaked into the air. He would like to think that Bob was right, that the fairy tales were a false trail, misdirection. And yet . . . the line of sweets in the snow, Annie's stories of death and sibling rivalry, Miss Young's voice as she enumerated the horrific plots . . .

Emma cut in. 'I found the story about the hedgehog. It's a Grimm's fairy tale called "Hans My Hedgehog".'

'Really?' said Edgar. 'It wasn't in my book.'

'It's not in all the anthologies. But I found it in an old book in my parents' library.'

Edgar tried not to look too interested. Emma rarely mentioned her family but it was obvious they were well off. A library, eh?

Emma took out a mottled book with roughly cut pages. She turned to the page marked by a piece of ribbon.

'A merchant and his wife are desperate for a child. The man says he'll be happy with a son, even if it's a hedgehog. Then he goes home and finds that his wife has given birth to baby that's a hedgehog from the waist up.'

'Painful,' said Bob. Emma ignored him.

'The hedgehog grows up to be a brave little boy and goes off to seek his fortune. He saves a king's life and, in return, the king promises his daughter. The king changes his mind so the hedgehog pricks his daughter till she bleeds. Then he saves a second king, who also offers his daughter but keeps to his promise. On the wedding night, Hans asks for a fire to be lit, steps into it, sheds his hedgehog skin and – *voilà* – a handsome prince.'

Emma showed them an illustration of a demonic little creature with snout and prickles, wearing red trousers and carrying a set of bagpipes. There's a second picture of a golden-haired prince and princess before a castle. A spiny mess in the background is obviously meant to represent the discarded skin.

'He played the bagpipes,' explained Emma. 'I'm not quite sure why.'

'So it's worse than they think,' said Bob. 'He's not just a hedgehog, he's a Scottish hedgehog.'

'It's got a lot of the traditional themes,' said Edgar. 'The longing for a child, promises kept and broken, retribution, transformation, rebirth.' He paused, wondering if he should go into the imagery of the hedgehog pricking the false princess until she bled.

'Of course, there's a Freudian interpretation too,' said Emma briskly. 'The wedding night, blood on the sheets and all that. It's a bit like the Little Mermaid bleeding as soon as she gets legs. I'm interested, though, that Miss Young read this story to her class, given that it's so hard to get hold of.'

'Yes,' said Edgar. 'We should certainly see Miss Young again.'

Bob was flicking through the pages of the book with a disgusted face. 'Thank God my parents never read to me. That's all I can say.'

Max walked to the theatre on Monday with a distinct spring in his step. The night with Joyce had been extremely enjoyable, so much so that they had repeated the experience on Sunday. Max was even thinking about ignoring his 'no landladies' rule and allowing the affair to continue until the end of the run. He had to admit that this thought was partly – but not entirely – influenced by the fact that Joyce's bedroom was miraculously warm *all night long*.

'The radiators upstairs don't work very well,' she told him airily, putting on her make-up at her kidney-shaped dressing table. 'I expect it gets quite cold at night.'

'It does,' Max assured her.

'Well, darling . . .' She gave him a bold look in the mirror. 'The temperature was certainly torrid in here.'

She was cool though. When the other lodgers were around, it was still 'Mr M' and not 'darling'. He'd even deigned to have breakfast this morning and Mrs M's presence certainly lent a frisson to the bacon and fried bread. So, all in all, things were looking up. The *Evening Argus* wasn't printed on Sundays but the pantomime had earned some very good reviews from the national press. Roger Dunkley would be delighted. The *Sunday Times* had called it 'everything a panto should be'. Max was sure that this line would find itself on the billboards before long.

Sure enough, he was met at the stage door by the director himself, waving an early copy of the *Argus*. 'It's a love letter,' he said. 'An actual love letter.'

'Really?' Max tried to edge past. He liked good reviews as much as the next pro but he liked to read them in private with a whisky or a black coffee to hand. He wondered if he could send one of the ASMs out for supplies.

'Listen to what it says about you, Max. Here it is . . . "Legendary magician Max Mephisto casts a powerful spell as Abanazar, the villain of the piece. His stage presence is mesmerising – I wondered if it was almost too sinister for his young audience – and the magic tricks performed with his usual aplomb. Altogether a sparkling production." '

Roger looked expectantly at Max.

'Almost too sinister?'

'Oh, that . . .' The director waved the words away. 'You're meant to be sinister. You're the villain. It's a humdinger of a review. And it's the local paper that brings in the local crowds. The reviewer even had a good word to say about old Diablo: "Veteran music-hall star The Great Diablo steals the first scene." He'll love that, the old ham.'

Roger exited chuckling. Max walked slowly towards his dressing room. Roger was right, it was an excellent review, but, even so, the faintest hint of criticism caught in his teeth like a piece of Mrs M's fried bread. Almost too sinister? Had he judged it wrongly for the family audience, so different from the normal variety crowd? Had scores of children gone home to nightmares about the tall green magician who could make people disappear beneath his magic cloak?

He sent Sid, an obliging ASM, to the Italian cafe to get him a coffee. Then he lit a cigarette and sat at his dressing table to read the rest of the reviews, thoughtfully left there by Roger. He could see why the director was so pleased. The production was praised on all sides; even Annette came away with nothing worse than 'the usual rather wooden Principal Boy' and 'seemingly rather overawed by the occasion'. He was variously 'brilliant', 'delightfully villainous' and 'the perfect Abanazar'. Even so, the local paper's words kept coming back to him. Almost too sinister. Should he lighten things for the matinee audience today? Come on beaming and shouting 'Hallo, boys and girls' like Diablo?

'Hallo, darling boy. Reading the ghastly old reviews?' The old ham himself was standing in the doorway.

'They're not ghastly at all. Have you read them?'

'Just skimmed through them, dear boy. At my age you don't take much notice of reviewers.'

Max didn't believe a word of it. He was sure that Diablo would like to get 'The Great Diablo steals the first scene' embroidered on his emperor's robes.

'Anyway Roger the Dodger is pleased.' Diablo sat down heavily on the small sofa (a perk for heading the bill). 'And it gets that tedious scriptwriter off my back.'

Max doubted this. He was sure that Nigel Castle would hound Diablo until the end of the run, waving the script in front of him.

'Did you have a good night on Saturday?' Max asked.

'Tolerable, dear boy. Tolerable. They're a nice crowd. Little Hilda is a sweetheart. A bit like your Ruby, don't you think?'

Max said nothing, although the resemblance hadn't escaped him. Diablo was still talking, stretched out at his ease, feet (in slightly threadbare velvet slippers) up on the sofa.

'And even Annette is a nice girl when you get to know her. And, of course, Denton and I go way back.'

Max remembered Diablo greeting the Dame with slightly ironical affection. 'Oh yes, I forgot that you knew each other. Have you been on the bill with him before?'

Diablo's eyes bulged slightly. 'Many times. But the first time was in the pantomime that I was telling you about. *Babes in the Wood* in Hastings. When that poor girl was killed.'

Max stared. Like many pros, Denton McGrew could be any age but he doubted if he was more than sixty.

'He was in that show with you? Before the first war?'

'Yes. He was the other Babe, you see. The boy Babe.'

And Max thought of Denton McGrew last night, dressed in his voluminous skirts, throwing sweets down to the audience, that cascade of glittering pink and white, caught by the children's eager hands.

CHAPTER 12

They hadn't warned Brian Baxter that they were coming but he was ready for them all the same, once again dressed in a suit and tie as if for a day at the office. Edgar saw Bob looking at the neat little man and coming up with the worst of conclusions. For his part he thought Brian odd but not exactly sinister. If anything, he looked sad, ushering them into the spotless sitting room and saying, 'I thought you'd be back.'

'And why was that, Mr Baxter?'

'Because they're dead, aren't they? This is a murder enquiry now.' Brian took out a neatly folded handkerchief and dabbed his eyes although, as far as Edgar could see, they weren't wet. When he spoke again, though, his voice was distinctly shaky.

'I kept hoping, you know, that you'd find them alive. That they'd . . .'

'That they'd what?' It would be interesting to know where Brian had thought the children might be. After a moment's pause, he said, 'That they'd gone to their grandparents or something.'

Edgar let it go, though he was sure that this was not what the man had meant. He said, 'As you say, Mr Baxter, this is now a murder investigation and we're talking to anyone who knew the children, hoping to throw some light on their movements on the night of the twenty-sixth of November.'

He had meant to frighten Brian slightly with the official language and with the presence of the silently glowering Bob but the speech seemed to have the opposite effect. Brian drew himself up, every inch the respectable citizen, and, putting away the handkerchief, looked him squarely in the eye.

'What is it you want to know?'

'When was the last time you saw Annie and Mark?'

'I told you, at the weekend.'

'They disappeared on the Monday. Did you see them on Saturday or Sunday?'

'It must have been Saturday. Annie's parents don't like her to go out on a Sunday. They're quite religious, I think.'

'So why did Annie come to see you that Saturday?'

'She had some homework she wanted to do. Like I said, it was difficult for her to work at home. I don't think there was much space. She liked it here because she could look at my encyclopaedias.' He indicated a set of red hardbacks that took up a whole shelf of the bookcase.

'What subject was she studying that Saturday?'

'History, I think. Yes. She wanted to look up something about the Romans.'

Volume eight, thought Edgar, RA to TR. His parents had owned a similar set and he never forgot the thrill of the arbitrary juxtapositions, Boadicea next to Bob Cat, Henry VIII on the same page as Henley Regatta. He understood exactly why Annie had wanted to study in this house.

'You said she wanted to tell you about her latest play. Do you remember what it was about?'

Brian frowned. 'I think it was something about a Witch. No, a Witch Man. It struck me as a bit dark for a child.'

'Her other plays hadn't been dark?'

'No, they were about fairies and goblins. You know, suitable things for children.'

You wouldn't say that if you'd read 'The Juniper Tree', thought Edgar. Aloud, he said, 'You said that it was a teacher who first heard about the theatre in your garage. Do you remember the teacher's name?'

He knew the answer already and wasn't surprised to see Brian's face infused with a schoolboy's blush. 'Yes. A lovely young woman. Her name was Young. Miss Daphne Young.'

The lovely Miss Young seemed a lot less lovely on a busy Monday morning. Emma interviewed her in the cloakroom and through the glass pane in the door Miss Young could see her class disporting themselves under the ineffectual control of the head boy and girl.

'The trouble is, they're the same age,' she said apologetically to Emma. 'The class hasn't got any respect for them. It's not like this with the younger children.'

Emma watched as paper darts flew through the air. The head boy was actually cowering under the desk. She doubted if even the infants held him in much respect.

'I've been reading Annie's play,' she said.

'Have you?' The teacher looked genuinely pleased. 'Don't you think it's terribly good?'

'I don't know about that,' said Emma. 'It's strong stuff.'

'But such impressive writing for a thirteen-year-old,' said Miss Young. 'I thought it was exceptional.'

'Weren't you at all worried by the content?' asked Emma. 'Gretel hating her brother and planning to kill him?'

'It's the genre,' Miss Young protested. As I said to you, fairy stories are very bloodthirsty.'

'How did Annie really get on with Mark?' asked Emma. 'Everyone said they were friends but was there ever any animosity? Did they ever fall out?'

Daphne Young stared at her. 'Do you mean to say that you've taken it literally? That you actually think that Annie wanted to kill Mark?' Her voice rose almost hysterically.

'Well, how did you take it?' asked Emma.

'It's a play.' Daphne spoke very slowly, as if to an idiot. 'A story. That's all it is.'

'And do stories never tell us anything about the writer's state of mind?'

'What do you think? That Annie killed Mark? Is that the official police theory?'

'We're just examining every line of evidence,' said Emma. 'And that play is evidence. She was halfway through writing it when she died.'

'She wrote it to be performed, not to be analysed like some undergraduate thesis.'

'I wanted to talk to you about that. I understand that it was you who introduced Annie to Brian Baxter.'

Daphne's eyes were bright with scorn now. She tossed back her Pre-Raphaelite hair. 'Oh, is he your number-one suspect? Well, it makes sense, I suppose. Lonely old man living alone. I know what the police are like.'

'Just tell me how you got to know Mr Baxter.'

Daphne took a deep breath, composing herself. A wodge of wet blotting paper hit the window with a splat.

'One of the dinner ladies here is a neighbour. She knew his wife, I believe. She told me about the theatre. I thought it would be interesting for the children so I took a small group along.'

'Including Annie?'

'Yes. She was already really interested in the stage. She wanted to be an actress and director.'

'Really? Her headmistress said she wanted to be a doctor.'

'Oh, for goodness' sake.' More hair-tossing. 'That's typical of the grammar school. No imagination. Annie was an artist. I could see her being a writer, an actress or a director. Never a doctor.'

'Did you know that Annie visited Mr Baxter often?'

'I think she mentioned it, yes. I thought it was nice. As I say, he was lonely.' She looked defiantly at Emma, daring her to see anything sordid in the relationship.

'Mr Pettigrew said that you and Annie were writing the Hansel and Gretel play together,' said Emma. 'Is that true?'

She had meant to jolt the teacher but Daphne just smiled. 'We said that we were writing it together but really it was all Annie. She wrote it all. I just listened to her ideas, suggested stories she might read. That sort of thing.'

'I've been reading some of the stories you mentioned the other day,' said Emma. ' "Hans My Hedgehog", for example.'

'Oh, you found that one did you? It's hard to track down. What did you think?'

'I thought it was weird,' said Emma. 'What did Annie make of it?'

'She loved it. It was very appropriate for Annie, that story.'

'In what way?'

'Well, she was a bit of a bagpipe-playing hedgehog, wasn't she?'

'What do you mean?'

'Oh, I'll leave you to work that one out,' said Daphne, smiling serenely as the noises from next door reached riot pitch.

*

On her way out, Emma thought to call on Mr Carew, the Class Five teacher, the man who could apparently give Daphne Young an alibi for the Wednesday night. She found him reading the *Manchester Guardian* whilst his class ran around the concrete playground.

'PT,' he said vaguely, 'or something like that.'

'Are they having a race?'

'Nothing so vulgarly competitive. It's like the Caucus Race in *Alice in Wonderland*.'

'All must have prizes?'

'That's right. I like a girl who knows her children's literature.'

You don't know the half of it, thought Emma. She realised immediately why Mr Carew had not left teaching to fight in the war. His left leg stuck out stiffly in front of him and a walking stick leant against his chair. He saw her looking and smiled.

'Lost it in August 1918. Any earlier and I could have saved myself a lot of bother.'

'How long have you been teaching here?'

'About twenty years. The head before Pettigrew was a real tartar. I felt I had to stay just to protect the children from him. Pettigrew's all right though. He wants to give these children a chance. Most of them will leave school at twelve or thirteen, half of them have parents who can't read; even today we have children take time off to help with the fishing boats.'

Emma looked at the children trotting around the

playground. Many had stopped running altogether and were walking along chatting but a few dogged souls were still running, round and round, kicking the wall to show when they'd finished a lap. Were they the ones who would succeed, pass the eleven-plus and go on to the oak-panelled world of the grammar school?

'I'm investigating the murders of Annie Francis and Mark Webster,' she said. 'Do you remember them?'

'Of course,' said Mr Carew. He folded his paper carefully but Emma noticed that his hands were shaking. One hand was missing a finger. Emma remembered her father telling her that many veterans had this injury. 'You light up a cigarette and – wham – a sniper's bullet gets you.' Mr Carew certainly looked like a smoker.

'They were both very bright,' he said. 'Annie especially. When I first met her, I thought, there's a girl who's born to succeed. Well . . .' He smoothed back his hair with his uninjured hand. 'God had a nasty sense of humour.'

'I've just been talking to Miss Young about Annie.'

'Ah, they had a real bond. I was too dry a teacher for her really. But Daphne, she's got a real imagination.'

I bet she has, thought Emma.

'I understand you saw Miss Young when she was working late on the night of Monday the twenty-sixth?'

Mr Carew gave her a sharp look. 'Yes. I looked in on her at about five-thirty. She was still marking books. She works very hard.'

'Did you talk to her?'

'I think I suggested that she might give the marking a miss and go for a quick drink in the Evening Star. She said no thank you.'

Mr Carew might be pushing sixty, thought Emma, as she said goodbye to the teacher and made her way out through the exit marked 'Boys', but he had a thing for Daphne Young all the same. But he had given her an alibi. It would have been hard for Daphne to leave the school after five-thirty, abduct the children and kill them. Hard, Emma reminded herself, but not impossible. As she headed off down Bristol Road, she could hear Class Five still running around the playground.

Back at the police station Edgar and Bob were in the subterranean CID room. The electric fire was on but there was a raw, dank feeling in the air. The smell of Bob's fish-paste sandwiches didn't help either.

When Emma came in, she brought a rush of cold air and a palpable sense of energy.

'I went to see Daphne Young again,' she said. 'And I saw Mr Carew, one of the other teachers, who confirmed that he'd seen her at the school on the night of the twenty-sixth.'

'Well, that's her off the hook then,' said Bob, through a mouthful of sandwich.

'Not necessarily,' said Emma, her face taking on her stubborn look. 'I still thought that Daphne Young was odd about Annie. She wouldn't admit that there was anything disturbing about the Hansel and Gretel play and she said that Annie was "a bit of a bagpipe-playing hedgehog". I asked her what she meant and she told me to work it out for myself.'

'What do you think she meant?' asked Edgar.

'Well,' said Emma, 'I thought it might mean that she was bit of a freak in her family. You know, clever, imaginative and all that.'

Edgar thought of the Francis family, of the house full of children, washing and the detritus of family life. There was no doubt that Annie had sometimes wanted to escape – to her grandparents or to Brian Baxter's house – but who was to say that she wasn't also happy with her parents and brothers and sisters? Edna Webster had said that Sandra Francis expected a lot of Annie but she had also voluntarily spent a lot of time with the younger children, organising them into her 'acting troupe'. There was probably affection there too.

'Didn't Mark's mother say that Annie's parents were strict with her?' said Emma.

'She did,' said Edgar, 'but we mustn't read too much into that. Remember, Mark was an only child. It was different in their house.'

'I'm an only child,' muttered Emma. 'That's no picnic either.'

Interesting, thought Edgar.

Bob finished the last of his sandwich. 'I just can't believe it was any of the parents. Brian Baxter, though,

I didn't like the look of him at all. Nasty, weaselly little man.'

'That doesn't make him a killer though,' said Edgar.

'He hasn't got an alibi for the Monday night,' said Bob.

'He hasn't got a motive either.'

'Did you ask him about his parents?' asked Emma. 'Just to rule out the son of Ezra theory?'

'Yes,' said Edgar. 'No go, I'm afraid. He's Brighton born and bred. His father only died last year.'

'Pity,' said Emma. Edgar saw Bob stifle a smile. He was about to say more when he noticed a shape lurking in the doorway. Either the ghost of Chief Constable Henry Solomon or one of the duty officers from upstairs.

'Sorry to bother you, sir.' Definitely not a ghost. 'But there's someone to see you.'

'I can't see anyone. I'm in a meeting.'

'He said it was important, sir.'

Edgar sighed. 'Does the visitor have a name?'

The PC exhaled with something like awe. 'It's that magician chap from the pier. Max Mephisto.'

'It might be nothing,' said Max. 'But I thought I should tell you.'

'It's a hell of a coincidence though,' said Edgar. 'Denton McGrew was appearing in a pantomime and a young girl was murdered. Forty years later, he's in a pantomime again and two children are killed.'

'Coincidence could be all it is, of course,' said Max.

'Yes,' said Edgar. They were in his office, another basement room with only a narrow strip of window showing feet going past. A WPC had brought tea, which Max had accepted with a charming smile. Now he looked at it dubiously. 'Haven't you got any coffee?'

'No.'

Max took out his hip flask and added something to both cups. Edgar took a sip and almost choked.

'How much did you put in here?'

'Just a splash of brandy. It's medicinal. Do you mind if I smoke?'

'Yes.'

They sat in silence for a moment, Max tapping his cigarette case meditatively.

'Tell me about Denton McGrew,' said Edgar at last.

Max looked up at the pockmarked ceiling. 'He's all right, I suppose. He's been in the business for ever. I wasn't surprised to hear that he used to be a child actor. He was a straight actor for a time – I heard that he even went to Hollywood before the war – but he never made it really big. He's really made his name as a Dame. He's one of the best and a good Dame can make a lot of money. It's the Dame who makes or breaks a pantomime.'

'Not the Demon King?'

Max grinned. 'Anyone can twirl a moustache but the Dame carries the show.'

'Is he married?'

'No. I've always assumed he was homosexual but that

may not be the case. Lots of happily married men make their living dressing up as women.'

They might do in your world, thought Edgar. His own upbringing had been rather more sheltered.

'What does Diablo think of him?' He had underestimated Diablo once before when it came to judging character. He wouldn't do it again.

'They insult each other all the time, the ways pros do. Denton can be very waspish – some of the younger cast members are quite scared of him – but Diablo says he's pleasant enough underneath it all. They go drinking together.'

'Diablo would drink with the devil if he knew a members-only club.'

'That's true.'

'I'd like to talk to McGrew,' said Edgar. 'Nothing official, just a chat. Do you think you could set it up?'

'I'm sure I could,' said Max. 'Why don't you come backstage tomorrow, before the evening show?'

CHAPTER 13

Edgar had never before interviewed a man who was wearing full make-up, a hairnet, tweeds and a false bosom. Of course, it wasn't, strictly speaking, an interview. It was just a friendly chat, brokered by Max, who had told Denton McGrew that Edgar wanted some background on past cases. What Denton made of this, Edgar couldn't tell. He was a hard man to read, even without the barrier of several layers of pancake make-up.

'It's very good of you to see me,' said Edgar. 'Especially just before a show.'

McGrew shrugged. 'It's the best time. I have to come early to get all this on.' He gestured at his outfit, which was half pantomime Dame, half man about town. It was odd seeing him at this stage, like watching a creature halfway through transforming. Edgar thought of the bagpipe-playing hedgehog in his red trousers. Did Denton too shed his skin at the beginning of the performance?

'I'm interested in a production of *Babes in the Wood* that

was performed on Hastings Pier in 1912,' said Edgar. 'I understand you appeared in the show as a child actor.'

Denton turned his mascaraed eyes in Edgar's direction. 'Max said you wanted to talk about that. I can't think why.'

'It's simply a line of enquiry,' said Edgar. 'One of the cast was murdered. What do you remember about that?'

'Betsy Bunning,' said Denton. 'She was a prize bitch but she didn't deserve to die.'

'You and Betsy played the Babes?'

'Yes. I was ten. It was my first pantomime. My parents were both in the business and it was just accepted that we'd all follow them. My sisters were dancing snowdrops in the same production.'

'Was Betsy a professional child actress?'

'God, yes.' Denton laughed harshly. 'She was a pro to her fingertips, was Betsy. She was fifteen and hard as nails but she had the whole little-girl thing off pat, skipping around in her frilly dresses, making eyes at all the men.'

'What do you remember about her murder?'

'I wasn't there that day. We weren't supposed to rehearse in the afternoon. I heard about it later, how Alice Dean had hysterics and Stan – the Great Diablo – was sick in the sand bucket.'

'Did you know Ezra Nightingale, the man convicted of the murder?'

'Oh, we all knew Ezra. He used to hang around the theatre all the time. You always get people like that. They're harmless, most of them. He was a writer, I think. Used to write poems to some of the girls in the cast. Always going on about the true sources of fairy tales like "Babes in the Wood". How they were all very gruesome really and we shouldn't make them all sweet for the audience. He said that's why he killed Betsy, to show that the story wasn't meant to have a happy ending. He was a nutter, of course. They still hanged him though.'

'Did you ever speak to him?'

'Maybe just hallo and goodbye. He wasn't interested in little boys.'

'Was he interested in little girls?'

Again the mirthless laugh. 'That's what they claimed in court. That he was obsessed with Betsy and that's why he killed her. But I don't think so. Betsy made up to him, calling him "Uncle Ezra" and all that, but I think she was just playing him for all she could get. He gave her a fur jacket and she was always prancing round the place in that. But he had a wife and child. I don't think he was interested in her sexually.'

If Denton thought having a wife and a child precluded a man from being interested in young girls, then he was more innocent than he looked, thought Edgar. Also, a fur coat is the kind of present that you give to a mistress, not to a child.

'I've been looking at the newspaper reports,' he said. 'It seems that Ezra confessed.'

'Oh, I don't think they even looked for anyone else,'

said Denton. 'Story was that Ezra was sitting in the stalls with blood on his hands. Like I say, he was a nutter.'

'Must have been awful for you all.'

Denton shrugged, causing the false breasts to rise alarmingly. 'Yes, it was awful. The show had to come off. A whole panto season wasted. My parents were furious. It was a nice little earner for them, with three children in the cast. Tony Billington, Bert's father, you know, was the producer and he wanted to press on with a new girl in the part but the rest of the cast, led by your mate Diablo, didn't want to.'

'Did you keep in touch with any of the cast over the years?'

'Oh, I saw some of them on the circuit,' said Denton. 'But I was in Hollywood for years, you know.'

'I know you were a big star there,' said Edgar. If he had learnt one thing about pros over the years, it was that you could never go wrong with a bit of flattery.

It certainly seemed to do the trick now. Denton positively preened himself, stretching his painted lips in the first genuine smile Edgar had seen from him.

'I did have rather a success, yes. This' – again he gestured at his outfit – 'is just a bit of fun really. I don't need the money.'

Of course you don't, thought Edgar. He couldn't imagine that anyone would cover themselves in greasepaint and squeeze themselves into a corset twice a day just for fun. But then, he wasn't an actor.

'Thank you,' he said. 'You've been very helpful. I don't suppose you've got a picture of Betsy, have you?'

He expected Denton to say no – after all, he didn't sound as if he had been particularly fond of his co-star – but the actor said, with surprising alacrity, 'I might have one somewhere. I'll dig it out and give it to Max.'

'Thank you. That would be very kind.' Edgar stood up to leave. 'Break a leg tonight. That's what you're supposed to say, isn't it?'

Denton turned and, rather alarmingly, switched into an entirely different voice. His Widow Twankey voice, Edgar presumed.

'Ooh, you're a cheeky one. Take care, dear. It's always the cheeky ones that get into trouble.'

And, with a regal wave, the Dame dismissed him.

Outside, Edgar took a deep breath. He wasn't sure whether the conversation had got him any further but, on the other hand, he had learnt a few things: Ezra Nightingale had been obsessed with fairy tales, Denton resented Diablo for insisting that the pantomime closed after Betsy's death, Denton still kept a photograph of Betsy. There were other things too, details that floated queasily through his subconscious. Betsy had called Ezra Nightingale 'Uncle Ezra'. Nightingale killed Betsy to show that stories shouldn't have happy endings. Denton McGrew could switch personalities in the blink of a false eyelash.

Max had invited him to stay for the show but, after

Denton's memories of *Babes in the Wood*, he didn't really feel like watching a pantomime. Backstage, the atmosphere was heating up. Men in overalls carried props to and fro. A flock of dancers in short Chinese tunics pushed past him in a multicoloured whirl of silk. He passed a man wearing a dragon's head and a harassed-looking musician carrying a double bass.

'Broken my bloody E string,' he said to Edgar.

Edgar wasn't sure of the correct response but the musician didn't wait for an answer. He hurried on through the twisting corridors, like the White Rabbit in search of a burrow.

Edgar knocked on Max's dressing-room door.

'Come in.'

Max was sitting in front of a mirror. He was wearing a poison-green robe with matching cloak and elongating his eyebrows with a black pencil. Edgar could never get used to seeing his friend in this environment. The face in the mirror, its handsome contours enhanced so as to seem almost grotesque, was Max and yet it wasn't. The voice, though, was the same.

'Get anything out of Denton?'

'It was interesting but there's really nothing concrete that links that case to this one.'

'Except Denton and Diablo.'

'Who's the producer of *Aladdin*?'

Max raised a villainous eyebrow. 'Bert Billington. Why?'

'His father produced *Babes in the Wood*, all those years ago.'

'Well, they're a theatrical family. Bert owns a string of theatres across the country. He lives in Lancashire, rarely comes south. He was down in Brighton for a night a week or so ago. Roger was summoned for a meeting. We won't see him again for the rest of the run.'

'I'd better go,' said Edgar. 'You'll be on in a minute.'

'Are you staying to watch the show?'

'I don't think so.'

'I don't blame you,' said Max, adding a streak of white to his cheekbone. 'I've had enough of it myself.'

Edgar didn't believe him. He could tell that Max was itching to go on stage, to become the creature in the mirror.

There was a knock on the door and a voice shouted, 'Fifteen minutes, Mr Mephisto.' Edgar judged that it was time to go.

The foyer was full of jostling crowds. A jukebox was playing 'Rudolph the Red-nosed Reindeer'. Edgar passed families clutching programmes and bags of nuts. There were also a few over-made-up women who had clearly come for a glimpse of the great Max Mephisto. Then, just as he had almost reached the doors, he saw a face he recognised: Daphne Young, very chic in a fur coat. Edgar looked to see if she was being followed by a crocodile of excited schoolchildren but she was on her own.

CHAPTER 14

Rather to Edgar's surprise, Denton delivered the picture of Betsy Bunning the very next day. It was handed in at the station in an envelope addressed to 'The good-looking detective inspector'.

'I'm assuming this is you, sir,' said the wooden-faced desk sergeant.

'Of course it's me,' said Edgar. 'Who else could it be?'

'Could be almost anyone, sir.'

In the incident room Edgar slit open the envelope. A black-and-white starlet grinned up at him. Edgar remembered Diablo's description: *She was fifteen, looked ten and acted like a thirty-five-year-old.* Betsy's hair was arranged in elaborate ringlets, and she was looking over her shoulder in a manner which was either charming or deeply disturbing, depending on your viewpoint. For some reason she was wearing Tyrolean costume and posing against a painted backdrop of snow-capped mountains.

Bob came to look over his shoulder.

'Who the hell's that?'

'Betsy Bunning, the girl killed by Ezra Nightingale in 1912.'

This made Emma come over. The three of them stared at the photograph.

'How old was she?' asked Bob.

'Fifteen when she died.'

'She looks very knowing for a fifteen-year-old.'

'She didn't know enough to stop herself getting murdered,' said Edgar.

'I think she looks sad,' said Emma.

Bob snorted but, looking more closely at the photograph, Edgar thought that he could see what Emma meant. The professional smile did not meet Betsy's eyes and there was something forced and unnatural about her pose. He thought of Denton, whose parents had been pleased because their three children were earning money on stage. Did Betsy have parents who had pushed her onto the boards before she could walk? Perhaps she was supporting them and a host of little brothers and sisters. She had called her murderer 'Uncle Ezra'. Maybe she had been lonely for a little adult attention. But Betsy, the child who had swaggered around in a fur coat looking grown-up before her time, had never had the chance to become an adult. There was definitely something sad about the thickly made-up little face.

'Do you really think there's a link between this case and ours?' That was Bob, who never gave up.

'There are links between *Babes in the Wood* and *Aladdin*,' said Edgar. 'Denton and Diablo were in both productions. The 1912 pantomime was produced by Tony Billington, the father of the man who's producing *Aladdin*. But I can't see anything that really links our murders with Betsy's death. Ezra Nightingale confessed. Denton said that he was literally sitting in the stalls with blood on his hands. Nightingale said he killed Betsy to show that fairy stories shouldn't have happy endings. The original story of "Babes in the Wood" had a tragic ending.'

'What happens?' asked Bob.

'It's pretty horrible really,' said Edgar. 'The children's uncle wants to kill them and claim their inheritance. He tells two ruffians to take the children into the wood and leave them there. One of the ruffians, "the 'milder man'" it says in the story, promises to come back with food but he never does. The children die and birds cover them with leaves.'

'Bloody hell,' said Bob. 'What happens in the panto version?'

'The uncle becomes the Wicked Baron and Robin Hood gets involved somehow. The children are rescued and everyone lives happily ever after.'

'Some people say the legend started in Wayland Wood in Norfolk,' said Emma. 'An uncle abandoned his niece and nephew in the wood so that he could claim their inheritance.'

'Did they die?' asked Bob.

'Yes and their ghosts haunt the forest. It's known locally as Wailing Wood.'

'Remind me not to go there for my holidays,' said Bob. He looked again at the photograph of Betsy Bunning, holding it up to the light as if expecting to see a message written in invisible ink. 'I don't see the connection,' he said. '*Babes in the Wood* is English; *Aladdin*'s all Chinese and genies and flying carpets.'

'Except that both stories feature a wicked uncle,' said Emma. She took the photograph out of Bob's hands and smoothed it protectively. 'Do you mind if I do a bit of background research into the 1912 murder?' she asked Edgar. 'I've got a friend in the Hastings police.'

'As long as it doesn't take your attention off this case,' said Edgar. 'It's been six days since the children were killed. The trail's going cold. We've got to get back out on the streets, retracing Annie and Mark's last movements, interviewing anyone who may have seen them.'

After Bob and Emma had left, determined to get back on the trail, Edgar stayed behind for a few minutes. He was looking at another publicity photograph, one which had been sent to him that morning. This one was in colour, showing an enchantingly pretty girl in a showgirl's outfit. Even so, the similarities with the pathetically grinning ingénue in the fake mountain scene made him feel uncomfortable. This photograph had writing across it, in a bold slanting hand cutting through the feathers and the fishnet.

Show opens on Saturday. Fancy coming to see me on Friday?

Love,

Ruby

Edgar had a frustrating day. He sent a team of officers to follow the route taken by Annie and Mark on 26th November. He had gone back over the witness reports and Emma, who was good at that sort of thing, drew a map of Freshfield Road and the surrounding streets. A blue line traced Annie's movements and a red line Mark's. Edgar wondered if she'd deliberately tried to avoid 'blue for a boy'. The two lines stopped though, a few inches from the square of green depicting Queen's Park.

On that Monday, the younger children had come home from school and played in the road, skipping and marking out a hopscotch grid. Then 'the big ones' came back at about four. 'I always watched them walking up the hill,' said old Mrs Rigby from number 11. 'All dressed up in their grammar-school uniforms, carrying all those books. The boy sometimes carried a violin too. The girl was always just a little bit ahead.' I bet she was, thought Edgar. Annie and Mark changed into old clothes and came back out to play with the others. 'Annie seemed to be telling them what to do,' said Tom Halloran, the butcher's boy, who was passing with a delivery. 'They didn't seem to mind though. She was a caution, that Annie. Always made me laugh when she came into the shop.'

The children had played – or rehearsed – until about

four-forty-five. Then Louise and Lionel had been called in for their tea. Annie had wanted to carry on, said Betty, but the others didn't think it was much use rehearsing without Louise. Betty and Richard had gone back into their house. 'It was cold,' said Richard defensively. Kevin took his little sister, Agnes, home. Then Annie and Mark must have taken the fatal decision to walk two hundred yards down the hill. Had they been on their way to buy sweets? Betty and Richard thought so. 'Mark always had sweet rations,' said Betty. 'His mum used to give him hers.' Had they been planning to spend Mark's money on gobstoppers from Sam Gee's shop? If so, they never got there.

They were last seen in St Luke's Terrace, a road that led from Freshfield Road towards Queen's Park. The sweet shop was at the end of the road. Annie and Mark had been seen standing on the street corner, talking or arguing. Arthur Bates, passing by with his sister, thought he had heard Annie say that Mark should 'go back to primary school'. If Emma was right and this was an intention rather than an insult, the quickest route to Bristol Road Juniors was back through the park. But no one had seen the children in the park. Admittedly it was dark but there had been a few dog-walkers around. Surely someone would have seen something? But the trail ended there, on the corner of St Luke's Terrace and Freshfield Road. Could they have gone back up the hill to Uncle Brian's house? Or back down towards Kemp Town? But none of the neighbours, all of whom knew the children by sight, had seen them walking up or down the steep hill.

Edgar felt as if he'd walked up and down the hill a hundred times that day. But they didn't get any further in tracing the blue and red lines. Edgar wondered if he should get two similar-looking children to walk the route to see if it would jog any memories. He had heard of this working in other missing-person cases. Reconstruction, they called it. Betty could play the part of Annie, or would this be too distressing for her? He'd ask Emma's opinion; she seemed to have got on well with the children.

It was dark when Edgar walked back to the station. He was passing the top of Upper Rock Gardens at five o'clock. Would Max be in? He said that he sometimes went back to his digs between shows. It would be extremely pleasant to have tea with Max and Mrs M. And he might finally be able to thank the landlady for her kindness last week.

As he approached the house, a man came out of the front door. At first Edgar thought it was Max but then he saw that this man was older, with grey hair visible as he adjusted his hat. Like Max though, this man was tall and well dressed, wearing a coat that looked expensive even from a distance. As Edgar watched, he descended the steps and got into a waiting car, not into the driver's seat but into the back. Who could be visiting Mrs M in a chauffeur-driven car? Maybe it was an agent or someone from a big London theatre.

Rather to his surprise, Max himself opened the door.

He was in his shirtsleeves and holding a cigarette. He looked, there was no other word for it, rattled.

'Ed.'

'Hallo, Max. I was just passing and . . .'

'Come in. Mrs M would like to see you.'

'Thank you.' Edgar stepped into the hall and saw that the landlady was standing in the background. She, at least, was looking her usual insouciant self.

'Who was your smart visitor?' he asked Max.

'My father,' said Max briefly.

Max still couldn't quite believe that he'd been there. Alastair, Lord Massingham, standing on the steps of a Brighton boarding house. Max and Joyce had been in bed. It was becoming his regular routine, to dash back to the house between shows for an hour in bed with Joyce. Sex, warmth, tea and biscuits afterwards. What could be better?

The knock on the door had been loud and peremptory.

'It's probably Walter,' said Joyce. 'He always forgets his key.'

Max put on his trousers and looked out of the window. 'It's a man. Not Walter though. Jesus, I think it's my father.'

'Your father? I thought he lived miles away.'

'He does. Yes, that's him. His car's parked on the road. What the hell does he want?'

'I think you're about to find out, darling. Give me a few

minutes, will you? It takes me hours to get back into that girdle.'

'I'll go down.' Max was buttoning his shirt. 'It won't take me long to get rid of him.'

The tattoo on the door was just starting again when Max flung it open.

'What took you so long?' That was his father's greeting.

'How did you find me?' That was his.

'I asked at the theatre.'

Wonderful. Lou Abrahams must have loved that. All the pros would know by tonight.

'How did you know I was at the theatre?'

Lord Massingham snorted. 'There are pictures of you all over the damn town. Can I come in?'

'I suppose so.' As his father stepped into the hall, Joyce was making her way downstairs. She paused on the bottom step, very much the landlady, despite the fact that she hadn't got her stockings on.

'Mrs Markham, my landlady. Alastair Massingham, my father.' He was damned if he was going to add the 'Lord'.

But he was pleased to see that Joyce was in no way overawed by the visitor. She looked him coolly up and down.

'Yes, I can see the resemblance,' she said. 'Shall I make some tea?'

She ushered them into the snug, not the big room where the pros usually ate and chatted but a stuffy little parlour at the back of the house, crammed with photographs and ornaments. Max's father examined a carved black elephant.

'Jolly little thing.'

'I'm sure she'd sell it to you if you asked her nicely.'

Alastair said nothing but he put the elephant down rather quickly. He sat opposite Max and took out his cigarette case.

'Want one?'

'Thanks.'

They smoked in silence until Max could bear it no more.

'Why are you here, Dad?'

He used to call his father 'Papa', maybe a legacy from his Italian mother. After her death, when Max was six, Alastair had instructed his son to call him 'Father'. When he was older, in retaliation Max had settled on the most déclassé appellation he could find. He had even considered 'Pop'.

Alastair's cheek twitched but he didn't react to the name. 'Came to see you. It's been a long time, Max.'

'Not that long.'

'Two years.'

Christ, was it that recent? He remembered a flying visit to the ghastly old pile in Somerset. He'd had a girlfriend with him. Was it Vicky or Gloria? One of the chorus girls from the Shepherd's Bush Empire. Even before then, contact had been sporadic: a few postcards, an occasional visit. Though his father did bother to check that he hadn't been killed in the war. Max remembered the telegram clearly. 'Have checked with war office. Stop. Understand you alive. Stop.' Clearly Alastair's paternal streak was making a reappearance.

Joyce came in with the tea tray. She put it down on the table between them but made no attempt to stay. Her blouse and skirt were neat but her hair was slightly disarranged at the back. She gave Max the shadow of a wink as she passed.

'Seems a nice woman,' said Alastair.

'Very nice,' said Max.

'I suppose you've seen all sorts in your time.'

'You suppose right.'

Another silence and then Alastair said, 'The thing is, Max, I've heard a rumour.'

'What sort of rumour?'

Alastair looked him full in the face for the first time. 'A rumour that you have a daughter.'

'How did you hear?' asked Max. He was genuinely fascinated to know. He wouldn't have thought that there was any place where his world and his father's overlapped.

'Shall I pour some tea?' said Alastair.

'Go ahead.'

At least neither of them mentioned being mother. Alastair drank his tea as though needing sustenance. Then he said, 'Every year there's a Christmas party at the golf club. Usually I don't go. Lots of ghastly people playing golf these days. But Bertie asked me if I'd come this year. Make a speech, that sort of thing.'

He took another sip of tea. Max thought he knew the sort of thing exactly. Bertie Bridges was Alastair's horrendous gun-toting, bridge-playing friend, a red-faced monster of a man, given to terrifying barks of laughter and to groping maids during meals.

'There's always entertainment of some kind,' Alastair continued. 'One year there was a fellow who could swallow razor blades. This year there was this magic chappie called The Great Raymondo.'

'Ah.' Max began to see the light.

'He wasn't much cop, to be honest, but he did a fairly good trick with some golf balls and a glass of port. Afterwards he came over to our table. I complimented his act, just to be friendly, y'know, and he said, "It's better with a girl. I used to have this gorgeous girl assistant." And I said – again, just being friendly – "Wish I'd seen her," or something of the sort. And this fellow Raymondo said, "I'm sure you will see her one day. After all, she's your granddaughter."

Bloody Raymondo, thought Max, he could never resist a cheap reveal. Raymondo had worked with Ruby once; he must have ferreted out this story and waited for his moment. Aloud he said, 'What did you say?'

'I said, "You mean she's Max's daughter?" After all, who else could she be?'

'First rule of magic,' said Max. 'Never ask a question if you don't already know the answer.'

'Well, I did know the answer,' said his father, with some asperity. 'Or I thought I did. So, is this girl your daughter?'

'Yes,' said Max.

'When were you going to tell me about her?'

Just for a moment, Max felt slightly guilty. He should have told his father. After all, as Raymondo had kindly pointed out, Ruby was his granddaughter. Was it because he couldn't bear to acknowledge their relationship? He had often thought that Ruby, with her dark eyes and hair, might resemble his mother. Was it just that he couldn't stand the thought that she also had a genetic link to Alastair, a man who pronounced golf 'goff' and talked about 'ghastly people'?

'I'm sorry,' he said at last. 'I should have told you.'

The apology seemed to blow away the last vestiges of Alastair's bluster. He sat back in Mrs M's overstuffed armchair, as if awaiting further revelations.

'She's called Ruby,' said Max. 'She's clever, she's determined and she's very pretty. She came to work for me as an assistant last year. I had no idea then that she was my daughter.'

'I suppose you could have any number of illegitimate children scattered around the country,' said Alastair.

'It's possible,' said Max. 'Ruby's mother was a snake charmer called Emerald.'

He thought that his father let out a faint groan.

'Anyway, Ruby was my assistant for a week, the summer before last, here in Brighton. It's her ambition to be a magician, by the way.'

This time there was a definite groan.

'The summer before last,' said Alastair. 'Wasn't that when there was that ghastly case of the girl who'd been chopped into three? Weren't you involved with that too?'

'I didn't do the chopping,' said Max. 'But I was involved, yes.'

Alastair put his head in his hands. 'I don't know,' he said. 'I did my best. It was hard after your mother died but I sent you to a good school. Money was no object. They all said you were clever. How . . . how has this happened?' His sweeping gesture seemed to encompass Max, the boarding house, the illegitimate daughter and a world where women could be chopped into three.

'I hated that school,' said Max. 'As you know very well. And I haven't done too badly for myself.'

'Oh, I know you're *famous*,' said Alastair, managing to make the word sound somehow disgusting. 'I know you're the great Max Mephisto. But you're my son, you're my heir, you'll be Lord Massingham one day. You shouldn't be wasting your time appearing in end-of-the-pier shows, sawing women in half or whatever you do. You should be at home, managing the estate. You're forty-one years old. You should be married to some nice girl, not having children with snake charmers. And my granddaughter wants to be a magician too! I despair, I really do.'

And he did sound despairing. Max felt almost sorry for him. His father had aged, he thought. His hands had shaken when he'd poured the tea and his hair was more white than grey. Max was touched, despite himself, that Alastair had got his age right.

'I'll introduce you to Ruby,' he said. 'You'll like her, I promise.'

Alastair took out a handkerchief and blew his nose loudly. 'Have you got a photograph?' he asked.

Only yesterday Ruby had sent Max a photograph of herself in full showgirl mode. 'When are you coming to the show?' she'd written across the picture. Something told Max that this was not the image to show his father. Instead he got a snapshot out of his wallet. It showed Ruby on Brighton pier, laughing as the wind blew back her hair.

Alastair got out a pair of glasses and looked at it intently. 'Pretty gel,' he said at last.

'Yes, very.'

'Clever too, you said.'

'Very clever.'

'She has a look of my mother,' said Alastair. 'She was said to be the prettiest girl in five counties.'

From what Max remembered of his paternal grandmother this was hard to believe, but he took the remark in the conciliatory spirit with which it was offered.

'I'll bring her to see you,' he said. 'Perhaps after Christmas.'

'I'd like that,' said Alastair. 'I'd better be off now. Matthews is waiting outside.'

'Aren't you staying to see the show tonight?' asked Max, not entirely joking.

'I don't think so, no,' said Alastair. 'My compliments to the lady of the house and thank her for the tea.'

Edgar had almost collided with Lord Massingham on the doorstep.

'He'd found out about Ruby,' said Max. 'He wanted a confrontation.'

'Did he get one?'

'Not really. He did rant on a bit about how I was wasting my life, having children with snake charmers and the rest of it.'

'I see you didn't spare him the detail.'

'No. I could tell the snake charmer went down well.'

'Is she the first snake charmer in the Massingham family?'

'Yes. Most of them have never done an honest day's work in their lives.'

Joyce brought in some more tea. She hovered, as if unsure whether to stay or not.

'Thank you,' said Edgar. 'And thank you for the other night. I hope you got the flowers.'

'Oh, were they from you? Lily just said they were from a strange man.'

'That's Ed to a T,' said Max.

'It's not the first time I've had flowers from a strange man,' said Joyce. 'I'll leave you two to have a chat.'

She was, in some ways, the most tactful woman that Max had ever met.

Edgar looked exhausted. He'd been tramping the streets all day, looking for clues. Max had seen the evening paper: 'Child killer still at large'. He didn't think that Edgar and his team had got the slightest idea who had killed Annie Francis and Mark Webster. 'They'll kill again,' Diablo had said yesterday, 'mark my words.' Max hoped not, for everyone's sake. Diablo seemed very upset by this case. Well, everyone in Brighton was upset. There was a pall of fear and unhappiness over the town that all the pantomimes in the world couldn't dispel. But Diablo was also thinking about that other pantomime murder, all those years ago. How strange that Denton had been there too.

'Did you hear any more from the great Dame?' he asked.

'He sent me a photograph of Betsy, the girl who was killed. Poor little thing, she was all dolled up with ringlets and a ridiculous costume. She can't have had much of a life. Then she was murdered by a madman at fifteen.'

'There were a lot of those acts before the war,' said Max. 'Little girls all dressed up singing "My Heart Belongs to Daddy". There was something very strange and disturbing about them.'

'Ezra Nightingale was certainly a strange and disturbed man.'

'And there's no madman on the scene this time?'

'It doesn't seem so,' said Edgar. 'Some strange characters around but no one with any real motive. Annie, the girl who died, she was interested in the stage. She wrote plays and got her friends to perform them. I keep thinking that the murder is connected to the theatre in some way. You should read some of the things she wrote. Talk about disturbing. I keep thinking that there's a clue there that I'm missing.'

'Beware of misdirection,' said Max. 'If something looks impossible, that's because it is.'

'What's that supposed to mean?'

'The audience thinks that the girl can't possibly be sawn in two,' said Max, 'and they're right. It's the magician's job to try to blur those lines between the possible and impossible. It's probably a killer's job too.'

' "Once you eliminate the impossible, whatever remains, no matter how improbable, must be the truth".'

'Who said that?'

'Conan Doyle. Sherlock Holmes.'

'There you are. He was a magician, if you like.'

CHAPTER 15

Edgar was back at Freshfield Road. He wished, more than anything, that he was calling to tell the families that he'd make a breakthrough in the case. But, instead, he was sitting in the Francises' tiny front room, telling them about the autopsy report on their daughter. In a few minutes he would have to go seven doors down and have the same conversation with the Websters.

Sandra and Jim sat close together on the sofa. The twins were at school and the baby was in a playpen in the corner. Outside they could hear the dustcart groaning up the hill. The snow had cleared and service was getting back to normal.

But the Francises' life was never going to get back to normal. Edgar told them, as simply and as gently as he could, that the coroner had found that death was by manual strangulation. The children's bodies had probably been stored somewhere warm and dry before being left out on Devil's Dyke. There were fibres in their hair that looked as if they had come from a blanket. The cold made it hard to tell time of death but it had probably occurred two or three days before the bodies were discovered.

'Two or three days,' said Jim. 'That means on Monday. On the day they went missing.'

'That's what we think,' said Edgar. 'We think the bodies must have been put there before the snow started on Tuesday night.'

Sandra crossed herself. Her face was greenish-white and she had her arms wrapped round her body as if she were literally trying to hold herself together. Jim, on the other hand, was becoming more belligerent.

'Have you got any leads? Any clues? Seems to me that you lot are doing nothing. Sandra says you were tramping up and down the street yesterday but you're no further forward than you were before. What about Sam Gee? Have you spoken to him? They were on their way to his shop, weren't they?'

'I have spoken to Mr Gee,' said Edgar. 'He says that he didn't see the children on Monday and we've no reason to disbelieve him.'

'Have you searched his flat? Questioned his wife? You said there were – what was the word – fibres on the children's bodies. Can't you find out where they came from?'

'I have questioned Mr and Mrs Gee,' said Edgar. 'I'd need a search warrant to search their house and at the moment I haven't got the grounds to ask for one. We will try to trace the fibres but they're very small, almost microscopic.' He looked at the two faces opposite him, one resigned, one angry. 'Believe me, Mrs and Mrs Francis, we are doing our best. I've got my whole team working on this case, day and night. We'll find the person who did this, I promise.'

There was a silence, broken only by the baby banging a wooden brick against the bars of his playpen. Eventually Sandra said, 'The funeral's tomorrow. At St George's. We arranged it as soon as we heard from the coroner.'

'I'd like to come,' said Edgar, 'and so would my team. Is that all right with you?'

'We'd like you to be there,' said Sandra. 'Are you a Christian?'

The question took Edgar by surprise. He remembered Brian Baxter saying that the Francises were religious. Sandra had made the sign of the cross too. Was it only Catholics who did that? But St George's wasn't a Catholic church. He tried to answer honestly.

'I was brought up in the Church of England,' he said. 'I was confirmed. I certainly believed as a child. But, when the war came, I suppose it made me question everything. My brother died . . . I suppose I'm trying to say that I don't know. I wish I did.'

To his surprise, Sandra smiled. It was the first time he had seen her smile and it completely transformed her face.

'If you want to believe,' she said, 'that's half the battle. God will see to the rest.'

'Sandra believes,' said Jim. 'It's a comfort to her. Me, I'm like you. I can't see why a God would let these things happen.'

'Would you do a reading at the funeral?' asked Sandra. 'It would mean a lot to us.'

Edgar was touched but he wished they hadn't asked. He hadn't read aloud since university and the thought of standing up in church, in front of the bereaved families and all his colleagues, made him feel hot and cold all over.

'I'd be honoured,' he said. 'Thank you for asking me.'

'I've asked Miss Young too,' said Sandra, 'Have you met her? She was Annie's primary-school teacher. She's a lovely lady, always so kind to Annie.'

'I have met her, yes.'

He was surprised they'd asked Daphne Young. For some reason he had thought the family might resent the teacher's interest in their daughter. But it seemed that they too had fallen under Miss Young's spell. He wondered why neither parent wanted to read at the funeral. Perhaps they just couldn't face it. He thanked them again for asking him and assured them that he'd see them at the church at noon tomorrow.

'I'm sorry about your brother,' said Sandra as she showed him out. 'What was his name?'

'Jonathan.'

'I'll pray for him.'

'Thank you,' said Edgar.

*

'The Francises are arranging everything,' said Reg Webster. 'We don't really have anything to do with the church.' He made it sound as if 'the church' was a sinister international organisation. Which perhaps it is, thought Edgar.

Reg didn't sound as if he minded his neighbours taking over. Edgar had not quite worked out the relationship between the families. When he'd first interviewed Edna Webster, he'd thought that she considered her husband superior to Jim Francis, because Jim was a labourer whilst Reg worked for the bus company. But she'd also sounded slightly disparaging about Sandra Francis, who was well spoken and clearly well educated. Both houses were neat and tidy but the Websters possessed ornaments and net curtains, which hinted at a desire for gentility. Maybe it was just that the Websters didn't have young children who would knock over china Alsatians and miniature cottages inscribed 'A present from the Lake District'. Perhaps the Websters just weren't the neighbourly sort. 'We keep ourselves to ourselves,' that's what Edna had said. It could be that this attitude also extended to God.

Edna didn't seem to have the energy to be disparaging about anybody today. She sat next to her husband, a thin wisp of a woman who seemed to have got thinner and wispier since the news of her son's death. Edgar had given the Websters the same information from the autopsy but, unlike the Francises, they hadn't queried anything. They hadn't told Edgar that he wasn't doing his job properly.

They just stared at him with a kind of dumb resignation that made him feel even worse.

'Mrs Francis asked me to read at the funeral tomorrow,' he told them. 'Is that all right with you?'

Please say it isn't, he begged them silently. Say that one of you is desperate to do the reading.

'That'll be very nice,' said Edna, as if he had offered to bake a cake for the Mother's Union Christmas tea party. There was an invitation to this event on the mantelpiece, next to Mark's photograph. Would Edna still go, now that she wasn't a mother?

Walking back down the hill, Edgar thought about Friday. Ruby had asked him to come to Worthing that day. Would it be unseemly to think of pleasure so soon after such a funeral? He imagined the newspaper report. 'Heartless policeman DI Edgar Stephens was seen in Worthing with his showgirl girlfriend on the very day that the tragic children were buried.' But, even as he imagined the headlines, he thought: Showgirl girlfriend?

He still wasn't sure if Ruby was his girlfriend. But she'd sent him the photograph and she'd asked him to come and see the show. He imagined taking Ruby home to see his mother. Surely even Rose would be won over by Ruby's beauty and charm? Actually he had a nasty feeling that his mother was immune to beauty and charm. At any rate she would think them unnecessary qualities in a girlfriend, not like respectability and a light hand with pastry. She would consider Ruby somehow 'flashy', like Max's Bentley or the check suits worn by his Uncle Charlie. 'You're over thirty now,' his mother had said on his last visit to Esher. 'About time you settled down with some nice girl.'

He should go and see his mother. He couldn't go now, in the middle of a case, but he knew that a visit was long overdue. It had been early autumn went he last went to Esher, a mild day because they'd gone for a walk on Ditton Common and Rose had remembered how he and Jonathan used to cycle there as children. 'You were always close. You left poor Lucy out sometimes.' At the time he'd thought that this was a typical Rose remark, wistful but at the same time wounding, but afterwards he had wondered if there was some truth in it. He had been close to his younger brother, who had the sort of sunny personality that was easy to love. Lucy had been altogether more difficult: the middle child, strident and combative. One of the first sounds Edgar could remember was Lucy's voice raised in protest, declaring that it just wasn't *fair*. Well, it probably hadn't been; he could imagine that his parents, neither of them exactly fans of female emancipation, might have expected Lucy to do more than her fair share of household chores. She had probably been helping their mother wash up while he daydreamed over his Latin. Even so, Lucy had done well at school, passing her exams with honours and going on to do a secretarial course, which had eventually led to a job as a doctor's receptionist and marriage to a GP. But Edgar had studied Modern Greats at Oxford.

He must go and see his mother at Christmas. The thought made his heart sink but he knew that it was his duty. And besides, what was the alternative? Sitting alone in Brighton with a bottle of whisky dreaming about Ruby? Lucy, Rupert and the boys would probably be at his mother's too and he'd make a special effort with them. He liked his three nephews, George, Edward and baby David, but he couldn't remember ever doing anything fun with them. He must try to be a jolly uncle, like Uncle Charlie had been to him, and not a miserable figure in the corner always moaning about work.

Without knowing it, he was back at the station. He had made his decision. He was going to see Ruby on Friday. The funeral was at noon; he'd work all afternoon and then set off to Worthing at five. It would give him something to look forward to at any rate. He was already dreading the service.

Friday was an appropriately overcast day, cold and grey with flakes of snow in the air. More snow was forecast and Edgar just prayed that it held off until he got to Worthing. Then he could be snowed in with Ruby. He worked all morning, putting off the moment when he had to set off for the church. Emma and Bob left at eleven-fifteen. 'We'll save you a seat,' said Emma, looking anxious. It was twenty to twelve by the time that Edgar left Bartholomew

Square. Outside he saw Frank Hodges getting into his chauffeur-driven car. He didn't offer Edgar a lift.

Edgar walked as fast as he could, his old army pace. It was further than he thought. He saw the tower of St George's from a long way off; it was a curiously Italianate affair, out of place against the December sky. Inside it was exotic too, dark and candlelit, with lots of gilt and statues of the saints. Sandra Francis, who was a regular worshipper here, must be quite High Church. Edgar thought of her crossing herself, of her offering to pray for Jonathan. Well, he hoped that her faith was comforting her now.

There were two solid-looking rows of policemen, most of them in uniform. Emma was sitting at the end of the second row. She moved up for him. 'Cutting it a bit fine, sir.' Frank Hodges, who was in the row in front, didn't look round but Edgar saw his moustache twitch.

The church was packed and the atmosphere sombre yet somehow expectant, almost like the moments before a wedding when you crane around to see a glimpse of the bride's white dress in the porch. But when the music started, and the vicar began to walk slowly up the aisle, intoning, 'I am the way, the truth and the life,' Edgar thought that it was as far from a wedding as anything he had experienced. A pall of complete and utter grief fell upon the church. The two small coffins, each bearing a wreath of white roses; the families following behind; the stifled sobbing in the congregation: it all seemed combined to test the human heart beyond bearing.

Sandra Francis, all in black, looked pale and dignified. Jim followed, looking surprisingly impressive in a dark suit. The Websters walked behind, smaller and less striking, Edna in a grey coat with a dipping hem, Reg in a greenish-black suit. The children were there too. Edgar could see Betty's red head in the front row beside her grandparents. The Websters, of course, had no other children.

The vicar, an effete-looking man in a snowy cassock, made some general remarks about life, death and resurrection and then it was Edgar's turn. He walked up to the pulpit, hearing his shoes echoing on the stone floor. He tried not to look at the congregation as he found his place in the open Bible but he did see Max and Diablo sitting in one of the back pews and was touched that they had come.

The reading was from the gospel of St Luke. People bring their children to Jesus to be blessed and the disciples protest. But Jesus says, 'Suffer little children to come unto me, and forbid them not: for of such is the kingdom of God.' Reading those words 'suffer little children' in this place and with the two small coffins in front of him seemed, to Edgar, a new and exquisite torture. He read too quickly, hardly daring to look up, conscious of his voice dying away at the end of each line.

When he had sat down, Daphne Young made her way to the front of the church for the second reading. Edgar had noted that there were quite a few teachers present – including the three heads, Patricia Paxton, Martin Hammond and Duncan Pettigrew – but Daphne hadn't been sitting with them. It was if she had materialised from the candles and the incense. She walked slowly, not looking to left or right, poised and elegant in a tight-fitting black velvet suit with her Titian hair piled up on top of her head. She scanned the congregation coolly before starting to read and, as soon as she opened her mouth, Edgar realised that she put him to shame. Her voice was low but clear enough to reach to the gilded ceiling. She spoke as if the words had just been revealed to her in a cloud of holy smoke. This reading was from John, the raising of Lazarus. Edgar wondered who had chosen it. It seemed tactless, somehow, to tell the story about Jesus raising Lazarus from the dead when nothing on earth or in heaven was ever going to bring Annie and Mark to life again. Lazarus is sick but Jesus takes His time coming to visit. When He arrives, Mary and Martha (Edgar had forgotten that they were in this story) tell him that their brother is dead. 'If you had been here,' says Mary, in what Edgar can't help but hear as an accusing tone, 'our brother would not have died.' Jesus answers: 'I am the resurrection and the life. The one who believes in me will live, even though they die.' Then Jesus goes to the tomb, asks for the stone to be rolled away and calls, 'Lazarus, come out.' The dead man appears, still in his grave-clothes. Lazarus is recalled to life.

As Miss Young sat down there was a low murmur in the

church. Edgar, too, felt strangely disquieted by the teacher's performance, for performance was how he thought of it. He thought of 'The Juniper Tree'. *Marlinchen might be a corruption of Mary Magdalene and the boy coming to life could be seen to mirror the Resurrection.* So satisfying, the justice meted out in these stories. But where was the justice for the children in their coffins below the altar steps? He looked at the families in the front row. Sandra Francis's head was bowed, her youngest child sat in her lap. He saw Jim Francis pat her shoulder and turn round to glance reassuringly at Edna Webster. Reg Webster was sobbing into his handkerchief.

The vicar spoke next and his words seemed to be deliberately dry and detached, as if to disassociate himself from the drama of stones being rolled away and dead bodies appearing trailing their shrouds. He said that the death of children was always particularly sad but that, as St Luke said, children had a special place in the Saviour's heart and that, even now, they were at his right hand in paradise. He said this as though paradise were an address in Brighton. Then the congregation rose to sing 'All Things Bright and Beautiful' and the coffins began their slow journey out of the church.

Max, watching from the back, thought that the vicar could have a future on the boards. His voice, though expressionless, carried effortlessly into the furthest rows, the cheapest seats. As for the previous speaker, the glamorous redhead, she was a thwarted thespian if he ever saw one. Edgar had been barely adequate, rushing through that rather beautiful passage as if he were reading a police report. Max was sure that Edgar had, in fact, been close to tears. He was too sensitive for police work; Max had told him so before now.

'Dear me.' Diablo dabbed his eyes as the coffins went past. 'How sad this all is. Those poor families. They'll never get over it, you know. My mother never got over the deaths of my two younger brothers in the first war.' It was the first time that Diablo had mentioned this loss to Max. Edgar had lost a brother in the Second World War, he remembered.

The police contingent marched past. Max recognised the gormless sergeant and the good-looking blonde plus a host of other uniformed plods. Edgar stopped at their pew.

'Thank you so much for coming. It was very good of you.'

'We wanted to show our respect,' said Diablo. 'This must be terribly hard for you, dear boy.'

'It's hard for the families,' said Edgar. 'I don't know how they'll cope.'

The doors were open at the back now and people were streaming out. The committal, the vicar had said, was for close family only.

'Who was the red-headed woman?' said Max. 'The one who read the Lazarus story?'

Edgar looked round quickly before replying. 'Miss Young, the children's primary school teacher. She's an interesting woman.'

'She looks it.'

'What about coming for a quick drink?' said Diablo hopefully. 'I'm sure we all need it.'

'I can't,' said Edgar. 'I've got to get back to work.'

'Tonight then.'

'I'm busy tonight. I'm meeting Ruby.'

Edgar could never quite say Ruby's name without blushing, thought Max. Aloud he said, 'It's her first night tomorrow, isn't it?'

'Yes.'

'Well, wish her luck from me.'

'I will.'

Edgar smiled rather nervously at them both before making his way out of the church. Max, waiting for the crowds to disperse, wondered why he minded Edgar seeing Ruby. He should be pleased, surely, that she'd found herself such an eminently decent man. Except that Ruby was twenty-one and Edgar ten years older. But Ruby was old for her years. To his surprise, he realised that he was more worried about Ruby breaking Edgar's heart than the other way round.

'Bloody hell,' said Diablo. 'Look who's here. It's Roger the Dodger and that fellow who keeps telling me that I'm getting the lines wrong.'

Max followed Diablo's pointing figure and saw Roger

Dunkley and Nigel Castle amongst the crowd at the doors. He'd told Roger that he'd be attending the funeral, saying that he'd be back in good time for the matinee. Why hadn't the director mentioned that he'd be there too?

'Shall we find a side exit?' said Diablo in a stage whisper. 'A little of those two goes a long way with me.'

Max acquiesced but he couldn't help looking back at the two theatricals as they mingled with the children's family and friends. He couldn't have said why their presence made him feel so uneasy.

CHAPTER 16

Edgar left the station promptly at five and arrived in Worthing early. He parked the car and walked along the esplanade. He was meeting Ruby by the bandstand on the seafront. He remembered Ruby writing that Worthing was 'so boring' but, after the events of the last week, he found the solid hotels and broad streets rather reassuring. It was nearly dark but there was a cheerful, wholesome feeling about the town that was quite a contrast to Brighton. The passers-by all looked respectable types, huddled up against the cold, hurrying home to blameless high teas and *Mrs Dale's Diary*. He thought of his old army major, who had also lived in Worthing. He had been thoroughly respectable. On the surface, at least.

By the time that Ruby appeared, he was frozen and had lost all feeling in his extremities. The sight of Ruby, though, was enough to warm his heart. She looked so pretty, her heart-shaped face framed by a fur hat, her black coat nipped in to show her trim chorus girl's figure.

'Am I late? Sorry.'

'No. You're exactly on time. I was early.'

He wasn't sure whether to kiss her or not but she presented her cheek like a child. Her skin was firm and cold. She smelt of a sharp lemony scent that was unfamiliar.

'It's lovely to see you, Ed.' She tucked her hand into his arm and briefly rested her head on his shoulder. His senses reeled. Was she treating him like a trusted friend of her father's or was this something else? He thought of the day at the ice rink. Then, when he'd kissed her, she had definitely kissed him back. He remembered the sensation of her lips against his, the scent of her hair. One way or another, he had to kiss her again. The moment was lost now though, they were walking briskly along the promenade and she was telling him about Worthing and her landlady and what Buttons had said to one of the Ugly Sisters.

He had asked her to suggest a restaurant for dinner and she'd chosen an Italian place just off the seafront. She had Max's gift for sniffing out a good meal, Edgar realised that at once. Toppolino's was both friendly and professional, just full enough to be exciting but spacious enough for them to have a corner table with candles and a red-checked tablecloth. The waiters made a discreet fuss of Ruby, taking her coat away to hang up and bowing as they pulled out her chair for her. Edgar felt both embarrassed and proud to be seen in her company. He hoped that they didn't look like father and daughter.

Under her coat Ruby was wearing a black-and-white check suit. When Edgar complimented her on it, she said, 'Thank you. Mummy doesn't really like me to wear black.'

This reference to her mother, the former snake charmer, threw Edgar off track. (On the way he had rehearsed things he could say; compliment her on her dress had been the first thing.)

Ruby saved him by leaning forward and saying, 'I've been reading about your case in the papers. It must be terrible.'

Her saying that made everything easier. He was even able to tell her about the funeral that morning without thinking that he sounded too morbid.

'Max . . . your dad . . . was there. With Diablo. It was good of them to come.'

'I love Uncle Stan,' said Ruby. 'He's so sweet.' She didn't mention Max. Edgar noted that Ruby was another one with an adopted uncle. Did she know about her grandfather's visit? Max said that he'd promised to introduce Lord Massingham to Ruby. What would Ruby make of that meeting? 'She'll have the old bastard wrapped around her little finger in minutes,' said Max. Edgar had no doubt at all that this was true.

'How's your show?' asked Edgar. 'Any last-minute panics?'

Ruby grinned. 'The dress rehearsal was so bad that the director cried. You are coming to the opening night tomorrow, aren't you?'

'I'll try,' said Edgar. 'It just might be difficult with work and things.'

'Max said he'd come one day when he hasn't got a matinee,' said Ruby. 'It's difficult when we're both in shows at the same time.'

Her tone was light but Edgar thought that she sounded put out all the same. The waiter was hovering and he chose lasagne at random. Ruby spent a long time deciding on saltimbocca and a side salad. Edgar recklessly ordered a bottle of red. He'd just have to drive home slowly.

'Are you nervous?' he asked.

'No,' said Ruby with a defiant tilt of the chin. 'I'm only in the back row of the chorus, after all.'

This was almost exactly what Max had said. Had he been stupid enough to say it to Ruby?

'Well, I know I'd be petrified,' he said. 'I was in a play at school once. I only had to say that someone "lies i' the second chamber" and I couldn't sleep for a week.'

Apparently the thought of Edgar the thespian cheered Ruby up. She laughed and accepted a glass of wine.

'It's quite good fun being a panto babe,' she said, 'and I'm learning a lot, but it's not what I want to do all my life.'

'Do you still want to be a magician?' asked Edgar.

'Yes. I suppose you think that's stupid?'

'No, I . . .'

She laughed. 'It's all right, Ed. Even I think it's stupid

sometimes. But it's all I want to do. I've been practising some new tricks. Shall I show you?'

Edgar nodded, dazzled by her.

'All right.' She fished in her bag for a piece of paper. It was torn from a letter, he couldn't help noticing. Who had been writing to her? Max? Her mother? Another man?

'Write something,' she said. 'Anything.'

Of course, then he couldn't think of a single thing. Not a single word in the whole English language. A is for apple. B is for bear. Think, man, think.

He wrote 'Ruby'.

'No, not my name,' said Ruby, without looking. 'Something more difficult to guess.'

She gave him another scrap of paper and he wrote 'Juniper'.

'Now fold it up.'

She took the folded paper and held it in the flame from the candle. It burnt quickly, the candle stuttering, the shadow wild on the stucco wall. Then she smiled at him and accepted her saltimbocca from the waiter.

It was only when they were drinking coffee that she told him to look at the screw of paper in his saucer.

He unwrapped it. One word, written in a slanting, foreign-looking hand: 'Juniper'.

He gaped at her. 'That's amazing. How did you . . . ?'

She smiled, her creamy cat's smile. 'That would be telling. Max says never to tell the audience how it's done.'

But on the way to her digs she relented. She had visited the restaurant earlier that day and primed the waiter. He had been standing behind Edgar when he wrote the word.

'That's cheating.'

'No,' she said seriously. 'It's making use of what you have.'

Afterwards he wondered a lot about that remark.

It was nearly midnight when he got home. It hadn't snowed but the roads were icy. He drove with his gloves on, leaning forward to see through the space carved by the windscreen wipers. When he'd kissed Ruby goodbye, in the doorway of her digs, she had clung to him but he didn't know whether that was just because of the cold. He had kissed her on the mouth, just lightly, and she had accepted it, her face tilted upwards. She hadn't joined in as she had that day on the ice rink.

He was glad to reach his flat, glad to escape the various turmoils of the day. Even though the house was likely to be as cold inside as out, he could at least have a whisky and get into bed. He let himself in, stepping over the post that always seemed to silt up in the communal hall. He was about to put the letters on the half-moon table when he realised that he was looking at his own name, 'DI Edgar Stephens', written in a clear hand on an expensive-looking envelope. No stamp or address. For a second he thought of Ruby and her trick. Had she somehow arranged for this letter to be here, waiting for him? No, that was impossible. Nevertheless the feeling remained, that this was a trick or a trap, something to be feared.

He opened the envelope. Inside was a single sheet of thick cream paper.

Dear Detective Stephens,

Can you come to the address above urgently? I think I've discovered something about Annie and Mark. I think it's important.

Daphne Young

CHAPTER 17

Edgar looked at his watch. It was ten to twelve. Too late surely to call on Daphne Young? It would be crass, almost amounting to misconduct, to knock on her door at midnight. He'd go round before work in the morning. Nevertheless he slept badly, dreaming of churches and juniper trees and bodies rising from the dead. He was up and dressed at six but thought he should wait until seven to make the call. He drank black coffee, looking out of the window. It was still dark but, as a watery sun rose over the rooftops, he could see the frost glittering on the pavements. Snow lay in dirty drifts at the side of the road. At seven he started up the police car and drove slowly down the hill, keeping in a low gear and trying not to brake too much. The address on Daphne's letter was Montpelier Terrace, a smart residential area near the Seven Dials. The road was quiet, just a milkman and his horse plodding slowly past the white terraced houses. Edgar came to a halt, skidding slightly, and consulted the letter. First-floor flat, number 14.

There was no answer from the first floor but Edgar didn't panic. It was still early, Daphne was probably in bed. He watched the horse disappearing around the corner, the milk-cart swaying behind him. A bus edged past on the road below. Edgar rang the bell again and counted to ten. Then he tried the bell below.

The door opened very suddenly and an elderly man in a dressing gown stood glaring at him.

'What do you want?'

Slightly taken aback, Edgar said, 'I'm Detective Inspector Edgar Stephens of the Brighton Police. I came to see Miss Young in the flat above but she's not answering her bell.'

'Well, she's probably asleep. As any decent person should be at this hour.'

'I really do need to see her urgently,' said Edgar. 'Do you have a key to her flat?'

A woman had joined the man. She was in dressing gown and curlers but seemed disposed to be helpful.

'We've got a key,' she said. 'What's this about?'

'He's from the police, Irma.'

'Well, all the more reason to help him, Morris. Come in. Come in.'

He had to wait in the black-and-white tiled hall for what felt like hours while Irma and Morris searched for the key. Eventually they emerged. Irma had taken her curlers out.

'Here it is. I'd put it in the spare tea caddy for safe keeping.'

'Except you forgot where you'd put it,' said her husband.

Edgar took the key and bounded up the stairs. The elderly couple followed, still arguing gently.

At least it was the right key. Edgar pushed open the front door, calling, 'Miss Young? Daphne?'

There was no sound but the heavy ticking of a clock. Edgar opened a door and saw a sitting room with blue-swathed sofas and an upright piano. The next room was the kitchen. He opened the door at the end of the passage.

He turned to Irma and Morris. 'Don't come any further!'

But they, of course, had followed him and were peering over his shoulder. Irma said 'Is she dead?'

'I'm afraid so,' said Edgar.

Daphne lay on her bed but, even to the inexpert eye, her pose was unnatural and grotesque. One leg was bent under her, the other stretched out to the floor. Her neck was back and, even from the doorway, Edgar could see the fingerprints around her neck.

'Has Miss Young got a telephone?' he asked.

'All the flats have telephones,' said Irma.

'Stay where you are,' said Edgar. 'Don't go into the bedroom.'

The telephone was on a small table by the front door. Edgar rang the station and asked them to send the coroner's van. 'And telephone Solomon Carter and ask him to meet me here. And when Sergeant Willis or Sergeant Holmes gets in . . .'

'Sergeant Holmes is here now, sir.'

'Is she? Well, tell her to meet me here too. Thank you.'

He went back to the bedroom. The elderly couple were still standing in the doorway. He hoped the experience hadn't been too much of a shock for them but Irma said, in a surprisingly strong voice, 'Shall I make us all a cup of tea?'

Edgar saw a chance of getting them out of the flat. 'That would be very kind. Thank you. Could you make it downstairs? I'll join you as soon as I can.'

Morris and Irma retreated, rather reluctantly. Edgar approached the bed. He knew he shouldn't touch anything – there could be fingerprints, clues, blood, anything. But he wanted to see the body. He wanted to see some sign that Daphne had been dead for hours, that he wouldn't have saved her if he'd driven round at midnight last night. He thought the body looked stiff but he couldn't tell without touching it. Daphne's red hair touched the floor; her lips were bared in something between a smile and a grimace. He thought of her yesterday, reading from scripture, her voice resonating around the packed church. *I am the Resurrection and the life. The one who believes in me will live, even though they die.* He wished that he was like Sandra Francis, that he believed in God. He wished he could pray for her.

He wasn't sure how long he stood there. The clock

ticked in the hall, otherwise the flat was silent. Edgar went back into the sitting room. This room, like Daphne's classroom, was a jewelled cave. No utility furniture here; everything seemed to belong to an older, richer age. Red silk curtains gave the room a pinkish glow. The sofas were covered with blue fabric embroidered with stars and moons. On the table between the sofas there was a pile of paper snowflakes. Edgar's throat contracted. Daphne had been making her Christmas decorations. Next to the paper shapes there was a cup. Just one. Daphne clearly hadn't been expecting visitors. He touched it. Cold. A lipstick kiss was imprinted on the china. There were two books on the table too. A Bible and a book of fairy stories. He wrapped a handkerchief around his hand and opened the fairy stories. It fell open at a place marked by a photograph. Edgar stared at the children in the picture, all of them now as familiar as his own nephews. Mark, Annie and her little sister, Betty. It was the only photograph he had seen of Mark smiling. He had his hand over his mouth as if trying to stifle a laugh. Annie looked at him, halfway between irritation and affection. Betty beamed into the camera, clearly delighted to be in such exalted company.

'Edgar! Fancy meeting you here.'

It was Solomon Carter, who had made his usual silent entrance.

'Where's the corpse?'

'This way.' Edgar led the way back to the bedroom.

*

Emma arrived just as he was leaving the house on Montpelier Terrace.

'You took your time,' he said.

'I had to walk.' Emma was pink-faced with exertion. It was uphill all the way from Bartholomew Square.

'I'll give you a lift back.'

'Aren't we going to examine the scene?'

'Solomon Carter's in there now. We'll go back when they've removed the body.'

He opened the car door. Emma got in beside him. Edgar started the engine but didn't make any move to set off. Exhaust smoke billowed around them.

'How did she die?' asked Emma.

'Strangled, Carter says. He thinks she's been dead about twelve hours.'

That meant he couldn't have saved her even if he'd gone round last night. Even so, if he'd gone home after work, if he hadn't driven straight to Worthing to see Ruby . . .

'Anyone see anything?'

'The neighbours, Irma and Morris Gold, have been very helpful. They're the sort who notice everything. They said that Daphne came in at about two in the afternoon yesterday. She must have come straight home after the wake. The school was shut all day. Then they heard her go out at about three.'

That must have been when she walked to his house. As briefly as possible, he told Emma about the note from Daphne.

'I've got it here. Look.'

She put on her gloves to touch it. Edgar was impressed, even though his prints must be all over the paper.

'She thought she'd discovered something about the children?'

'Yes. It must have been after the funeral. She came home and thought of something. She walked round to my place with the letter. She was back at four. Solomon Carter thought she must have been killed a few hours later.'

'How did she know where you lived?'

'It wouldn't have been hard to find out. I'm in the book.'

'Do you think she was killed because of this piece of information, whatever it was?'

'I have to think that. She wrote to me. Who else did she tell? Someone thought it was important enough to silence her.'

'I wish she'd just told you in the letter,' said Emma.

'So do I. But that was Daphne Young. She liked a mystery. She liked a good story.'

'And it killed her,' said Emma. They were silent for a minute and then she said, 'Did the neighbours see anyone coming to the house?'

'That's the frustrating thing. They have their supper at six and weren't at their usual spot by the window. Irma did say she thought she heard a man's voice upstairs but, as Morris said, that could have been the wireless.'

'Have you any idea what she thought she'd discovered?' Emma tapped the cream envelope.

'No. I've been thinking and thinking about it.' Daphne must have come back from the funeral, made herself a cup of tea and sat on the sofa. Was she reading the book of fairy stories? Did that give her the clue? He told Emma about the photograph.

'It was just a picture of Annie, Mark and Betty, that's all?'

'That's all. No writing on the back. Nothing.'

'You said it was marking a place in the book. Which story was it marking?'

The funny thing was, Edgar thought he didn't know but he did. He could see the page as if it was imprinted on his eyelids, the little figure cavorting in its red trousers. ' "Hans My Hedgehog" ' he said.

'Daphne said that Annie was like Hans,' said Emma. 'It must mean something.'

'Yes,' said Edgar. 'But what? Come on, let's go back and brief the team.'

CHAPTER 18

'Murdered children's teacher found dead.' Lou Abrahams was reading the paper in his cubbyhole. Max, on his way to change for the evening show, looked in and saw the headline.

'Christ,' he said. 'What's that about the teacher?'

'What?' Lou was deep in the sports news.

'On the front page.'

'Oh. Those poor kiddies, the ones who were found up at the Dyke. Their teacher's been found dead.'

'How was she killed?'

'Paper doesn't say. They have to be careful about stuff like that. At first I thought she'd done it and topped herself but it says "suicide has been ruled out". Here, you can have a look. You know the policeman, don't you?'

'Yes, I served with him in the war.' Max found that this explanation always tended to be accepted at face value. He took the paper.

MURDERED CHILDREN'S TEACHER FOUND DEAD

Miss Daphne Young, aged 25 and a teacher at Bristol Road Junior School, was found dead at her Montpelier Terrace flat this morning. Miss Young taught the murdered schoolchildren Annie Francis and Mark Webster and had yesterday attended their funeral at St George's Church, Kemp Town. Police declined to comment on the cause of death but did disclose that suicide had been ruled out. Mr Duncan Pettigrew, the headmaster at Bristol Road Juniors, said, 'This is a terrible shock. Miss Young was a wonderful teacher. The children loved her.' Miss Young was the daughter of the Hon. Basil Young and his wife, Laura Young, née Asherton-Smythe.

Max thought of the mesmerising figure in black reading from scripture. He had thought then that she was an interesting woman and it seems that he was right. Uninteresting women, in his experience, didn't get murdered. He noticed how the paper homed in on Miss Young's mildly aristocratic background. He had suffered from this fixation himself. In the early days, no review had been complete without calling him The Hon. Max or mentioning his father. All the same, he wondered how Daphne Young had ended up teaching in a backstreet Brighton school.

'Max, have you seen Diablo? I just want to go over his scenes with him.'

It was Nigel Castle, the scriptwriter, looking as harassed as ever. Max knew that Diablo would be drinking gin in the chorus girls' room and would welcome seeing Nigel as much as Nigel would welcome Diablo's ad-libs later that night.

'I don't know,' he said. 'Have you tried the Green Room?'

But Nigel had caught sight of the *Evening Argus*. 'What's this?' He almost snatched the paper and began reading. 'My God. That's terrible.'

'You were at the funeral yesterday, weren't you?' said Max.

Nigel looked at him, still pale with shock. 'Yes, I was.'

Max tried to think of a subtle way of asking the question but eventually settled on a bald, 'Why?'

Nigel didn't seem to resent his curiosity. 'Roger and I went into a few local grammar schools to do some drama with them. It was all part of some community project. I met the children then.'

'You met Annie and Mark?'

'Yes. I remember them because they were so talented. Annie, in particular, had a real gift for story-telling.'

'I've heard.'

'I was so shocked when I heard that they had been killed. It brought on an attack of nerves. I was in bed for a day.'

Nigel's nerves were already notorious amongst the cast.

'Did you go into this Miss Young's school?'

'No. We went into the grammar schools. I remember Mark's headmaster in particular. He was very interested in the theatre.'

Max wanted to ask more but Nigel staggered away still clutching the paper and looking at if he'd seen the theatre ghost.

There was no chance of getting to Ruby's first night. In fact Edgar didn't even think of her until he looked at the station clock and realised that it was seven o'clock. It had been a long and stressful day. After briefing the team, Edgar had driven to the morgue, where Solomon Carter confirmed that Daphne Young's death had occurred from manual strangulation. He put the time of death at about seven p.m. on Friday night. So Daphne was killed only a few hours after she had delivered her letter to Edgar. Who else had she contacted on her way? He sent officers door-to-door and went back to Montpelier Terrace with Emma and Bob.

Irma Gold was waiting for them.

'I thought you'd be back. I've been thinking about the man.'

'Which man, Mrs Gold?' asked Edgar.

'The man I heard upstairs last night. I think he may have been Irish.'

'Irish?'

'Yes. Morris doesn't agree but I think I heard a definite Irish lilt.'

Morris shouted from inside the flat, 'You couldn't even hear his voice, let alone a lilt.'

'I've been thinking about it and there was definitely a musical quality.'

'Josef Locke was on the wireless singing "Danny Boy".'

'If you'll excuse us,' said Edgar, 'my officers and I need to go upstairs.'

'Shall I make you some tea?'

'That's very kind but we don't want to put you to any trouble.'

'No trouble.' Irma retreated but Edgar had no doubt that she would appear again, ten minutes later, with a laden tea tray.

Daphne's flat already had the stale, sad air of a place that has been abandoned. There was post by the door and Edgar flipped through it. A gas bill, a flyer for a women's clothes shop and a postcard showing Edinburgh Castle. Edgar turned it over.

Darling Daphers,

It's jolly cold here in bonny Scotland. Hope you're having fun by the sea. I hear your pal is doing the panto there. Give him my best.

Toodle-oo, pip pip,

Bootsie

'Toodle-oo, pip pip, Bootsie,' repeated Bob. 'What the bloody hell does that mean?'

'The upper classes speak a different language,' said Edgar.

'Who's her pal in the panto?' said Emma, reading over Edgar's shoulder.

'*Doing* the panto,' said Edgar. 'He might not be an actor.'

'You can ask *your* pal,' said Bob, who seemed to harbour a deep resentment of Max.

'Yes, I can,' said Edgar. 'Bob, you look in the kitchen. Look for any signs of recent meals, anything unusual. Don't touch anything. Emma, you do the sitting room. I'll do the bedroom.' He was dreading the bedroom but, because of that, knew that he couldn't delegate it.

There was nothing surprising in the room. A double bed, still with its rumpled lacy cover, a wardrobe, a chest of drawers. Carter thought that Daphne had been killed in the sitting room and carried into the bedroom. There were fibres from the sofa on her hair, he said. Edgar agreed. Daphne was not the sort of girl to have brought a man into her bedroom. Even so, the sitting room had shown no signs of a struggle. Had the visitor just leant over and strangled Daphne where she sat, not even knocking over her teacup?

Edgar opened the wardrobe. Daphne's black velvet suit, the one she'd worn for the funeral, was there on its hanger. When she died, she'd been wearing a tweed skirt and lavender jumper. She'd changed before she set out with her letter, which made sense because it was a long walk and her black shoes, placed neatly on the wardrobe floor, were very high. He thought of the body on the bed, the stockinged foot touching the floor. He called out to Emma, 'Any shoes in the sitting room?'

'Yes,' she answered, 'a pair of brogues by the door.' A sudden picture of Daphne, curled up on the sofa reading her fairy tales, came into Edgar's mind. For a moment he felt almost angry with her. Why hadn't she screamed? Why hadn't she run? Why hadn't she told him more in her letter?

He went into the hall again. 'What time was Josef Locke on the wireless last night?'

'No idea.' Bob emerged from the kitchen. 'I hate that sort of singing.'

'There's a *Radio Times* here,' called Emma from the sitting room. He heard her turn the pages. 'Six-thirty.'

Edgar went back into the bedroom. At six-thirty, while Josef Locke was singing 'Danny Boy', Irma had heard voices upstairs. By seven o'clock, Daphne was dead.

Edgar was looking through the chest of drawers – underwear, scent, scarves, gloves – when he heard a tentative tap on the door. That would be Irma with the refreshments.

But when he opened the door, the downstairs neighbour was there but she was accompanied by a smartly dressed middle-aged couple.

'Detective Stephens?' said the man. 'We're Basil and Laura Young.'

It wasn't how Edgar would have planned it, meeting

the bereaved parents in their daughter's flat. He was actually grateful to Irma for fussing around with tea and biscuits and saying how fond she had been of Daphne.

'She was a real lady, that's what Morris and I always said.'

Laura Young dabbed her eyes. 'She told us how kind you both were.'

When Irma finally left, Edgar asked Bob and Emma to wait in the kitchen. He didn't want to overcrowd the Youngs but he also wanted his officers within earshot, just in case.

'I'm sorry,' said Edgar. 'This must be a terrible time for you.'

'Yes,' said Basil. 'We've driven straight down from Shropshire. We left as soon as we spoke to you on the telephone.'

'We couldn't take it in,' said Laura. 'You said that Daphne had been murdered?'

'I'm afraid it looks like that,' said Edgar.

'But who would . . . ?' Laura started crying again. Basil glared accusingly at Edgar. He was a large man with sparse gingery hair. Daphne might have inherited his colouring but, in all other respects, she resembled her mother.

'Can we see her?' asked Laura, looking around the room as if she expected to find her daughter's body there.

'Of course,' said Edgar. 'I'll take you to the . . . to the place myself. I just wondered if I could ask some questions first.'

'Why?' asked Basil. 'What could we possibly tell you?'

Edgar sat opposite them. 'We want to find your

daughter's killer and any little thing might help. I promise you, we won't rest until this person is found.' He seemed to be saying this a lot these days.

Basil muttered about the police not having done much so far, but he sounded mollified all the same.

'The thing is,' said Edgar, 'we can't discount the possibility that Daphne's death may have been linked to the deaths of the two children, Annie Francis and Mark Webster. As you probably know, Daphne taught the children in primary school.'

'I always said she shouldn't have become a schoolteacher,' exploded Basil. 'She should have stayed at home and found a husband, like her sister did.'

So Daphne had a sister, thought Edgar. Aloud he said, 'When did you last speak to Daphne?'

'She telephoned the night before last,' said Laura. 'I spoke to her every week.'

'How did she sound?'

'A bit down, a bit sad. It was the funeral the next day and she was dreading that. She'd been asked to do a reading and she was very nervous. And she loved those children. She got fond of all the children she taught but she always said that Annie was special.'

If Daphne had been nervous in the church, thought Edgar, it hadn't showed. He had been the one who gabbled and stuttered and looked an idiot. Daphne had been all coolness and grace.

'Did she talk to you about Annie?' he asked.

'Yes. She said she was really clever. That she deserved a better life than her parents could give her. Some of those children come from very poor families, Detective Inspector, very poor indeed. And when she died, Daphne was heart-broken. She felt . . . I don't know.'

'She felt what?'

'She felt as if she should have saved her.'

'What do you think she meant by that?'

'She had some crazy idea about adopting the child,' Basil cut in. 'Madness, and we told her so.'

'Daphne wanted to adopt Annie?'

'It was only an idea,' said Laura. 'Daphne always had these impetuous ideas. She felt that Annie didn't . . . didn't fit in with her family, though I'm sure they were very decent people. Daphne thought she could give her a better life, one filled with music and art and stories, that's what she said.'

'Did she speak to Annie's parents about this?'

'Oh no,' said Laura. 'As I say, it was only an idea. She soon saw that it was impossible. Anyway, Annie passed her eleven-plus, she was on the way up. She didn't need Daphne any more.'

Interesting, thought Edgar. He asked Laura Young if she'd heard anything from her daughter on the Friday. No, said Laura firmly, they always spoke on Thursday, that was their routine.

Edgar picked up the postcard, which was lying on the table.

'Have you any idea who this is from?'

Laura's eyes filled with tears. 'It's from Daphne's sister, Sarah. We always call her Bootsie.'

Why? thought Edgar. As he had told Bob, it's a different language.

'Bootsie lives in Edinburgh,' said Laura. 'Her husband's a doctor.'

'Sarah . . . er, Bootsie . . . mentions Daphne having a friend in the pantomime. Have you any idea who that could be?'

To his surprise, Laura smiled mistily. 'Oh, that will be Nigel. Nigel Castle. He writes plays. He was a friend of Daphne's from university. Such a nice boy.'

CHAPTER 19

'So what sort of man is Nigel Castle?' asked Edgar.

Max frowned into his coffee. It was Monday morning and they were sitting in a seafront cafe. Freezing sleet battered the windows but there was a warm fug inside and a comforting smell of frying. Edgar was looking forward to his eggs and bacon. Max had – of course – rejected food with a shudder.

Edgar had called at Max's digs at an hour which felt like midday to him but he was sure would count as breakfast time for the pros. Sure enough, Mrs M answered the door wearing a frilly apron and Edgar could hear sounds of a meal in progress.

'Oh, it's you,' said the landlady. 'Is it Mr M you want?'

'Yes, please.'

Mrs M smiled and beckoned him into the hall. Then she shouted upstairs, 'Mr M! Visitor for you.'

'If it's the bailiffs, I'm out,' Max shouted back. Edgar

was surprised to find him so jocular in the morning. Max appeared a few minutes later, tucking in his shirt.

'Ed! What are you doing here?'

'I wondered if we could have a talk.'

'Well, we can't talk here, the place is full of actors. Let's go to the Sea Spray. They do a decent coffee there.'

'Your coat, Mr M,' the landlady held it out to him.

'You're a diamond, Mrs M.'

'Mr M and Mrs M,' said Edgar as they made their way along the seafront, heads down against the wind. 'You could be a married couple.'

Max didn't reply, but then it was an effort talking at all. Inside the cafe it was easier. Max drank some coffee and lit a cigarette.

'Nigel? He seems harmless enough. Always fussing about the script. Most panto writers accept that the cast will make it up as they go along but Nigel seems really hurt if we don't stick to his words. Diablo is driving him insane.'

'I can imagine.'

'It seems odd, though, that Nigel didn't tell me that he knew this Daphne Young. He just said that he'd been at the funeral because he'd visited the school and met the children.'

'He did? Bristol Road Juniors?'

'No. The grammar schools, he said. Nigel and Roger Dunkley, the director, went to do some work with the children, teach them about acting. Not that Nigel knew anything about acting.'

'I'll follow that up. Apparently Daphne met Nigel Castle at university. How old is he?'

Max shrugged. 'I don't know. About twenty-five or twenty-six, I suppose. I know he was too young for the draft.'

Edgar always felt ashamed of the slight resentment he felt for men like Nigel and Bob who had been too young to fight. Added to that, Nigel had completed university while he had had to leave after two terms and been sent to freeze to death in Norway. Jonathan had gone straight from school to the army and had been dead within the year.

'Do you seriously think that Nigel might be a suspect?' asked Max.

'I don't know,' said Edgar. 'But I have to consider it. Nigel knew Annie and Mark and he was a friend of Daphne's. And then there's the writing. Annie wrote plays; Daphne seemed obsessed with fairy tales; you say that Nigel is pretty obsessive too.'

'Yes. And of course most pantomimes are based on traditional tales. Nigel keeps going on about that.'

'Denton McGrew said that Ezra Nightingale was always talking about the true sources of fairy tales. How they were all very gruesome really and shouldn't be made sweet for the audience.'

'Ezra? Oh, Diablo's killer. Do you still think there's a link?'

'There are a lot of links. Denton, Diablo, the Billington

family, the murder of children. It's just whether any of them mean anything.'

Edgar's breakfast arrived, steaming and beautiful. He plunged his knife into the egg and tried not to think about Diablo's description of Betsy's blood running down from the stage.

'How was Ruby?' asked Max.

Edgar was taken aback. 'She seemed very well,' he said. 'I meant to go to see the show last night but I couldn't really get away.'

'Well, she's only in the chorus anyway.'

Edgar was stung on Ruby's behalf by the dismissiveness in Max's tone. 'She still wants to be a magician.'

'Really?'

'Yes.' Edgar told Max about the trick with the piece of paper in the restaurant. To his surprise, Max enjoyed it hugely.

'Very clever. A waiter makes the perfect stick. They're always there and yet you never see them. Classic misdirection.'

Edgar knew that 'stick' was a magician's word for a stooge or plant. He found Max's praise as irritating as his indifference.

'I'll walk with you to the theatre,' he said. 'And then I can speak to Nigel Castle.'

'All right,' said Max. 'I'm sure he'll be there. He seems to sleep in the place.'

*

Max was right. They found the scriptwriter sitting in the foyer, reading the programme. Surely he must know what's in it by now?

'Max.' Nigel looked up. 'You're early.'

As it was now past twelve Edgar found it hard to believe that anyone could call it early. But the matinee started at two and there were no other actors to be seen, so maybe Nigel was right to look surprised. Max smiled, rather grimly.

'Nigel, this is my friend Edgar Stephens. He's a policeman. He'd like to have a chat with you, if that's all right.'

Edgar had thought that Nigel looked nervous before. Now he positively quailed, literally shrinking away from them.

'Talk to *me*? Why?'

'I understand that you were a friend of Daphne Young's.'

'Who told you that?'

'Her parents.'

'Oh.' Nigel's eyes darted from Max to Edgar and back again. Then he seemed to make a huge effort to compose himself. 'Well,' he said. 'Yes. It's a terrible thing. Poor Daphne. I must write to Laura and Basil.'

'I'm sure they'd appreciate that,' said Edgar. 'I'm just trying to get some idea about Daphne as a person. That's why I wanted to talk to you.'

'You can use my dressing room,' said Max. 'I'll go and see Lou.'

'No,' said Nigel. 'Please stay, Max.'

Max raised his eyebrows. 'If you want me to.'

They sat in Max's dressing room amongst the telegrams and empty champagne bottles and scraps of paper with girls' names on. Nigel perched on the sofa and Edgar sat next to him, trying not to seem confrontational. Max took his dressing-table chair, which he pushed back against the wall.

'I understand you knew Daphne from university,' said Edgar.

'Yes. We were both at St Andrews. In Scotland, you know. Both doing English. We hit it off immediately.'

'Were you romantically involved?'

Nigel laughed. Edgar would not have believed him capable of making such a cynical sound. 'Oh no. Daphne was much sought-after. She could take her pick of boyfriends. No, I was cast as the best friend, the confidant, safe and sexless.'

Edgar noted the theatrical terminology. Also the bitterness.

'And was it pure coincidence that you both ended up in Brighton?'

'Yes. I sent some scripts on spec to Bert Billington. He liked this one and he signed me up. He told me that I didn't have to be here for the run but I wasn't going to miss seeing my pantomime in rehearsal. I took digs near Brunswick Square.'

Brunswick Square was not far from Montpelier Terrace.

Also, *my* pantomime. 'What did Daphne say when you told her?'

'She was happy for me. She knew how long I had been waiting for my chance.'

'What did you do before this?'

'I was a teacher. I only went into it because you could get out of National Service if you agreed to teach for five years after graduation. To make up for the shortage of teachers after the war. I hated it. The kids made my life hell. Not like Daphne; she was a natural.'

Edgar felt another wave of resentment. He was sure he would have hated National Service but he would have done it, in the same dogged, conscientious way he'd gone to war. Why should Nigel – sitting there in his corduroy trousers and cravat – escape all the horrors of life? He found himself hoping that Nigel's pupils really had made him suffer.

'I understand that you and the director, Roger Dunkley, went into some local schools,' he said. 'Can you tell me about that?'

'It was an idea the Local Authority had, to encourage creativity and what have you. We went into the schools and did some basic drama and writing exercises. I was worried about it at first but it seemed to go quite well.'

'You went into both grammar schools?'

'Yes.'

'And you met Annie Francis and Mark Webster?'

Nigel looked at Max as if asking for his help. 'Just

briefly. Annie had rather a good idea for a script. It was a version of "Hansel and Gretel". Quite dark, quite funny.'

'What about Mark?'

'He was more interested in the technical stuff. I thought he would have made a brilliant stage manager.' Nigel rubbed his eyes. 'So tragic. When I heard they'd died . . .'

'Mr Castle,' said Edgar. 'I'm asking everyone this. What were you doing on the night of Monday the twenty-sixth of November?'

He had tried to soften the blow but Nigel still goggled at him. 'You can't think . . . This is madness . . . I . . .'

Max said. 'As I understand it, the police are simply trying to eliminate people from their enquiry.'

His voice seemed to have a calming effect on the writer. Nigel's voice still shook, though, when he said, 'I can't remember. I was here, I think. Then I went back to my digs, listened to the wireless . . .'

'Did you see Daphne?'

Nigel blinked. 'No. I think she was working late. We didn't see that much of each other. She had her own life.'

'Did she have a boyfriend? You said she could take her pick.'

'I don't think so. There was a man at St Andrews but, when that finished, she said that she was going to concentrate on her career. She was going to live for the children, she said.'

Did Nigel know that Daphne had thought about adopting one of those children? wondered Edgar. Once again there was something cynical in his tone, as if he hadn't believed in his friend's vision of a selfless life devoted to education.

'What about Friday night? Where were you then?'

Nigel blinked rapidly but he answered fairly calmly. 'I had a drink with a few members of the cast. Diablo was there and Denton and some of the girls. Then I went home at about nine.'

'What time was this drink?'

'About seven. In the Colonnade Bar, next to the Theatre Royal.'

Edgar knew the bar, a famous hang-out for theatricals. If Daphne was killed at six-thirty, whilst Josef Locke was singing, it was possible that Nigel could have killed her and still made it to the bar for seven. Possible but not entirely probable.

'Can you let me know if you remember the name of the man in Scotland?' he asked.

'It was Douglas something. I'll think.'

'That would be very helpful. Thank you, Mr Castle.'

Nigel stood up. 'You mean I can go?'

'Of course.'

Nigel did not need telling twice. He shot out of the door so quickly that Max's champagne rattled in its ice bucket.

CHAPTER 20

'He was nervous,' said Max.

'Yes,' said Edgar. 'But the police make most people nervous. It needn't mean anything.'

'I still think it's funny that he didn't say anything to me about knowing the woman.'

'Do you suspect him then?' It was a serious question. Like many people who deal in illusion, Max was a hard man to fool.

'I don't know.' Max moved his chair back to the dressing table. 'I can't quite see him as a killer. What motive would he have?'

'He seemed to be pretty bitter about Daphne. It was obvious that he was in love with her and she never gave him a moment's notice, except as a friend.'

'No motive for the children though.'

'No.' Edgar thought of the little bodies lying on the snowy ground, a picture that never seemed to fade no matter how hard he tried to banish it. 'He could have killed them to spite Daphne, but it's a long shot. And it was a brutal crime. Both children were strangled, they would have struggled . . .'

Max raised a hand to stop him. 'Spare us the details, Ed, please.'

There was a silence. Edgar could hear footsteps running up and down the corridor. The show was starting in an hour.

'Was the teacher strangled too?' asked Max.

'Yes, but keep it to yourself. We don't want the press finding out.'

'So you think it was the same person.'

'I do, yes.' He told Max about the letter.

Max frowned at his reflection in the mirror. 'She just said that she had discovered something, not that she knew who the killer was.'

'Whatever she discovered was enough for someone to murder her.'

'All the same,' said Max, 'if she'd thought, say, that her old university pal was a murderer, she'd have said so.'

'Yes,' Edgar conceded. 'But I don't think she knew who the killer was. The note said "I've discovered something about Annie and Mark". She knew it was important but maybe not why.'

'Any idea what it could have been?'

'None at all,' said Edgar. That wasn't strictly true, he realised. He had an idea but it was to do with dancing hedgehogs, with brightly coloured sweets in the snow, with bones buried under a juniper tree. He knew that if he said any of this aloud the pieces of the puzzle would shatter and he would be left with nothing.

Max was reaching for his make-up. It was time to go.

Emma was on her way back to the grammar schools. DI Stephens, having vanished all morning, turned up at one-thirty, just as she and Bob were grabbing a quick sandwich in the CID room, and asked if she'd do another interview with the two head teachers, Dr Hammond and Mrs Paxton.

'I've just found out that two members of the theatre company went into the children's schools about a month ago. Nigel Castle, the writer, and Roger Dunkley, the director. If you remember, Nigel Castle was Daphne's old university friend.'

'Has he got an alibi?' asked Bob briskly.

'Not for the children's murder,' said DI Stephens. 'He's got one for Friday night although it's a bit shaky.'

'Hang on,' said Emma. 'Aren't we going a bit fast here?'

The DI smiled. Rather patronisingly, Emma thought. 'Possibly. But he's an odd character. And he's a writer with a particular interest in old stories. Then there's the pantomime link. I saw Daphne Young there last week. And Brian Baxter was going to take Annie and Mark as a treat.'

'I still think Baxter's our man,' said Bob.

'I'm not ruling anything out,' said the DI with what

seemed to Emma to be exaggerated patience. 'I just think we should look into Nigel Castle's past.'

'What about the other chap?' asked Bob. 'Dunkley.'

'Him too,' said DI Stephens. 'I'm going to interview him tomorrow. I can't see what motive he'd have though.'

'Motiveless malignity,' said Emma, more to annoy Bob than anything.

Sure enough: 'Speak English,' growled Bob.

'It's what Coleridge said about Iago,' said the DI, 'and not, strictly speaking, relevant here. Emma, you go and see the grammar-school heads. Find out what they remember about the visits, in particular any interaction with the children. Bob, you go back to the primary school and talk to the headmaster there. See if you can find out any more about Daphne Young, both her professional and private life.'

'I see I get the little kids,' said Bob. 'Is that because I won't be clever enough to understand them up at the grammar school?'

'No, it's because that's the way I want it,' said DI Stephens, acerbically for him.

Now, as Emma trudged up the gravel drive towards the boys' grammar school, she wondered what was behind Bob's resentment. He'd failed the eleven-plus, he told her the other day. Was that really all it was? She hadn't taken the eleven-plus because her parents had her name down for Roedean, probably from birth. They lived near the school and, all through her early childhood, it had loomed in the background, half threatening, half reassuring. She'd been embarrassed to be a day girl because, although the boarders clamoured for invitations to her home (all that food and central heating too!), they seemed to have a bond which she couldn't share. That was why she had been so pleased when the school was evacuated to the Lake District. It was her chance of freedom, her chance to be like everyone else. So why was she now back living at home, within sight of her alma mater? You wanted to join the police, she told herself as she stepped through the double doors and entered the fusty academic world, and that's why you're still here, in Brighton, when all your friends are either married or partying. She hadn't wanted to go to university and the only other options seemed to be finishing school, being presented or marriage. Her parents had wanted her to go into teaching but Emma had had enough of school at eighteen. She had chosen the police force because it had seemed exciting and, besides, with her name, what could she do except solve crimes?

What about the DI? He had recognised the Coleridge quotation. Where did he go to school? Did he go to university? They all knew that DI Stephens had served in the war and rumours about the shadowy group called the Magic Men abounded at the station. But he did have rather an academic look, come to think of it. Emma could imagine him teaching English literature or history somewhere. Instead of which, he was hunting down murderers in Brighton. Maybe there's something about the south coast, she thought; everyone gets washed up on these shores. DI Stephens, Daphne Young, Nigel Castle. You run away until you can't get any further because there's nothing else, only the sea.

You could see the sea from Dr Hammond's office, a thin line of blue behind the Regency hotels and Victorian terraces. Emma stared out of the window as the secretary set off in search of the headmaster. 'I think he's taking the Remove for Latin today.' Schools really are short-staffed, thought Emma. Duncan Pettigrew taking the boys for football, Dr Hammond teaching Latin. She looked around the room with its wooden panelling and framed photographs of Cricket elevens and thanked God for the police force.

'I'm so sorry.' Dr Hammond bustled in, gown off one shoulder. Emma thought what a stereotypical figure he cut, like something from a comic book. Were there still teachers like this in 1951? Obviously so.

'Thank you for seeing me, Dr Hammond.' Emma waved his apology aside. 'I just wanted to ask you about something that has come up in our enquiry.'

Dr Hammond sat opposite her and peered over his spectacles in a comic-strip kind of way.

'I understand that two members of a theatrical company visited the school in early November,' said Emma. 'Their names were Nigel Castle and Roger Dunkley.'

'I'm not sure I . . .'

'They visited the school in early November as part of a Local Authority initiative.'

'Oh yes.' Dr Hammond looked vaguer than ever. 'I think I remember. They acted out plays in the school hall.'

'We believe that Mark Webster was one of the boys involved.'

Emma watched understanding and . . . what was it? . . . yes, *fear* . . . blooming on the headmaster's face.

'He might have been,' he said slowly. 'I seem to remember it was the younger boys. First and second years. They did some writing exercises and acted out little plays.'

'Did you attend the sessions?'

'I may have been there for some of them.'

'Were you there for Mark's session? Do you remember him chatting to the two theatricals?'

'No.' Dr Hammond drew himself up. 'I don't think I was there for Mark's session and I cannot imagine any of our boys *chatting* to a visitor. I'm sure Mark spoke when spoken to, that's all.'

Dr Hammond was hiding something, thought Emma, as she made her way to the girls' school next door. But what? It occurred to her that Martin Hammond, who seemed a hundred in his dusty gown, was probably only in his early fifties.

Mrs Paxton was less defensive but hardly more helpful. Yes, she remembered the visit. She'd mentioned it last time, if Sergeant Holmes remembered. The theatre people had seemed jolly nice chaps. Yes, Annie had been one of the girls involved. She hadn't been to any of the sessions herself. No, she didn't know anything about a 'Hansel and Gretel' play. Sounds a bit young for a thirteen-year-old. Annie was a very mature young lady, good at science, wanted to be a doctor.

Emma set off towards Brighton feeling frustrated. Why did both the heads want to play down the significance of the visit by the theatricals? Was it simply academic bias against the arts? Emma was sure that the answer to this crime lay in the stories, particularly 'Hansel and Gretel' and 'Hans My Hedgehog'. That was why she had suspected Daphne Young. Well, she had been right; Daphne *was* involved, just in a different way. Although, as she told a sceptical Bob that morning, Daphne could still have killed the children. Getting murdered herself was no guarantee of innocence.

It was very cold; the snow was still on the ground in some places, icy and treacherous. Emma put up the hood of her duffel coat and walked faster. Her footsteps seemed to beat out a series of slightly jarring couplets. Annie and Mark. Hansel and Gretel. Martha and Mary. Flanagan and Allen. Abbott and Costello. Emma and Bob. Emma and . . . She changed step, skipping past the peace statue on the sea-front and causing a passing errand boy to whistle at her appreciatively.

It was dark by the time she reached the station. DI Stephens was in a meeting with Superintendent Hodges. Emma made a cup of tea and sat down to read through the witness reports from the night that the children disappeared.

Bob came in at about five.

'Got something for you,' he said. He put an envelope in front of her. Emma looked at it curiously. It was addressed, in slightly wavery capitals, to 'The Lady Policeman'.

'Little girl at the primary school gave it to me. She didn't say her name but I think it was Annie's little sister.'

Emma opened the envelope. 'You Are Invited,' she read, 'To A Show. Come and see The Stolen Children at Uncle Brain's House on Friday 14th December. 5p.m. Do Not Be Late.'

'Uncle Brain!' Bob was reading over her shoulder.

But apart from that it was beautifully written and spelled, thought Emma. How old was Betty again? And why were they putting on the play without Annie?

'Will you go?' asked Bob.

'I certainly will,' said Emma. She looked at the invitation, which was decorated with stars and flowers that brought to mind Annie's exercise books.

Do Not Be Late.

CHAPTER 21

The meeting wasn't going well. Edgar had always known that Superintendent Hodges resented him, thought him a posh university boy who had been promoted through the police ranks via some sinister old boys' network. The truth was that Edgar had progressed fast because the police force, like teaching, was short of men after the war. He owed his commission to his army rank and he'd only got that because, whilst recuperating from the Norway campaign, he was recruited by MI5 on the strength of his way with a cryptic crossword. To Frank Hodges, who, because of childhood polio, had been forced to sit out two wars, Edgar was the epitome of modern softness and lack of backbone. Now, with two children and a woman dead, his so-called brilliant detective inspector was no nearer to catching the culprit. Frank was not going to miss out on a fight this time.

'What about the teacher?' he said. 'There must be a boyfriend somewhere. Remember thinking at the funeral what an attractive woman she was.'

'There's no current boyfriend on the scene,' said Edgar. 'I'm on the trail of her old university boyfriend though.' He would have to chase Nigel Castle for the name.

'Girl like that,' said Hodges. 'What was she doing teaching in a dump like Bristol Road Juniors?'

'I think she wanted to do good, sir,' said Edgar. He was pretty sure that this would be an alien concept to Hodges.

Hodges chewed his moustache furiously. 'You say the girl wrote to you just before she died?'

'Yes, she sent me a note saying that she'd discovered something about the children, Annie Francis and Mark Webster.'

'And you've no idea what that was?'

'No, sir.'

'Seems to me,' said Hodges, 'that you haven't got many ideas at all. I thought that was what you university chaps were good at, ideas.'

Edgar wanted to say that he had many ideas, some of them as fanciful as the fairy tales so beloved of Miss Young and her pupils. That was the trouble. The truth was there, he was sure of it; it was just hard to see. Smoke and mirrors, Max would say. What was real and what was illusion?

'We're following up some leads,' he said. 'We're going to interview everyone who was at the wake. It's possible that Daphne Young's discovery about Annie and Mark was triggered by something she saw or heard there.'

The wake after the children's funeral had been held in

the local Scout hall. Edgar hadn't attended; he'd wanted to get back to work because he felt guilty about going to see Ruby that evening. He regretted it now.

'It seems to me that all you've got is guesswork,' said Hodges. 'We've got to get some answers on this case. It looks bad for us, you know.'

It didn't look too good for the parents of the dead children either, thought Edgar. But he said nothing. He knew that the superintendent was working himself up to the big threat.

'If this case is too much for you, Stephens . . .' Hodges puffed out his chest importantly. 'I might have to bring someone in above your head.'

Edgar imagined a shiny new detective inspector floating about amongst the pipes and peeling paintwork of the ceiling. The way he felt at the moment, the new man was welcome to it. But he promised Frank Hodges that he would redouble his efforts on the case.

'You'll see some results soon. I promise.'

'I hope so, Stephens. I really hope so.'

Edgar left the super's office feeling depressed. He'd promised results but he really wasn't sure what to do next. No one had seen the children disappear and it seemed that no one had seen the killer enter and leave Daphne's house. It was a vanishing trick worthy of Max himself. That reminded him that he was going to interview Roger Dunkley, the pantomime's director, tomorrow. There might be something more in the visit of the two theatricals to the children's schools. Nigel Castle had certainly been nervous when Edgar had spoken to him. It was worth a shot anyway.

He walked past the cells and down the stone stairs to the CID room. Emma and Bob were both there, at separate desks, going through files. They were good officers, thought Edgar. Whatever happened, he must make sure that they weren't affected by his failures on the case.

Emma blushed when she saw him, as if he'd caught her having a tea break rather than conscientiously going through the paperwork.

'Find anything?' He gestured towards the files.

'Just checking eyewitness reports, just to see if we've missed anything. And look . . .'

She was holding out a piece of card with a child's drawings on it. *You Are Invited To A Show.*

'It's Annie's sister, Betty,' she said. 'She's putting on Annie's play, the one they were rehearsing when she died.'

'And it's at Brian Baxter's house?'

'Yes.'

'Interesting,' he said. He turned the card over in his hand. The bright crayon and wobbly capitals seemed to be reproaching him. This child, Betty, was carrying on her sister's work but he had failed to bring her justice.

'Isn't it?' said Emma. 'It seems like Betty is determined to put on Annie's play. I wonder why?'

'I'm glad she invited you,' said Edgar. 'You must have gained her trust.'

He handed the card back and Emma said, without looking at him, 'Do you want to come too?'

'No,' said Edgar. 'It's probably better if you go alone. You're the one who has forged a relationship.'

He turned to Bob, who was shuffling papers with a rather sour expression on his face. 'Find anything useful at the primary school, Bob?'

'Not really. They're all very cut up about Daphne Young's death. I spoke to Mr Carew, the Class Five teacher, and he was almost in tears. Didn't seem the sort of bloke who cried easily either. First World War veteran.'

'I thought he had a soft spot for Daphne,' said Emma. Despite everything, Edgar noted that she still sounded rather disparaging about the dead teacher.

'They all loved her,' said Bob. 'The headmaster hasn't been able to get a replacement either. He was taking Class Six himself. That's where I saw the little girl, Betty.'

'I've been talking to the super,' said Edgar. 'He's very impressed by your work on this case, both of you.'

Bob and Emma looked at him sceptically, as if they knew this was a lie.

'It's six o'clock,' said Edgar. 'You should both go home. Lots of work to do tomorrow.'

Even if Frank Hodges hadn't said so, Bob and Emma had worked well, thought Edgar, as he trudged up the hill towards his flat. They made a good team. Bob was steady, a little unimaginative perhaps, but a good hard-working officer. Emma was more prone to sudden enthusiasms but she too was a grafter, meticulous about detail. The two sergeants had managed well together on this case – interviewing the children, for example – but he knew that Bob was apt to be slightly resentful of Emma, the newcomer who had been promoted from the ranks. Did the resentment mask something else? Emma was a very pretty girl. Could Bob be harbouring warmer feelings towards his colleague? For some reason, Edgar didn't like to think so.

The house was quiet. Even the neighbour who fed the seagulls at all hours was sensibly inside. Edgar let himself in and poured a whisky without taking his coat off. Then he sat on the sofa and contemplated his evening. He had saved three days' worth of cryptic crosswords from *The Times*, the whisky bottle was half-full and he was sure he had some spam in the meat safe. He was just wondering if he dared face the freezing kitchen when the telephone rang.

'Ed. It's Lucy.'

'Lucy. Is anything wrong?'

His sister snorted down the phone. 'You're getting just like Mum. Why should anything be wrong?'

Because you never normally ring me, Edgar wanted to say. Instead he asked after his nephews.

'Well, it's them I'm ringing about really.'

'Is it?'

'Yes. It's the Christmas holidays soon and I thought – what would be a nice treat for them?'

'What would be a nice treat for them?' Edgar took a surreptitious sip of whisky.

'The pantomime, of course!'

'Which pantomime?' Though he thought he could guess.

'The one in Brighton. The one with your friend in it.'

'*Aladdin*.'

'Yes, that's it. I thought I'd bring the boys down on Saturday. Just George and Edward; I'll leave the baby with Rupert. We could go to the evening show and stay the night with you.'

Edgar mouthed hopelessly at the phone.

'Don't start making problems, Ed,' said Lucy, although he hadn't. 'The boys and I can have your bed. You can sleep on the sofa.'

'The bed's not that big.' When he last saw them, his older nephews, aged six and eight, seemed roughly the size of young elephants.

'Rubbish. It's a double, isn't it?'

'Yes.'

'What's the problem, then? They're little boys. Don't you want to see your family, Edgar?'

'Of course I do. It's just, it's a bit of a difficult time.'

'You mean with those poor children getting killed?'

'Yes. I'm in charge of the case.'

'Well then, you're probably working far too hard. You need a break. Seeing George and Edward will put everything in perspective.'

And that, thought Edgar, putting down the receiver and massaging his ear, was almost certainly true.

Emma had never told her colleagues where she lived. There was nothing to be ashamed of about still living with your parents at the age of twenty-three; it was just that she didn't exactly want to broadcast the fact. Or the fact that her parents lived in a thirties mansion big enough to have a swimming pool (covered now for the winter) in their garden. They also employed a maid, a motherly woman called Ada, and a cook-general. It was Ada who opened the door to Emma as she stood panting in the porch after the long walk from Bartholomew Square.

'You're freezing, Miss Emma. Let me take your coat.'

'Thank you, Ada.'

Ada held the duffle coat at arm's length. 'You should have a proper coat, not this thing.'

Emma knew that, to Ada, proper meant fur.

'Is Mummy in?'

'Yes.' Ada nodded towards the drawing room. 'But she's got people.'

People meant dinner guests. Emma tiptoed towards the staircase, anxious to avoid them.

'Emma?'

Damn. She put her head round the door, observing that the room contained three unnecessary bodies. Alderman and Mrs Stanway and Mrs Rita Headland.

Emma called out a general hallo and tried to withdraw her head.

'Come in and say hallo properly, Emma.'

Emma's mother, Sybil, beautiful in some floaty blue garment, held court on the sofa. Emma's father, Archie, stood, at bay, behind the cocktail cabinet.

'Here's my little princess,' he informed the room.

Emma stood with her feet at ten to two, looking less like a princess than it is possible to imagine.

'Stay and have a cocktail, Emma,' said her mother. Thank God. Cocktails must mean that the people weren't staying to dinner.

'I've just got in,' said Emma. 'I'd really like to go upstairs and wash.'

'It must be so hard,' said Mrs Headland, round-eyed. 'Your mother was telling us that you were dealing with that dreadful murder.'

Emma glowered at her mother, who shrugged in a 'someone has to keep the conversation going' way.

'I'm afraid I can't talk about that,' said Emma stiffly.

This announcement only seemed to further electrify the guests. They stared at her as, giving in, she accepted a martini from her father.

'Come and sit by me, darling,' said Sybil. Emma sat, determined not to be won over. Unfortunately her mother was very charming and it worked on her daughter as well as on the Alderman Stanways and Mrs Rita Headland.

'We won't talk about the police any more,' said Sybil.

'Guess where Gloria and Larry have been?' Emma identified Gloria and Larry as Alderman and Mrs Stanway but her powers of deduction were not up to guessing their afternoon activities. Luckily her mother did not wait for an answer.

'They've been to the *pantomime*,' she breathed, as if this was an exotic and slightly risqué pastime.

'We don't usually go.' Gloria Stanway also seemed to feel that it needed explanation. 'But I'm a big fan of Max Mephisto.'

'Aren't we all?' said Sybil. 'I can't imagine him in a pantomime though. What part does he play?'

'He's Abanazar,' said Gloria. 'And the tricks he does, you wouldn't believe. He makes Aladdin disappear. Just like that.'

'Good thing too,' grunted Larry Stanway. 'Girl couldn't act at all.'

'My boss is a friend of Max Mephisto's,' said Emma. 'They served together in the war.'

She had just meant to say something (her mother's early training: 'It doesn't matter what you say at parties, just *speak*, darling.'). She hadn't counted on this remark being quite so fascinating.

'Really?' said Sybil. 'Old Inspector Stephenson?'

'It's Detective Inspector Stephens,' said Emma, 'and he's not old.'

'I can't imagine Max Mephisto in the army,' said Gloria Stanway. 'He looks foreign to me.'

'There were plenty of foreigners in the war,' said Emma. 'On both sides. Anyway, they were both involved in some hush-hush espionage group. I think it had to do with magic.'

'Magic?' Rita Headland laughed, making the ice cubes in her drink jingle. 'Making Hitler disappear?'

'Something like that,' said Emma. 'Max Mephisto came into the station the other day to talk to the boss. I think they're pretty close.'

'Really, darling,' said Sybil, 'I'm starting to see Inspector Stephenson in a different light.'

Emma didn't correct her about the name. Her mother was already starting to look at her in an uncomfortably knowing way.

Later, in her room, woozy after two martinis, Emma looked at her lists.

The Children
Annie
Mark
Kevin
Agnes
Betty
Richard
Lionel
Louise
Betsy (d. 1912)

<u>Teachers</u>
Daphne Young
Patricia Paxton
Martin Hammond
Duncan Pettigrew
Nigel Castle
Peter Carew

<u>Writers</u>
Annie
Daphne Young
Nigel Castle
Ezra Nightingale

<u>Involved in 1912 pantomime</u>
Stan Parks (the Great Diablo)
Denton McGrew
Ezra Nightingale

<u>Men the right age to be Nightingale's son</u>
Sam Gee
Martin Hammond
Duncan Pettigrew
Brian Baxter

Often she found that if she looked at her lists long enough they started to merge and overlap, providing possible leads and connections. Tonight, though, the names seemed irritatingly separate, refusing to cooperate. And, instead of making brilliant Holmes-like deductions, Emma was irritated to find herself writing, almost unconsciously and with loops and swirls worthy of Annie herself, one name over and over again.

Mrs Emma Stephens.

CHAPTER 22

Roger Dunkley was a burly man, more like a PT instructor than a theatre director. The impression of action was compounded by Dunkley's inability to sit still. During the course of the interview he rocked to and fro in his chair, twice got up to answer an imaginary knock on the door and, whilst up, performed a series of squats and knee-bends as if preparing for a race.

'Sorry,' he said, seeing Edgar watching him. 'I get a bit stiff if I stay still. Old age, you know.'

Roger Dunkley didn't look old, thought Edgar, but maybe things were measured differently in the theatre. It was, once again, about an hour before curtain-up on the matinee. Dunkley had denied having any nerves ('When you've been in the business as long as I have . . .') but he certainly seemed jumpier than any man had a right to be at one o'clock in the afternoon. However, he answered Edgar's questions calmly and without extraneous details. Yes, he had visited both schools with Nigel, the writer.

Nigel had been a teacher, only it had given him some sort of nervous breakdown. Had he ever done anything like that? No, the theatre was in his blood (banging his chest and bringing on a brief coughing fit); he couldn't see himself as a schoolmaster. But he'd enjoyed the afternoons with the students. No, he couldn't remember Annie and Mark specifically but he'd been very upset to hear what had happened to them. That's why he and Nigel had gone to the funeral, to show their respect.

Roger didn't show any disquiet on being asked about his movements on the twenty-sixth. In fact he laughed and stretched out his arms as if preparing to lift weights.

'I had a meeting with the producer. The great Bert Billington. We had dinner at the Grand. Now, that's not something you forget.'

Edgar remembered Max saying that Bert had made a rare visit south to see the director. As alibis went it was pretty good.

He asked, without much hope, if Roger had any photographs of the drama sessions at the school. To his surprise, the director jumped to his feet.

'I'm a bit of a devil with a Box Brownie. I've got some here.' He dug in his desk drawer and bought out a Kodak envelope. He spread the pictures out and Edgar moved his chair forward to look.

All the pictures seemed to be of the boys' school. There were a group of boys making hammy gestures to each other. Was that Mark in the glasses holding a spear? He couldn't be sure. Another photograph showed the masters in the audience, laughing and applauding.

'Is this a private party or can anyone join in?'

Edgar had recognised the voice so he wasn't too shocked to find himself looking into the florid face of a fully made-up Denton McGrew. The Dame, in his hooped skirts, made his way forward, uninvited.

'What's this? Photos? Goodie . . .'

'Shouldn't you be getting ready for the beginners' call?' asked Roger, rather feebly. Edgar remembered Max saying how important the Dame was to a pantomime. Roger clearly didn't want to offend his star.

'Just taking a peek. Oh my God.' Denton was shocked back into his normal voice. 'That's Marty Hammond, the old tart, all dressed up as a teacher.'

'I knew he was hiding something,' said Emma.

'Let me get this straight,' said Bob, with the stubborn look that meant he was finding something difficult to understand. 'Denton McGrew, Widow Twankey, says that he's seen Dr Hammond, Mark's headmaster, in a club for queers.'

Edgar winced slightly at the terminology. 'Yes. Apparently Martin Hammond was a frequent visitor to a private club near the Seven Dials that's popular with homosexuals.'

'But he's a headmaster.'

Emma laughed. 'Homosexuals are real people, Bob,

doing real jobs. And it's not that surprising really. Brighton's famous for that sort of club. What about the Star of Brunswick and the New Pier Tavern?'

'According to Denton,' said Edgar, 'when the navy were billeted at Roedean School during the war, so many sailors used to go to the Star of Brunswick that it was declared out of bounds.'

He expected Emma to laugh but, to his surprise, she blushed and looked away.

'I'm not from Brighton,' said Bob, implying that he thanked God every night for his good fortune in this respect.

'The point is,' said Edgar, 'being homosexual does not make Martin Hammond a suspect. In fact, this could explain his rather furtive behaviour when Emma interviewed him.'

'But if he lied about this, he could have lied about other things.'

'He didn't lie,' said Emma. 'He just didn't mention it and I don't blame him. He must be terrified of losing his job. He's taking a real risk, you know, going to a club like that.'

'Maybe not that much of a risk,' said Edgar, 'Denton said the place was very discreet.'

'Well, Denton wasn't very discreet,' retorted Emma. 'No wonder Dr Hammond didn't mention the theatre people coming to his school. It must have been far too close to home.'

'Did Widow Twankey say anything else about Hammond?' asked Bob.

'His name's not Widow Twankey,' said Edgar. 'And he said that Martin Hammond was well known but he wasn't one of the more outrageous club members. He would have a few drinks, chat to his friends, then go home.'

'Did he have any special friend?' asked Bob. Edgar sighed. Bob's attitude was starting to annoy him, even though it was probably shared by people like Frank Hodges. In the past, the police had raided clubs like the one at the Seven Dials, seeking out men whose heinous crime was loving other men. Well, that wouldn't happen while Edgar was in charge.

'Denton didn't know if Hammond had a lover,' said Edgar. 'They move in different circles anyway. Apparently Denton dressed up as Marlene Dietrich for the Sussex Arts Ball at the Aquarium. I can't imagine Martin Hammond doing anything like that.'

'No,' said Emma. 'He seemed rather frightened by the flamboyant side of the theatre. He kept saying that Mark wasn't "that sort". It was almost as if he was trying to distance himself from it.'

'Maybe he does,' said Edgar. 'Maybe he feels very torn by the two sides of his personality. Maybe that's why he works so hard to keep them separate.'

'Are we going to talk to him again?' asked Bob.

'No,' said Edgar. 'He hasn't committed any crime. It's part of the picture, that's all. This afternoon we're going to interview people who were at the children's wake, find out who Daphne Young spoke to. Then you two should go home at a decent time. I don't want you cracking up.'

'I won't crack up,' said Bob. 'I'm a man.'

Edgar sighed. 'Come on, let's get to work.'

Back at the theatre Max was in the wings, watching Denton McGrew push Wishy Washy (a gangling young actor called Kenneth Neil) into the washing machine. A few turns of the mangle and a cardboard cut-out Kenneth would emerge, to the delight of the audience. Then it was Max's cue.

Twankey: I wish I could find myself a real man.
Abanazar: You called? (*Flash of green light*)
Twankey: Oh heavens above, it's the Lone Ranger.

Max thought about Denton, who as a boy had been in a pantomime where a girl had died horribly on stage. Why would you carry on in the business, if that was your beginning? He watched Denton timing his double take perfectly. 'Ooh, Wishy. You *have* lost weight.' He was a pro, all right. Roger had told Max about Denton identifying the dead boy's headmaster as one of his clubbing friends. Roger had been quite upset ('He could lose his job, Max'). Well, Ed wouldn't be jumping to any stupid conclusions but there was no doubt that the teacher would find himself in a distinctly awkward situation. Why had Denton done it? Because, if an actor knows anything, he knows when to make his move.

'I wish I could find myself a real man.'

The green smoke billowed and Max entered, stage left.

CHAPTER 23

In the next few days there was a distinct dip in energy amongst the team. Edgar had experienced this before in murder investigations. You can only keep up the frantic pace for so long, however terrible the crime or however much you long to find the perpetrator. Edgar saw Daphne's parents once more and then they departed for Shropshire, taking their daughter's body with them. The funeral would be in Daphne's home village and none of the police officers were invited. So that was another ending, of a sort. Rather to Edgar's surprise, Nigel had come up with the name of Daphne's university boyfriend: Douglas McPherson. Edgar had contacted him and found that McPherson was a doctor, working in Glasgow. He had unimpeachable alibis for both murders and was, in any case, very far from being a suspect. Would Daphne have done better to marry a doctor, as her sister had, and bury herself in domesticity? There was no doubt that her parents thought so.

The team had interviewed everyone who had been at

the wake. It seemed that Daphne had, very properly, spoken to both sets of parents and to those of her pupils who had attended the funeral. She'd spent a lot of time talking to Annie's siblings. 'So sweet, it was,' said one onlooker. 'You could see how she really cared for them.' And Edgar thought she had cared. Much as he suspected that Daphne liked doing things for show, liked being seen as the perfect, caring teacher, he thought that she had genuinely been fond of the children, especially Annie. She had told her parents that she wanted to adopt Annie and, even if she hadn't gone any further with this idea, it showed a strength of feeling that went beyond the usual teacher/pupil relationship. What had Daphne's mother said? *Daphne thought she could give her a better life, one filled with music and art and stories.* Well, music and art and stories hadn't got Daphne very far. Had they even contributed to her death? Edgar asked if Daphne had spoken to the two theatricals – Roger and Nigel – at the wake but no one could remember her doing so.

By Wednesday night Edgar felt so low that he succumbed to temptation and went for a meal with Max and Diablo. Because of the evening performance, they didn't set out until ten and then Diablo insisted on popping into the Colonnade Bar 'for a snifter'. It was nearly eleven by the time they got to the restaurant but it was one of Max's secret, backstreet Italian places and so, although the sign said closed, the owner was only too happy to lay a table for them. As Enzo poured them home-made wine and offered them food that didn't appear on the menu, Edgar thought how little the austerity years had seemed to affect Max. Even in the days of powered egg and spam, Max always seemed to find be able to find a place where he could be served *melanzane parmigiana*. Diablo too, in his ancient fur coat, seemed to belong to a more glamorous and decadent age, swirling the dark-red wine in his glass and talking about the vineyards of Montepulciano. These days, when people spoke about Italy, it was usually just because they'd served there in the war. Diablo and Max remembered the years when you could travel for pure pleasure. Maybe that's why Edgar always found it fascinating when Max spoke Italian, as he was doing now, his face more mobile than usual and his hands in constant motion. Diablo might have been thinking the same thing because, when Enzo had left, he said, 'I always forget that you're half-Italian, dear boy. It explains a lot.'

'What does it explain?'

'Well, your good looks for one thing.' Diablo took a generous swig of his wine. 'And a certain pessimism. People always say that the Italians are so jolly – those crowds happily cheering Mussolini and then just as happily cheering his murderers – but it always seems to me that they're a people in love with death. That's what Catholicism does to you, of course.'

Once again, Diablo surprised Edgar. He was right, there was a deep ingrained pessimism about Max. It was probably this that made him so determined to enjoy himself.

'We can't all be as cheery as you,' said Max.

'And Edgar, of course, is an incurable optimist.' There was no stopping Diablo now.

'Am I?'

'Of course you are, dear boy. That's why you always get so upset by these tragic cases. You expect people to be better than that and so you're disappointed. Me, I always expect the worst of people. That's why I'm so cheery.'

Edgar remembered Diablo saying something very like this once before. He said, 'What about Denton McGrew. Do you expect the worst of him?'

'Do I expect him to be a scene-stealing, upstaging old ham? Yes. But I don't expect anything worse of him, if that's what you mean.'

Diablo leant back as Enzo put three plates of delicious-looking pasta in front of them. He tucked his napkin into his shirt and prepared to dive in.

'What was Denton like as a child actor?' asked Edgar. He thought of the changeling creature in the dressing room, the glee in his voice when he'd recognised Martin Hammond in the photograph.

'Oh, the usual sort,' said Diablo. 'Pushy parents. There were three of them in the cast, I remember, Denton and his two younger sisters. Denton wasn't a bad little actor, though. I remember he could cry on cue. He was very proud of that.'

'How did he get on with the little girl, Betsy?'

'Betsy wasn't a little girl,' said Diablo. 'She was as tough a pro as any I've seen. She'd been on the boards for ever. None of us really liked Betsy much, to tell you the truth, but when she died like that . . . it was such a shock . . . The management actually wanted us to go on with the show. Can you imagine?'

'Denton said that you were one of the main people who wanted the show taken off.'

'Yes, well . . . it wasn't decent, was it? That poor girl hardly cold, her parents grieving. Besides, who would have come to see it? The papers were full of the murder. It was the worst possible publicity.'

Is all publicity good publicity? wondered Edgar. He had read some of the newspaper reports and it was true that they were prurient in a way he would not have thought possible in 1912. The conversation seemed to have depressed Diablo, though his appetite was unaffected. He buried himself in his pasta.

'Anyway . . .' Max was obviously trying to lighten the mood. 'Denton's a bloody good Dame.'

'I'm coming to see the show on Saturday,' said Edgar. 'My sister and my nephews are coming down specially.'

Diablo brightened perceptibly. 'I didn't know you had a sister. You must introduce us.'

'I will,' said Edgar. He had a sinking feeling that Lucy and Diablo would get on very well.

'And tell me the boys' names. I'll mention them in one of my speeches.'

'Nigel Castle will love that,' said Max.

'That boy has to learn to lighten up,' said Diablo. 'He'll give himself an ulcer one day.'

It was well after midnight when they left the restaurant. Even though Diablo said he knew of an all-night club where they could go for a nightcap, they began a circuitous route home that took in Diablo's digs near the Steine, then Max's on Upper Rock Gardens and finally the long walk up the hill to Edgar's lodgings. It was very cold and fresh frost crackled under their feet.

'Always loved the stars,' said Diablo, reeling across the Pavilion Gardens. 'Used to lie there and look at them when I was a boy. Orion and the Bear and the Great Dolphin.'

Edgar was confused. *Was* there a constellation called the Great Dolphin? But it was a lovely clear night, the stars as bright as stage lights, spelling out the celestial names.

Diablo stood in the middle of the lawn, transfixed. Edgar allowed his policeman's eye to roam around the gardens. There was usually some crime in this area, though tonight it was probably too cold for even the most hardened pickpocket or prostitute. The Pavilion loomed in the background, a monstrous bloated shape. There were rumours that Brighton hadn't been bombed in the war because Hitler planned to make the Pavilion his summer palace. Edgar couldn't quite see how this fitted with Hitler's Aryan delusions but there was no doubt that the building was impressive, a farmhouse that became an Indian palace, a transformation scene worthy of any pantomime.

They walked past the shadowy minarets. At the gate Max stopped to light a cigarette. Diablo was still babbling about the heavens. But Edgar saw, like a scene-changer caught out when the curtain comes up, a dark figure moving across the light to disappear into the darkness of the shrubbery. And he was almost sure that it was Roger Dunkley.

CHAPTER 24

Emma began Friday by interviewing Annie and Mark's school friends. It was very different from talking to the acting troupe in the primary-school hall. Annie's grammar-school friends were trying hard to be sophisticated, tossing their hair and calling things 'feeble'. Emma had to put in a lot of work, and a little hair-tossing herself, before they relaxed and began to talk about Annie as if she was a real person and not the heroine of a wireless melodrama.

'She always made me giggle in worship,' said Felicity. 'She could keep her face really serious and still make you laugh.'

'She did that to me in history,' said Sally, 'and Miss Drew sent me out.'

'Did she ever show you anything that she'd written?' asked Emma. 'I heard that she wrote plays.'

'I don't know about plays,' said Jean, 'but she wrote poems sometimes.'

All three girls started to giggle. Emma smiled encouragingly.

'There was the one about Monsieur Jones,' said Sally. She turned to Emma. 'He's our French teacher.'

'Can you remember any of it?'

Felicity assumed a declamatory position.

'Oh, Monsieur Jones, your passé composé makes me feel warm and rosy, and your barbe noire makes me go ooh là là.'

'*Barbe* is French for beard,' explained Sally kindly. 'Monsieur Jones has got this really feeble little beard, like it's been painted on.'

'So he didn't really make Annie go "ooh là là"?'

'Nooo.' A long, contemptuous syllable. 'She thought he was feeble.'

'Did she ever talk to you about her friends outside school,' asked Emma. 'Did she ever mention Mark Webster, for example?'

'Mark? Oh . . .' Felicity's face, which had relaxed for the poem, became tight again. 'The boy who was killed. No, I never heard her mention him.'

'Did she ever talk about her family?'

'I knew she had a baby brother,' said Jean. 'She said she had to babysit for him sometimes.'

'Did she ever mention her sister, Betty, or her brother Richard?'

'She said that Betty would probably be coming here next year,' said Sally. 'She said we'd all better watch out.'

'Why?'

'She said that Betty was cleverer than her and worse than her.'

'Worse?'

'Worse behaved, I think she meant,' said Felicity. 'But Annie wasn't naughty, not really. All the teachers liked her. Because she was so clever.'

This was said without any resentment. All three girls nodded solemnly and suddenly Emma felt very fond of them.

'Did any of you ever go back to Annie's house?' she asked.

The girls looked at each other. 'Well, no,' said Felicity. 'She lived in Kemp Town. That's almost in Whitehawk.'

At that moment they all seemed a lot less lovable.

Taking the forbidden route across the field to the boys' school, Emma thought about Annie, the girl remembered for her laughter and for her poems about poor Monsieur Jones. But there was obviously a lot that Annie didn't share with her school friends: her home life, her plays, her friendship with Mark. She had been good at keeping a straight face, at keeping the most important part of her life hidden. And Emma was sure the plays and the acting had been significant. She would have to see if she could pick anything up tonight, at the performance of *The Stolen Children*.

Mark, too, had kept his head down at school. Emma met his friends Simkins Minor and Warburton (no first names here) in the chapel, which might have contributed to their subdued demeanour. Mark had liked cricket and history, he hadn't been so keen on rugby or mathematics. He played the violin in the school orchestra but they thought it sounded like cats being tortured; they'd told him so. Mark liked books by H. Rider Haggard and had been hoping for a cricket bat for Christmas. He didn't talk much about his 'people' but then no one really did at school.

'Did he ever talk to you about Annie?' asked Emma.

To her surprise, Simkins, an earnest-looking boy with glasses and a squint, said, 'Yes.'

'We met her once,' said Warburton. 'On the bus into town.'

'What did Mark say about Annie?'

'He said she was his best friend, more like a sister. I said that I've got three sisters and I wouldn't want any more but Webster was an only. He didn't know what sisters can be like.'

'I'm an only too,' said Emma. 'I always wanted a brother.'

'I've got a brother in the Remove,' said Simkins. 'You can have him, if you like.'

That was presumably Simkins Major, thought Emma. It was interesting that Mark had been more forthcoming with his friends than Annie had been with hers.

'Did Webster, Mark, ever tell you about the plays Annie used to write?'

Again, the boys surprised her. 'Yes,' said Warburton, 'he told us about the plays they put on with these little kids acting all the parts. He said that they had a proper theatre in someone's house. Mark's uncle, I think it was.'

Brian was everyone's uncle, thought Emma. But, again, Mark had been more open about the plays than Annie had been. He was proud of them, she realised, proud of his friend who was almost a sister, proud of their acting troupe and their 'proper theatre'.

'Did he tell you what the plays were about?'

'No, but he said that one of the plays they were putting on, *The Stolen Children* I think it was called, he said that it would frighten a lot of people.'

'Not frighten,' said Simkins. 'Shock.'

Emma sat up straighter. The choir were filing into the stalls at the front of the chapel. She hoped they weren't about to sing and put the boys off their stride.

'He said that *The Stolen Children* would shock a lot of people?'

'Yes. I don't know why. Maybe it had monsters or something in it.'

There was a Witch Man, Emma remembered, but he hadn't been the baddie. That had been the parents because 'Annie likes twists'. Why was Mark so sure that this play – written before any children went missing – would shock people? And why was the troupe putting on *The*

Stolen Children tonight? Was Betty – who was reputedly even cleverer than Annie – trying to tell her something? After all, she had gone to great lengths to ensure that 'the lady policeman' knew about the performance.

But the boys didn't seem to know anything else about the play. They were fidgeting now, sniggering at the choir as they performed their warm-up exercises.

'Do you remember some theatre people coming into the school a few weeks ago?' asked Emma. 'They took small groups and did play-writing and acting?'

'I didn't go,' said Warburton. 'I had a rugby match that day.'

'I went,' said Simkins. 'It was a bit silly really.'

'Did Mark enjoy it?'

'I don't know. I remember we were laughing because Old Hammer, sorry, Dr Hammond was going on about them being like Shakespeare.'

So Martin Hammond, who had claimed hardly to remember the visit, had likened Nigel Castle and Roger Dunkley to Shakespeare. Was this because he knew Denton McGrew from his shadowy double life? But the boys were getting restless. Emma asked one last question. 'When you met Annie on the bus, what did you talk about?'

'Her French teacher,' said Warburton. 'Apparently he's got a really stupid beard.'

In the end Emma left it a bit late to get to Brian Baxter's house. After visiting the schools, she had gone back to the station and written up her notes. Then she'd read back through her interviews with the younger children She'd never seen a script of *The Stolen Children*, if one existed, and she had to rely on the synopsis given by Kevin and co: 'The Witch Man steals children and eats them,' Agnes had said. 'He steals children and keeps them in a cage until they get fat enough to eat. All the villagers are scared of him. At night they say to their children, "Children, children, say your prayers . . ."' There were definite echoes of 'Hansel and Gretel' here, but without Annie's nasty twist of Gretel wanting to kill Hansel. 'Annie likes twists,' Betty had said. According to Bob's notes, Brian Baxter hadn't thought *The Stolen Children* suitable for children. Had he been shocked by it?

Bob and the DI had gone to the Devil's Dyke to follow up on a possible sighting of a man on 29th November. 'We'd better go today,' the DI had said. 'It might snow again tomorrow.' And when Emma finally set out, she could feel the snow in the air, a dense grey presence that seemed to press her closer to the earth. She'd forgotten what a long slog it was to the top of Freshfield Road. How many times had the children taken this route, walking back from school or visiting Uncle Brian's house at the top of the hill? Emma imagined Mark and Annie, weighed down by school books, Mark carrying his violin, Annie regaling her friend with stories about Monsieur Jones. Seeing their school friends had made the children seem very close somehow. Emma pushed on up the hill, head down. Halfway up, the streetlamps stopped and it was very dark with just the occasional flash of car headlights and the orange glow from a factory over towards Whitehawk. *She lived in Kemp Town. That's almost Whitehawk.*

There were lights on in Brian Baxter's house though, and an actual queue of people waiting for admission into his garage theatre. Emma, who had only heard about the place from the DI, was amazed to see proper seats and a glimpse of velvet curtains. The garage doors were open and a man in a dinner jacket was taking tickets. This must be Baxter, variously described as 'weaselly', 'strange' and 'suspicious'. When Emma approached him, he gave her a curious but not unfriendly smile.

'I'm Emma Holmes,' she said. 'The lady policeman.' She pointed to her invitation.

'Ah. Well, you've got the right name for it, at all events.'

Emma smiled politely. She was immune to comments about her name, except when they came from Bob. 'I was surprised they were putting on this show,' she said. 'I mean, without . . .'

'It was all Betty's idea,' said Brian Baxter. 'She organised everyone, made sure they learnt their lines, wrote out the invitations. I think it's her way of paying tribute to Annie.'

His voice broke a little when he said Annie's name but, unlike Bob, Emma didn't think this was sinister. He was sad, that was all. A sad little man in a dinner jacket, pretending to be a front-of-house manager.

'Have you seen the play?' asked Emma.

'I saw some rehearsals,' said Brian. 'They often come here to rehearse.'

'What did you think of it?'

'It seemed a bit dark for a children's play,' said Brian. 'But Betty said you need dark and light in a story.'

'Betty said you need dark and light in a story?' Betty, it seemed, was another girl to be reckoned with. Emma thought she could detect Daphne Young's influence. She wondered how Betty would get on at the grammar school next year, this girl who was 'worse' than her sister.

'She's a caution, that Betty,' said Brian. 'Another Annie.'

Emma felt a sudden chill that had nothing to do with the weather. But Brian's face only showed simple pride in his protégés. He obviously wanted her to move on so she smiled and walked into the garage. Brian Baxter shut the doors behind her.

The curtains were drawn but, behind the scenes, someone was playing Christmas carols on the piano. There were two rows of seats, occupied by solid parent types. Emma recognised Edna Webster but couldn't see Sandra Francis. Not many fathers. Presumably they were all still at work. Despite a strong smell of Calor gas, the room was very cold. Emma kept her coat on and surreptitiously blew on her hands.

'Parky, isn't it?' said her neighbour, a large comfortable-looking woman wearing a hat like a squashed mushroom.

'I'm Mareid O'Dowd,' the woman introduced herself. 'Kevin's mother.'

'I'm Emma Holmes. I've met Kevin.'

Mareid O'Dowd smiled complacently. 'Oh, everyone remembers Kevin. He's got a big part in this play. He's the Witch Man.'

The Witch Man. Why not a witch? Was it just to appease Kevin? She was willing to bet that he was one of the best actors.

'Have you seen the play before?' she asked.

'No.' Mareid dabbed her eyes. 'They were going to put it on . . . you know, before . . . It was Betty who wanted to go on with it. She said she found the playscript amongst Annie's "effects". That's how she talks, such a clever little thing'

'It must be hard for Annie and Mark's parents, coming here today.'

'Poor souls,' said Mareid. 'It's been such a terrible few weeks. Annie and Mark dying and then that lovely Miss Young. I've tried to help Sandra and Jim as much as I can. It's hard for her, with the baby and all. But she was determined to come today. Said that it was important to Betty. And I must say, we need something, like, to cheer us up.'

From what Emma had heard, *The Stolen Children* was unlikely to cheer anyone up. And if Sandra Francis had been determined to come, where was she now? She was about to ask when the curtains started to move back, jerkily, as if pulled by a string. The piano was revealed and the pianist – Sandra Francis.

'It's starting,' whispered Mrs O'Dowd, sounding genuinely excited.

But there was a dramatic pause. Sandra played a few more bars and then looked at her hands uncertainly. The gas heaters hissed, the mothers looked at each other, the curtains billowed in a sudden gust of wind.

And a red-haired boy rushed onto the stage. 'Someone's taken Betty,' he wailed. 'She's gone!'

At first Emma even thought that it might be part of the play. Then Sandra Francis crashed both hands down on the piano and screamed, 'Betty!' The boy – was it Richard, Betty's twin? – stood in the centre of the stage with tears rolling down his cheeks, waiting for someone to do something.

Emma climbed onto the stage and put her arm round the boy. 'It's OK. Do you remember me? I'm a policewoman.'

Behind her, Sandra said, 'The police?'

'Yes.' Emma turned back to the boy. 'Richard?'

He nodded, still crying silently.

'Richard, when did you last see Betty?'

He took a gulping breath. 'We were just getting ready and Betty realised that we hadn't got any sweets for the Witch Man scene so she went to Mr Gee's shop to get some. We'd saved our rations.'

Emma heard Sandra's sharp intake of breath. She tried to keep her own voice steady. 'Yes? She went to Mr Gee's shop and then what happened?'

'She didn't come back,' said Richard. 'So Kevin went to get her. Mr Gee said he'd never seen her.'

'He's got her,' screamed Sandra. 'That horrible little man in the sweet shop. He killed Annie and now he's got Betty.'

There was pandemonium amongst the audience now. Mothers grabbed their children, several of whom started crying. Emma saw Brian Baxter standing just below the stage, ridiculous in his bow tie.

'Let's try to keep calm,' said Emma, still with her arm round Richard. 'Betty could be at home. She could be all sorts of places. Mr Baxter, have you got a telephone?'

'Yes.'

'I've got to speak to my boss.'

She prayed that the DI would be back from Devil's Dyke and her prayers were answered. He answered on the second ring. She told him what had happened, trying to be as brief and professional as possible. She could hear the shock in his voice but he, too, was the model of calmness.

'Go to the house, see if she's there. I'll meet you there. Get names and addresses of everyone at Brian Baxter's house.'

Emma left Brian Baxter, who seemed relieved to be

given something to do, taking names and addresses and she walked with Sandra and Richard back down the hill to the Francises' house. Where was the baby? Who was looking after him? She tried not to think that the Francis family was getting smaller by the second.

When they got closer, Sandra started to run. She flung open the (unlocked) front door and shouted, 'Betty! Betty!' They could hear the echoes rebounding through the empty house. 'Betty! Betty!' Richard started to cry again.

At the doorstep, Emma knelt down to him. 'Richard, have a really good look for Betty in the house. I bet you two have got all sorts of secret hiding places, haven't you?' A small smile flickered. 'Go and look in all those secret places but don't leave the house. OK?'

Richard bounded upstairs as his mother emerged from the kitchen.

'She's not here,' she told Emma, wild-eyed. 'She's not here.'

'Come and sit down.' Emma led her into the tiny front room. 'Can I telephone your husband?'

'I haven't got a telephone.'

Emma was just wondering whether to go to the neighbours for help when heavy boots sounded in the hall. Jim Francis, looking larger than ever, appeared in the doorway.

'What's happening?'

'Jim.' Sandra threw herself into his arms. 'Betty's gone.'

'Betty? What are you talking about? She was doing that show up at Uncle Brian's.'

'She went for sweets and she never came back. Oh, Jim, she's gone. Just like Annie.'

Jim's fists clenched and, before Emma's eyes, the man seemed to swell into something altogether more alarming. He almost pushed his wife aside and made for the door. 'That little bastard shopkeeper! I'll kill him.'

Emma interposed herself between Jim and the door.

'Mr Francis! Stop.'

'Who the hell are you?'

'Emma Holmes. I'm a police officer.'

'What are you doing here?'

'I was at the play. We'll find Betty but we have to take things calmly. Jumping to conclusions won't help. Let's just wait until . . .'

Jim's face suggested that he was not about to wait for anything but, just as Emma was wondering if she could restrain him any longer, she heard a welcome voice calling her name. She went to the door and saw the DI, Bob and two uniformed policemen coming up the path. In the background were Mrs O'Dowd, Kevin and another woman holding a red-haired baby.

Sandra pushed past Emma and grabbed the child. 'Jimmy!' This must be her youngest, named after his father. The older Jim stood scowling in the doorway.

DI Stephens was quick and to the point. 'Bob, you go down to the sweetshop.'

'It'll be shut,' said Bob. Emma looked at her watch. It was nearly six.

'He lives over the shop,' said the DI. 'Knock on the door. Do you know the way?'

'Kevin can take you,' offered Mrs O'Dowd.

Kevin looked up at the policemen, trying to keep his face appropriately serious. Emma could tell that he was dying to go.

'Very well,' said DI Stephens. 'Kevin, you show Sergeant Willis the way to Mr Gee's shop. Sergeant McGuire and PC Andrews, you knock on all the doors in the road, ask if anyone's seen Betty.'

'I'll go with you,' said Emma.

'No, I want a word with you first,' said the DI. 'I want to get all the facts straight. Where's the child who reported Betty missing?'

'Richard!' Sandra put her hand to her mouth. 'Where's Richard?' Emma hoped for Richard's sake that he never realized how long it had taken his mother to notice his absence.

'I'm here, Mum.' Richard appeared at his father's side. Jim dropped a hand on his head.

'Let's go inside,' said the DI. Already there was a small crowd forming in the street.

The front room seemed even tinier when they were all crammed inside. Richard sat on his father's knee, Sandra cradled the baby. Emma found herself squashed up next to the DI on the sofa. She edged her leg away so that it didn't touch his.

'Richard,' said the DI. 'Can you tell us when you last saw Betty?'

But Richard seemed to be struck dumb. He looked at the ground, tears running down his cheeks.

'Speak up, Richard,' said Jim, not unkindly. 'Tell the policeman what happened.'

Emma leant forward. 'You're not in any trouble, Richard. Just tell us what happened. That way we'll be able to find Betty.'

Richard took a deep breath and, addressing himself to Emma, said, 'We was getting changed at Uncle Brian's, in his front room, and Betty was checking the props. You know, what we need for the show. The sweets weren't there, the ones what they use to get the Witch Man. Betty said she'd go to Mr Gee's to get some. We'd saved our rations so we had enough. Uncle Brian give us some of his as well. She went out . . .'

'On her own?' interrupted the DI. 'In the dark?'

'Yes,' said Richard, as if this was a stupid question. 'We went on getting ready but she didn't come back so Kevin went to look for her. He's the fastest runner. He came back and said he'd been to Mr Gee's but Mr Gee hadn't seen her.'

Jim made a sound like a growl. Richard looked up at him apprehensively.

'Go on,' said the DI.

'Then I got scared,' said Richard. 'And I ran into the theatre.'

'You did the right thing,' said the DI. 'The quicker we know about these things, the quicker we can do something about them. Richard, do you know what time it was when Betty went to get the sweets?'

But Richard, it seems, was vague about time. He muttered something about the big hand.

'The show was due to start at five,' said Emma. 'It could only have been a little while before that. I got to Baxter's house at about five to and I didn't see Betty. But it was very dark. There are no streetlights at the top of the hill.'

'I told them not to go to that man's shop,' said Sandra. Richard started to cry again.

The DI raised his hand. 'Is there anywhere else where Betty might go? Richard, you're her twin, aren't you? You must know her the best. Is there anywhere she could be?'

'She,' Richard nodded at Emma, 'told me to look in all our secret places and I did. Betty wasn't anywhere. I think he's got her.'

'Who?' asked DI Stephens.

'The Witch Man,' said Richard and broke into renewed sobs.

The DI had asked for reinforcements and, after Emma had made the Francises a cup of tea and left them in the care of Mrs O'Dowd, the two of them waited by the gate.

'Do you think she's been abducted?' asked Emma.

DI Stephens looked at her. She saw the dark circles

under his eyes and the lines at the sides of his mouth. 'Yes,' he said quietly, 'I do.'

They watched as Bob came jogging up the hill, Kevin slightly ahead of him. Richard was right, Kevin was a good runner.

'Well?' asked the DI.

Bob was breathing hard. Kevin ran past him into the Francises' house. 'Gee hasn't seen her. Said he hadn't left his shop all day.'

'Any witnesses?'

'No.'

'We'll get a warrant and search his house,' said DI Stephens.

'Do you think it's him?' asked Emma.

'I don't know but all three children disappeared in the vicinity of his shop. That's pretty suspicious, don't you think?'

'Last sighting of Betty was halfway down the hill here,' said Bob, 'Just by that bus stop. She was doing up her shoelace.'

'Who saw her?'

'Neighbour. Number seventy-two, I think. McGuire's got the details.'

'All right,' said the DI. 'She's only been missing about an hour. We need to talk to everyone in the vicinity, search every inch of ground. We need to search Baxter's house too. It's possible that she did get back there and that he spirited her away somewhere.'

'He was in sight all the time,' said Emma. 'He was taking tickets.'

'Even so. Let's not leave anything unchecked. And we must be methodical, no chasing off after hypothetical leads.'

He was talking to both of them but Bob was staring up at the sky. 'Damn,' he said.

It was the first time Emma had heard him swear. She looked at him in surprise.

'Damn,' said Bob. 'It's snowing.'

CHAPTER 25

They searched all night. As the snow fell, the police teams followed the route from Brian Baxter's house to the sweetshop, looking under hedges and in gutters, tramping through allotments and forcing open the doors of outhouses. At midnight the warrant came and Edgar, accompanied by Bob and PC McGuire, searched every inch of Sam Gee's house and garden. They found nothing but, when they left, with Sam's threats of legal action ringing in their ears, they found a small group of vigilantes standing outside, ankle-deep in snow.

'Go home,' Edgar told them. 'We've got no reason to suspect Mr Gee.'

'You searched his house though,' said someone.

'Go home to your families,' said Edgar. 'They need you now.'

Maybe this veiled warning worked, or maybe it was just the snow, which was falling heavily by then, but after a few minutes the knot of men dispersed and were soon lost in the swirling whiteness.

Edgar sent Emma back to look after the Francis family. Partly this was because he could see that she had formed a relationship with them, partly because he just wanted to spare her the freezing hours of fruitless searching. Bob worked alongside him, tireless and uncomplaining. At first light they walked back to Bartholomew Square. The streets were once again transformed by snow, every sharp edge rounded, every dark corner suddenly frosted and glittering. And, once again, Edgar saw absolutely nothing beautiful in the sight. They walked in silence until they reached the police station. In fact, Edgar felt as if he was almost too cold to speak; every muscle in his face seemed to be in spasm.

The night sergeant let them in, his craggy face sympathetic.

'I'll make you both a nice hot cup of tea.'

As they descended the stairs to the CID rooms, Edgar said, 'I've got a fresh team coming in at nine. We'll start again on the park.'

'I'll help,' said Bob.

'No,' said Edgar, 'you go home and get some sleep.'

Edgar walked up to the incident board. The photographs of Annie and Mark looked down on him, Mark smiling shyly, Annie staring challengingly into mid-distance. He remembered the picture in Daphne Young's flat: Annie, Mark and Betty.

He was surprised to feel Bob's hand on his arm.

'She could still be alive, sir. Don't give up now.'

Edgar turned away to hide his sudden tears. He was sure that Betty was dead.

Emma woke up on the Francises' sofa, conscious of a comforting warmth beside her. She opened her eyes. Someone had covered her with a blanket but the warmth was coming from Richard, who was cuddled up next to her.

She touched his shoulder. 'Richard?'

He muttered, not opening his eyes, 'I didn't like it in the room without Betty.'

'That's all right,' said Emma. 'You stay here.' She pulled the blanket over him.

She looked at her watch. Five o'clock. She should let Richard sleep for a bit longer. The doctor had come last night and administered a sedative to Sandra. So she at least would know a few hours of forgetting. Jim had refused to take anything. As far as Emma knew, he was still out with the search team.

It was odd. Emma was an only child. She had no young cousins and none of her friends had had children yet. She didn't think that she had ever held a younger child in her arms. Richard's acceptance of her as a place of refuge seemed an almost miraculous thing. She thought of Annie, who, at thirteen, was already an experienced big sister. She never thought that she would envy Annie but now, curled up on the sofa with Richard as the morning light filtered in through the curtains, she did.

She heard boots in the hallway. Emma got up, careful not to wake Richard, and padded to the door. Jim Francis stood there, shaking the snow off his jacket. He didn't seem surprised to see Emma but she was acutely conscious of her untidy hair and crumpled clothes.

'I was sleeping on the sofa,' she said. 'Richard's there too.'

Jim grunted. 'Poor little sod.'

Emma didn't have to ask if there was any news. One look at his face was enough.

'I'll make you some tea,' she said.

She walked into the kitchen and put the kettle on the hob. Jim followed her and stood there awkwardly for a moment before edging past her and going out through the back door. Emma realised that he was going to the outside lavatory. She thought of her own pink-tiled bathroom at home. She would certainly put off going to the lav until she got to the station.

She made the tea as strong as she could and when Jim came in again, they stood there drinking in silence. He was such a big man that he made the tiny kitchen seem like a dolls' house. There was a force about him too, something strong and slightly dangerous. Emma could see why Sandra Francis had married him.

Eventually she said, 'I'll get back to the station in a minute. DI Stephens will be sending new men to search.'

'He searched Gee's house last night. Didn't find anything.'

'I know.'

Jim looked at her, his heavy brows knitted together.

'If it's not Gee, then who is it?'

'I don't know,' said Emma, 'but we'll find him, whoever it is.'

Now Jim was looking at her almost pityingly. 'You don't believe that, love. Any more than I do.'

Jim Francis went out again as soon as he'd had his tea. He didn't even wait for breakfast. With Sandra still deeply asleep, Emma thought that she should wait until Richard had woken up, at least. Should she make the family some breakfast? The kitchen was extremely tidy but there was no fridge or twin-tub or any of the gleaming paraphernalia that made Cook's lair at her parents' home so mysterious. In the awful limbo after school, Emma had actually been on a cordon bleu cooking course but she couldn't really see herself rustling up *oeufs en cocotte* or kedgeree in this utilitarian sliver of a room. Opening the back door, she found a small pantry outside, cold enough to contain milk and eggs. There was a packet of porridge too. Should she make some for Richard? She was still standing, uncertain, in the doorway when a voice said, 'I don't like porridge.'

It was Richard, flushed from sleep, hair standing on end, determined to be difficult.

'What about a boiled egg?' said Emma. Surely she could manage that after six weeks with Madame Duvalier?

Richard didn't actually say no, so Emma fetched an egg from the pantry, shut the door (the kitchen was now freezing) and found a small saucepan. She also grilled some rather stale bread for toast. She was desperate for coffee but made do with black tea.

The egg was too runny ('I like the yellow bit hard') but Richard consented to eat. As he did so, Emma asked, 'You know the play you were going to do?'

'*The Stolen Children.*'

'Yes. *The Stolen Children*. Was there a script?'

Richard finished his mouthful. He was a neat but thorough eater. 'What's a script?'

'Something with all the words the actors say written down.'

'Annie told us what to say.'

'But did Annie have it written down somewhere? Mr Baxter, Uncle Brian, he said that Betty had taken over with the play. Did Betty find a book of Annie's with the words written down? Mrs O'Dowd, Kevin's mum, said something about Betty finding it with Annie's things.'

Richard pondered. 'There's a box under Betty's bed. It could be in that. She doesn't let me look in it.'

'Could we look now, do you think?'

'Will it help us find Betty?'

'It might,' said Emma, trying to sound confident. 'It really might.'

Richard led the way upstairs. A few minutes earlier Emma had heard the baby crying and Sandra moving about but her door stayed shut and Emma didn't want to disturb her. There were only two rooms upstairs and the children seemed to have the bigger room, at the front of the house. Even so there was hardly room to move, as it was crammed with a double bed and a single, so close that they almost touched. The only other piece of furniture was a chest of drawers. Emma thought back to her childhood bedroom, the white-painted bed, the desk, the bookcase. How had the clever Francis children ever managed to work in this house? Why wasn't she, with all that privilege on her side, a brain surgeon at the very least?

Richard bent down and pulled a wooden box out from under the double bed. Very carefully, Emma lifted out the contents, one by one. A broken doll ('Her name's Amelia'), a pink teddy bear ('I had a blue one but I lost it'), three books, worn with rereading – *Little Women*, *Good Wives* and *Black Beauty* – and a small pile of exercise books. One was tantalisingly labelled 'My Dairy' (Betty clearly had trouble with 'ai' and 'ia') but, when Emma looked inside, it was empty apart from the words 'Ellie Blackmore will always be my best friend' written in green ink. But the next book was covered with swirls and turrets and the title was *The Stolen Children*.

It was an extraordinary little play. Like *The True Story of Hansel and Gretel*, the play Annie had been working on with Miss Young, it was laid out like a proper script, with stage directions ('Star jumps up in surprise') and descriptions of scenery ('The forest can be Uncle Brian's rubber plants with a green screen behind them'). The play began with children playing, chanting their sinister little rhyme.

Children, children, say your prayers.
Children, children, stay upstairs.
Children dear, don't stay out late,
Or the Wicked Witch Man will be your fate.

Star is playing on her own. She tells the audience that she has an imaginary little brother. Later her mother is impatient with her, 'You can't imagine things all your life, Star. You have to get on with real life.' Had Sandra ever said this to Annie? But Star, like Annie, is resourceful. She ventures into the Dark Wood and finds a little boy called Leaf. The boy says he was stolen away from his real parents by the Witch Man. Star and Leaf prepare a trap made out of sweets for the Witch Man, hence Betty's trip to Sam Gee's shop. There was a very good scene where the children are waiting for the Witch Man and wondering what he'll be like. But when the Witch Man is caught in the trap, he turns out not to be the villain they imagine. He rescued Leaf when he was lost in the forest and has been secretly feeding him ever since. It turns out that Leaf is Star's brother but their mother (played, Emma remembered, by Betty) had abandoned Leaf because she didn't want a little boy. The policeman arrests the mother and the children live happily ever after with the Witch Man as a kind of live-in nanny. On the last page, Betty had written, with her distinctive green pen: 'They join hands and sing a song, "Brothers and Sisters, Friends For Ever".'

Emma sat back on her heels. The song was like the jig that was meant to have been played at the end of all Shakespeare's plays. It was to remind the audience that this is all make-believe and that evil mothers and Witch Men don't exist in the world. But what if they did exist?

Richard was reading over Emma's shoulder. 'It's good, isn't it?'

'Yes, it's very good.'

The song had a jaunty end-rhyme that reminded Emma of songs that she used to sing in the Brownies.

Brothers and sisters,
Friends for ever.
Brothers and sisters,
Friends together.
Let's form a ring
And play and sing,
Friends for ever, friends together.

What did it all mean? Why was Betty so determined to perform this play and to invite the 'lady policeman'? Emma stared at the exercise book, willing it to give up its secrets. The round green handwriting stared back up at her.

There was one other item in the box, a photograph. Emma held it up to the light. It was the same photograph that Daphne Young had kept in her fairy-tale book. Annie, Mark and Betty. The three faces smiled at her. Three children, two dead and one missing.

Richard looked at the photograph without interest. 'I'm not in it.'

Thank your lucky stars, thought Emma.

Max heard the news from Kenneth Neil (Wishy Washy), who had digs in Freshfield Road.

'There were coppers everywhere when I got back from the show last night. They say another kid's gone missing.'

'It's the sister of the first one,' said Ron Hunter-White (Chief of the Peking Police). 'That's what I heard.'

'There's a child-killer out there,' said Annette with a shudder. 'I won't be able to sleep tonight.'

'Well, you're hardly in danger, dear,' said Denton, whisking past on the way to his dressing room.

Max thought about Edgar starting another desperate hunt in the snow. He wouldn't rest until this child was found, alive or dead. Could it really be the sister of one of the other children? He couldn't imagine how a family could survive something like that. Plenty of families lost children in the war – Diablo's mother had lost two sons – but somehow that was different. They were adults and you could kid yourself that their sacrifice was worthwhile, but this . . . this felt like punishment from some sadistic God.

He saw Nigel Castle hovering on the edge of the gaggle of actors.

'Did you hear the news?' he asked.

'Another child's gone missing,' said Nigel. 'It's just too horrible.'

Nigel really did look upset, thought Max. His skin, always pale, now had an almost greenish tinge.

'Is it true,' said Nigel, 'that it's the sister of the girl, Annie?'

'I don't know,' said Max, 'but I think I heard something like that.'

'Another one of Daphne's pupils then,' said Nigel.

Max hadn't seen it quite like that. He supposed that the loss of his friend could account for Nigel's haggard look.

'Daphne's death must have been a terrible shock for you,' he said.

'Yes,' said Nigel, 'it was. I spoke to her parents, said how sorry I was, but they've gone back to Shropshire. I don't think I'll ever see them again. I won't even be able to get to her funeral.'

Again, that seemed a rather self-centred way of looking at things.

'Well, let's hope they find this little girl,' said Max.

He hadn't heard the director approaching. Roger Dunkley was looking even more distracted than usual.

'What's everyone doing?' he said. 'Overture and beginners in ten minutes.'

'We were talking about the girl that's gone missing,' said Nigel. 'They're saying it's Annie's sister.'

Roger seemed not to have heard him. 'The show must

go on,' he said, shepherding his cast along the corridor. Somehow he made it sound more like a threat than a promise.

'Go home and that's an order.'

'I'm not tired. I can carry on.'

Frank Hodges sighed. Edgar wondered if he was going to threaten, once again, to bring someone in above his head. But instead, the super just looked at him steadily. If it had been anyone else, Edgar would have thought that he was trying to be kind.

'DI Stephens,' said Hodges. 'You've been up all night. You're going to fall asleep on your feet in a minute and that won't help anyone. Go home, get a few hours' sleep and you can come back here in the evening.'

'But I need to coordinate the search . . .'

'I will personally take charge of operations while you're away. Does that satisfy you?'

God help the team, thought Edgar. But he could hardly argue. He didn't feel tired but he had started to enter that dreamy fugue state where nothing seemed quite real. He had sent Bob and Emma home but he knew that they'd be back later. Maybe he should go back. He could do with a hot bath too. He hadn't been dressed for snow last night and his shoes were still drenched. His left foot, which was missing a toe after frostbite in Norway, was completely numb. 'Thank you, sir,' he said. 'I'll be back by six.'

The walk home was hard going. The snow didn't seem

quite as heavy as last time but his feet were frozen and his face stiff with cold. He'd wear his Russian hat tonight. Halfway up Albion Hill he could see the teams working on Freshfield Road, tiny black figures against the white. Frank Hodges could at least be trusted to keep the search running smoothly. If there was any news, though, Edgar must be the one to break it to the Francis family. For a second he allowed himself to imagine the sensation of sharing good news. 'She was here all along . . . Yes, staying with a friend . . . She ran to her grandparents' house . . . Just wanted to get away for a while.' Sadly, none of these scenarios were likely to come true. Officers had visited the grandparents last night and again this morning. Neither set had seen Betty. They had visited all her known friends, everyone in her class at school and everyone involved in the play. They had searched Brian Baxter's house and found nothing. Baxter himself seemed on the verge of nervous collapse. Now they were back to trawling the streets.

Thank God the hot water was working. Edgar made himself a sandwich while the bath was running. He wasn't hungry but he supposed he had to eat. The sensation of lowering himself into the steamy water was amazing. When he had heard that Betty was missing, he had, for one brief but heartfelt minute, wished that he were dead. But he supposed that he was thankful to be alive, able to feel hot and cold, grief and happiness. He lay there until the water cooled, then he got out, dried himself, dressed in his warmest clothes and lay down on the bed. He wouldn't sleep, just rest for an hour and get back to the station.

He was woken from a deep, dark sleep by a pounding on the door. Who the hell could that be? He would bet on one thing: it wouldn't be good news.

A smartly dressed woman stood on the doorstep accompanied by two boys in duffle coats and woolly hats.

'What a journey!' she said. 'But at least we're here now. Say hallo to Uncle Edgar, boys.'

CHAPTER 26

'What the matter, Ed? Weren't you expecting us?'

Edgar shut his eyes. Perhaps when he opened them, they wouldn't be there.

'Why have you got your eyes shut? Do you need glasses? Wipe your feet, boys.'

This last as his nephews powered past him into the flat. Edgar shut his eyes again.

'Well, you don't seem very happy to see us,' said Lucy.

'I am,' said Edgar, standing aside to let her come in. 'It's just . . . it's a bad time. Another child has gone missing.'

'Another child?' Lucy was peeling off her gloves. There was snow on her boots but not on her hat. Thank God; that must mean that it hadn't started again. 'What do you mean?'

'A girl has gone missing,' said Edgar. 'The sister of one of the children who was murdered.'

'Oh my God.' Lucy looked genuinely shocked but was

almost immediately distracted by George and Edward, who had started a game of jumping off the sofa.

'Boys! Stop it. Don't mess up Uncle Edgar's house.'

'It's not a house,' said George, 'it's a flat.'

For some reason this word seemed to strike both boys as incredibly funny. Shouting 'Flat! Flat! Flat!', they began charging round the sitting room, knocking over a small table and a pile of books.

'We're still searching for her,' Edgar went on. 'I just came home to catch a few hours' sleep. I was up all night. I should be getting back to the station now.'

'So you're not coming to the pantomime with us?'

'No. Sorry.'

Edward, the six-year-old, suddenly transformed himself, with the magical ease of a young child, into a lovable moppet.

'Please come with us, Uncle Edgar.' A small hand crept into his.

Edgar remembered his resolution to be a fun uncle. He certainly wasn't making a very good start. 'I'm sorry.' He crouched down to his nephew's level. 'I'd love to come but I've got some important work to do. I'll walk to the pier with you.'

'Mum says you know Abanazar.' This was George, less cute. 'She said we could go backstage afterwards.'

Edgar looked at Lucy, who shrugged apologetically.

'I'll see what I can do,' said Edgar. 'And I'll give you some money to buy ice creams.'

'I've had ice cream before,' said Edward with a world-weary sigh. 'I was sick.'

Emma got back to the station at four. She hadn't wanted to go home at all but the DI had insisted. 'You'll be no use to me if you're dead on your feet.' So she'd walked to Roedean – the buses didn't seem to be running – to face the aggressive concern of her mother, father and the trusty Ada.

'You're not going back there,' said her father. 'You were out all night. It's not right.'

'I am going back.' Emma set her jaw. She would fight him if necessary. Perhaps her father realised this because he subsided into angry muttering. It was left to Ada to run her a bath and search for her Fair Isle jumper and warmest slacks. 'You might as well be warm while you're about it.'

Lying in the scented water, Emma thought about Jim Francis trudging out in the snow to his outdoor privy. The Francis house was clean and home-like but it still represented a level of poverty that Emma hadn't encountered before. The tiny kitchen, the overcrowded bedroom. What were they doing now, the shell-shocked family? She was sure that Jim would still be out there somewhere, searching. What about Richard, the little boy who had cuddled up to her in the night? It must be a terrible thing, to lose your twin. She thought of the bedroom with the double and the single bed. Would Richard soon be sleeping there alone? She shut her eyes, trying to rid herself of the image.

She must have fallen asleep because she was woken by her mother calling from the landing.

'Are you all right in there, Em? Ada's made you some hot soup.'

The soup was an olive branch, she knew. She ate in her dressing gown, watched by her mother, from across the table, and Ada, from the doorway.

'You should get some sleep now,' said her mother.

'Just two hours,' said Emma. 'Promise you'll wake me at four.'

But, in the end, she hadn't slept well. Voices echoed in her head. The DI, in answer to her question about Betty being abducted: *Yes, I do.* Richard: *I didn't like it in the room without Betty.* Daphne: *Children's imaginations are dark, Sergeant Holmes. That's why they like fairy stories. Parents killing their children. The stone falling on the bad mother and crushing her. The parents who want a baby and get a hedgehog instead. Life, death, birth, pain, happiness. It's all there.*

She woke with a start, thinking that she was still in the Francises' house. It was half past three. No point trying to get back to sleep. She dressed in the Fair Isle jumper and slacks. By the front door she found hiking boots and her mother's fur coat, plus a Thermos flask. She put on the coat. It was slightly too big but wonderfully warm. She dreaded to think what Bob would say when he saw it.

Her mother appeared as she was lacing up the boots. 'You will be careful, won't you, darling?'

'I won't be doing anything dangerous,' said Emma. 'I'll just be at the station, using my brain.'

It was an old joke, the Holmes brain. Her mother laughed, 'Now that really is dangerous, darling. I do hope you find her.'

Emma gave her mother a quick kiss. 'So do I, Mum.'

It was quiet at the station. Bob and the DI weren't back yet and everyone else was out with the search teams. Emma could hear Superintendent Hodges in his office yelling at someone about getting reinforcements from other forces. 'We can't cope any more. Don't you understand?'

Emma sat down with the case files. That was what the DI always said: 'Go back through the paperwork. The answer's probably there all along.' Bob and the others hated paperwork but Emma secretly rather liked it. She prided herself on her comprehensive notes and careful cross-referencing. She looked at the timeline stuck on the front of the file.

Monday 26th November: Annie Francis and Mark Webster reported missing.

Thursday 29th November: Annie and Mark's bodies found on open ground on Devil's Dyke.

She wrote, 'Friday 14th December: Betty Francis reported missing.'

She read through the witness reports from the 26th and 27th, she read the interviews with Patricia Paxton, Martin Hammond, Duncan Pettigrew and Daphne Young. Also in the file were the exercise books containing Annie's story,

'The Wicked Stepdaughter', and her unfinished play, *The True Story of Hansel and Gretel*. Emma opened the play, supposedly written with Daphne Young. The teacher had been right, it was extraordinarily good for one so young. But Emma had been right too; it was extremely disturbing. Gretel hates her brother because he's slow and stupid. She plans to murder him and blame 'the wicked witch'. Gretel doesn't believe in the witch but she plays on Hansel's fears, telling him that the witch will 'kill him in his dreams'. Hansel vows to stay awake for ever and there was a rather funny scene where he keeps falling asleep at school. Eventually Gretel persuades him into the forest (shades of the Dark Wood in *The Stolen Children*), where she proceeds to abandon him so that he'll be eaten by wolves. The play ends there. What had Annie planned for the denouement? Would the witch appear like a deus ex machina and restore justice? Or would the children join hands and sing, 'Friends together, friends for ever'? Emma doubted it somehow.

She was so absorbed in the story that she didn't, at first, notice the phone ringing.

'Call for you, Sergeant Holmes.'

'Hallo, Emma. I thought you'd still be there.'

It was Rosalind Macateer, a WPC in Hastings. They had trained together and Emma had asked Ros, as a favour, to look into the records for the 1912 pantomime murder.

'I heard about the other girl going missing,' said Ros. 'Tough luck.'

Tough luck. Ros was from a similar background to

Emma, which was why they had become friends, but it didn't make the stiff upper lip any more lovable at times like this.

'You asked me about Ezra Nightingale,' said Ros. 'Are you still interested?'

'Yes,' said Emma although, in truth, those suspicions seemed very far away now. She couldn't think beyond Betty and her walk down the hill towards the forest and the witch's cottage.

'Well, his son was called Gunther,' said Ros. 'Poor little sod. You can tell it was before the war. Gunther Adolf, if you can believe it. His wife was Elizabeth, maiden name Dunkley. They lived at . . .'

'Wait,' said Emma. 'What was the wife's maiden name?'

'Elizabeth Dunkley.'

Roger Dunkley was forty-eight, according to their records. He had changed his name, probably glad to swap those Germanic forenames for the quintessentially English Roger, but had reverted to his mother's maiden name. And Roger Dunkley had known both children, had visited their schools.

Emma thanked Ros. As she said goodbye, Bob came in wearing his fisherman's coat

'Bob,' said Emma. 'What was Roger Dunkley's alibi for the children's murder?'

'Who?' Bob was starting to take off the coat.

'Roger Dunkley. The director of *Aladdin*.'

'Oh, him. He was having dinner at the Grand with some bigwig. What are you doing?'

Emma was feverishly going through the telephone directory. Bob watched suspiciously as she picked up the phone and asked to be put through to the Grand. After a brief exchange and a long wait, during which Bob removed his boots, she was put through to the maître d'hôtel.

After a few minutes' conversation, some of it (to Bob's disgust) in French, she put the receiver down, eyes bright with excitement.

'Put your coat back on, Bob. We're going out.'

'What are you talking about?'

'The maître d'hôtel said that Bert Billington, the theatre impresario, stayed at the hotel on the twenty-sixth of November. He had a guest for dinner and the table was booked for eight.'

'So?'

'So Dunkley would have had plenty of time to kill Annie and Mark and make it back to the hotel for dinner. Come on, we've got to tell the DI.'

CHAPTER 27

George and Edward enjoyed the slip, slide and stagger down the hill to the pier. At first Lucy shouted at them not to throw snowballs or slide on the patches of grey ice, but after a while she gave up, more concerned with not falling over herself. She clung onto Edgar's arm, insecure in her high-heeled boots, and this, together with the dark and the snow, gave them an unaccustomed feeling of intimacy. Edgar couldn't remember the last time his sister had taken his arm. The Palace Pier Theatre looked magical, lights sparkling on the dark sea. The pier itself, with its domes, archways and pavilions, was snow-covered but someone had sprinkled salt over the gangplanks and a muddy path led to the theatre at the end, past the shuttered booths and the What the Butler Saw machines. Lucy stopped at a poster showing Max at his most Mephistophelean.

'Look, boys! That's Uncle Edgar's friend.'

But the boys, thrilled by the night and the snow and the prospect of a treat, had run on ahead.

A crowd was gathering in the foyer. Edgar pushed his way through and bought a programme. In the crush he was surprised to see Roger Dunkley, looking rather scruffy next to the theatre manager in his dinner jacket and bow tie.

'Mr Dunkley!'

Roger started and looked to see where the call was coming from.

'Edgar Stephens.' He didn't want to give his rank and lowered his voice when he added, 'From the police.' Even so, Dunkley looked rather shocked. 'It's nothing official,' said Edgar. 'It's just my sister and her sons are here to see the show tonight. I can't stay and I'd promised them that they could go backstage and see Max . . .'

'Of course.' Dunkley seemed to pull himself together with an effort. 'I'll take them through myself. Anything to keep the police happy, eh?' He laughed, rather loudly. Edgar could see Lucy looking over. He beckoned.

'Lucy, this is Mr Dunkley, the director. He's going to take you backstage afterwards to see Max.'

'Really?' Lucy's eyes lit up and the boys cheered. For a moment, Edgar really was the uncle of the year. Not counting Uncle Abanazar, of course.

'My pleasure.' Dunkley gave a bow, the most stagey gesture Edgar had ever seen him make. 'Meet me at the pass door afterwards. I'll show you where it is.'

'Have a great evening,' Edgar told his nephews. 'Here,

Edward. Here's some money for ice creams in the interval.'

'You don't need to do that,' said Lucy.

'A promise is a promise,' said Edgar.

'Don't worry, Detective Inspector Stephens,' said Roger Dunkley. 'I'll look after them.'

Max heard the opening number as he played patience in his dressing room.

Boys and girls of Peking,
Hallo!
Boys and girls of Peking,
Hurrah!
Boys and girls, boys and girls, boys and girls of Peking,
Come in!

It wasn't exactly Irving Berlin but it had a habit of worming its way into your head. Max often found himself humming it when he was shaving. He wasn't on until the third scene, where Widow Twankey is doing her washing and is surprised by the mysterious stranger claiming to be her brother-in-law and wanting to meet her son. Max always enjoyed this time before his first appearance, listening to the pantomime relayed through the loudspeakers, knowing that he was going to take the stage very soon. That mixture of nerves and anticipation, played out to the tune of terrible songs, was – in his mind – the very essence of the theatre. So he was mildly irritated when a knock on the door interrupted the ritual.

'Come in.' He had to stop himself singing it.

It was Roger Dunkley. This was odd in itself. The director usually spent the entire performance in the wings, making frantic winding-up gestures if he felt the actors were going too slowly.

'Roger. This is a surprise.'

'I've just seen your friend, the policeman, front of house.'

'Edgar?' Max was amazed. He would have thought that Edgar would be working flat out tonight. 'Is he coming to the show?'

'No. He couldn't stay, he said. His sister's here with her boys. Your friend wanted me to bring them to meet you backstage after the show.'

'Oh, I see.' Edgar had mentioned something about his sister on Wednesday. Max had never met any of Edgar's family. He was mildly intrigued.

'What's she like?'

'Quite attractive. Not your type though.'

Max would be interested to know what Roger thought his type was.

'I'll look forward to seeing her later,' he said.

Roger stood there for a while as if he wanted to say more but in the end he took himself off, humming 'Boys and Girls of Peking'.

*

Emma and Bob quarrelled all the way up the stairs.

'I still say we should tell the super.'

'We need to tell the DI first.'

'Why are you always running to the DI?'

They had reached the lobby now and Emma's angry retort was cut off by the desk sergeant saying, 'Sergeant Holmes, Sergeant Willis. There's a lady here to see DI Stephens.'

For one crazy moment Emma thought it would be Betty, even though she would hardly be described as 'a lady'. The woman waiting by the desk was not very old, probably slightly younger than Emma, but she was most definitely grown-up. She was also extremely pretty. Emma sensed Bob standing up straighter and puffing out his chest.

'How can I help?' asked Emma with a bland, professional smile.

'I'm sorry.' The woman's smile was warmer. She was beautifully dressed in a black coat with a fur collar. She was also wearing slightly more make-up than Emma's mother would think appropriate. 'I was just wondering if Detective Inspector Stephens was here.'

'He's out but he's due back very soon. Can I ask what it's about?'

That charming smile again, a dimple appearing and a flutter of eyelashes. 'It's not important. It's not to do with work or anything. Sounds silly but I found myself with the evening off unexpectedly. I wondered if he'd like to come to the pantomime with me.'

'Detective Inspector Stephens is in the middle of a murder enquiry,' said Emma. 'I hardly think he'll have time to go to the pantomime.'

'Of course not.' The woman looked duly chastened. Then Bob spoke up, like a fool. 'Can we give him a message? I'm sure he'll be sorry to have missed you.'

'Can you tell him that Ruby called?'

'Ruby.' Bob repeated it like it was the most wonderful name in the world.

'If you'll excuse us,' said Emma, 'we've got work to do.'

'Of course. Thank you. You've been very kind.' She made her way to the door and the desk sergeant sprang up to open it for her, like a commissionaire. With a half-wave, she disappeared into the night, leaving Bob staring after her like the village idiot.

Edgar, taking a short cut through the Lanes, met them at the corner by the Bath Arms, incidentally very near the spot where a fourteenth-century nun was meant to be bricked up. They both looked agitated and excited. Emma was wearing a fur coat, slightly too long for her, that made her look like a child dressing up.

'Bob, Emma. What are you doing here?'

'Looking for you,' said Bob.

'Sir.' Emma looked as if she wanted to grab his arm. 'We've found out something about Roger Dunkley.'

'Roger Dunkley? What?'

'He's Ezra Nightingale's son.'

'Are you sure?'

'Not entirely, but Ezra's wife's maiden name was Dunkley and he's the right age. And I've checked his alibi and it doesn't hold up. He had dinner with Bert Billington at eight. He could easily have killed the children before that. And he knew them, he went into their schools.'

Edgar thought of the director saying that the theatre was 'in his blood'. He thought of Roger Dunkley's photographs, so carefully saved in their envelope. Every picture had been of the boys' grammar school. *I'm a bit of a devil with a Box Brownie.* He thought of Roger, every inch the theatrical, ushering Edgar's nephews into the theatre. *Don't worry, Detective Inspector Stephens. I'll look after them.*

'We'd better go and talk to him,' he said.

He meant to send Bob back to the station but somehow the three of them were running through the narrow streets towards the Palace Pier. The night was darker now and the light from the theatre seemed to blaze. Could it really be Roger Dunkley? thought Edgar. Being the son of a murderer didn't make him a murderer, of course, but he had undoubtedly been nervous when Edgar had interviewed him. Betsy, Betty. Even the names were very similar. And if it was Dunkley, might he still have Betty hidden away somewhere? Might they actually be in time to save her?

They thundered through the archway welcoming them to the Palace Pier, galloping along the wooden gangplanks, slipping in the gritty snow. When they crashed through the doors into the foyer, Edgar was so out of breath that he could hardly speak. It was left to Emma to say, briskly, 'We're from Brighton CID. We'd like to speak to Roger Dunkley.'

The theatre manager gaped at them. 'Mr Dunkley will be backstage. The performance has started.'

Edgar waved his warrant card and panted, 'Unless you want me to stop the performance, you'll take me to Mr Dunkley as quickly as possible.'

The man paled and, with no further argument, led them towards an unobtrusive door by the sign saying 'Stalls'. Edgar remembered Roger pointing out the same door earlier.

'This way.'

They were in a long tunnel. It must have run alongside the auditorium because they could hear roars of laughter from the audience and, when they got closer, they could hear the performers themselves, as clearly as if they were standing beside them.

'Honestly, boys and girls, I despair of Wishy Washy.' That was Denton McGrew as Widow Twankey. 'You'd never believe that he's Aladdin's brother. Well, between you and me . . .' – anticipatory giggles – 'I did have a bit of hanky-panky with a handyman from Tonypandy. Ah yes, Handy Andy from Tonypandy. He's Wishy's father all right. Neither of them any good with tools . . .'

They reached another door. The manager opened it slowly and, to Edgar's surprise, he saw that they were actually in the wings. They could see the stage, Widow Twankey in her monstrous striped dress pushing Wishy Washy, in limp yellow satin, into a large washing machine. From across the stage he thought he could even see a glimmer of green where Max waited to make his entrance.

Roger Dunkley was standing watching the performers. He started when he saw the door open. The manager beckoned and Roger came out into the corridor, looking furious.

'What's going on, Tom?'

'These people' – Tom, the manager, jerked his thumb accusingly – 'want to talk to you urgently.'

'You again.' Roger glared at Edgar. 'This had better be good.'

'Is there somewhere we can talk in private?' said Edgar.

'My office. This way.'

The three police officers followed Roger Dunkley up a short staircase and into a room marked 'Director. Please knock'. There Bob shut the door on Tom. Roger faced them across his desk, still looking angry rather than afraid.

'Mr Dunkley,' said Edgar. 'Was your father called Ezra Nightingale?'

He didn't know what he expected. Tears, collapse, angry denial. Instead, Roger smiled thinly. 'I thought you'd find out eventually. So that's your case, is it? I'm the son of a murderer so I must be a murderer myself. Congratulations. You must be getting desperate.'

'You had dinner with Bert Billington at eight o'clock on the twenty-sixth of November,' said Emma. 'What were you doing between five and eight?'

Roger's face changed but Edgar couldn't tell exactly what the new expression signified. There was still anger and scorn there but they seemed to be overlaid with something like relief.

'I was with my lover,' he said.

'What's her name?' Emma wasn't about to give up so easily.

'His name,' said Roger, very slowly and clearly, 'is Martin Hammond.'

'Martin Hammond,' said Emma. 'Dr Hammond?'

'Yes,' said Roger, 'Dr Hammond the headmaster, which is why it's so important to keep our relationship secret. It's against the law for one thing. No one cares about actors like Denton but there are people around – probably people like you – who would think a homosexual man shouldn't be in charge of a school.'

That explained a lot of things, thought Edgar. It explained why Roger had kept the photographs, not because the children were in them but because Martin Hammond was. It probably explained why he had visited the school in the first place and why he had come to the funeral. Dr Hammond had been there too, he remembered.

Emma was momentarily speechless so Edgar said, 'I'd like to contact Dr Hammond to see if he corroborates your story.'

'Be my guest,' Roger scribbled a number on a piece of paper. 'But, please, be discreet.'

'I will,' said Edgar.

'Mind you,' said Roger bitterly, 'once Denton gets to hear about it, it'll be round the whole town. I sometimes think my father killed the wrong child all those years ago.'

It was a black joke, thought Edgar, if it was a joke. But maybe Roger Dunkley was entitled to his bad taste. For him it was, quite literally, gallows humour. Did Denton McGrew know that Ezra Nightingale was Dunkley's father? Edgar thought that he didn't but once the secret was out, that too would be known by the whole of Brighton. Yet Dunkley had deliberately entered his father's world; he employed two actors – Denton and Diablo – who had been involved in the 1912 production. He must have known that his secret couldn't stay buried for ever.

They walked in silence back down the tunnel. From the auditorium came the sound of Max, in full Abanazar mode. 'You're not my real uncle.' 'Of course I'm your uncle. Just look how alike we are . . .'

Edgar stopped. He remembered the exchange between Window Twankey and Wishy Washy earlier. 'I despair of Wishy Washy. You'd never believe that he's Aladdin's brother.' Abanazar wasn't Aladdin's real uncle, Wishy Washy wasn't his full brother. A woman had longed for a child and given birth to a hedgehog. A woman had killed her stepson and laid the blame on her daughter. Mary and Martha had wept at the death of their brother Lazarus.

'Emma.'

'Yes?' She had been subdued since the scene with Roger Dunkley. Edgar knew that she felt embarrassed about the collapse of her theory. He would tell her later that it hadn't been her fault. But now he had more important things on his mind.

'Do you remember what the children said, the ones who saw Annie and Mark by the park?'

They had reached the foyer again. The attendants were standing with trays of ice cream, waiting for the interval. Great 'Oohs' and 'Aahs' were coming from the theatre. Max must be performing a trick.

'They didn't know the time,' Edgar persisted, 'but said they'd just seen the number twelve bus go past.'

'Yes.' Emma and Bob were both looking at him.

'Do you remember where Betty was last seen?'

'By the bus stop,' said Bob.

'Do you know which route Reg Webster drives?' asked Edgar.

CHAPTER 28

It took one phone call to establish that Reg Webster drove the number 12 bus on a route that went all the way from Queen's Park to the Devil's Dyke. It was a Southdown bus and the depot was at the bottom of Freshfield Road.

Edgar asked for a squad car to meet them at the garage but he thought that they'd be quicker on foot. It had started snowing again and the roads were becoming icy and dangerous. They jogged across the Old Steine, heading towards Edward Street and the road up to Queen's Park. The fountain was frozen, the water held in mid-air as if it was part of one of Max's illusions. As they ran, Edgar explained his theory.

'You know everyone said that Annie and Mark were like brother and sister? Well, I think they were brother and sister. I don't think that Mark was Reg's son. I was thinking of the photograph in Daphne Young's book. Annie, Mark and Betty. Two sisters and a brother. I think that's what she had discovered. I think she realised when she read the lesson at the funeral. Martha, Mary and Lazarus. Two sisters and a brother.'

'Betty had that picture too,' said Emma. 'It was in a box under her bed.'

'So you think that Mark is Jim Francis's son,' said Bob. 'Why didn't he have red hair then?'

'The red hair comes from Sandra's side,' said Edgar. 'Her mother has it.'

'And that was the significance of *The Stolen Children*,' said Emma. She was less out of breath than either of the men. Edgar was quite impressed at how fit she was. 'It was about finding a long-lost brother. "Brothers and sisters, friends for ever." That's what Betty wrote. I think she knew. I think that's why she wanted me to see the play.'

'And you think that's why Webster abducted her,' said Bob.

They stopped at the bottom of the hill to catch their breath. Bob and Edgar bent double, Emma pawing at the snow like a reindeer, a shaggy reindeer in her big fur coat. Edgar was relieved that Bob used the word 'abducted' and not 'murdered'. Please, God, make Betty still be alive.

They started up the hill. 'We've got no evidence,' muttered Bob from the back.

'No,' agreed Edgar. 'Do you want to go back?'

No one spoke as they continued the climb, heads bent against the snow.

*

Ruby came to see Max in the interval.

'You were good,' she said. 'I was quite scared of you.'

'Not too sinister?'

'No, just right, I'd say.'

Max looked at her, neat and perfect as ever in a tightly fitting green dress. The theatre manager had bowed almost to the floor when he'd shown her into Max's dressing room. He was surprised that Roger Dunkley hadn't popped round to see the visitor. He was usually everywhere in the interval, telling people how well they were doing, urging everyone to get through the business quickly 'so that we'll be in good time for the bar afterwards'.

'I called on Edgar,' said Ruby, 'but a very stuck-up policewoman told me that he was in the middle of a murder case and couldn't be bothered with trivial things like pantomimes.'

'He is a bit busy,' said Max, marvelling slightly at Ruby's self-absorption. Mind you, it was probably a necessary trait in an actress. 'Another child has gone missing. His sister and nephews are here tonight though.'

'I didn't know he had a sister.'

Would you have remembered if he had told you? thought Max. Aloud he said, 'Why have you got the evening off?'

'Oh, the director lets all the chorus have the odd night off,' said Ruby. 'There are all these stage-school children from Chichester just dying to step into our shoes.'

'Our director never lets anyone have time off,' said Max.

'Even if you were dead, you'd probably have to go on.' Surreptitiously he searched for some wood to touch.

'But you're the star,' said Ruby. 'People come because of you. You should hear them talking about you in the audience. I wanted to tell everyone that I'm your daughter.'

'You'll be a bigger star than me one day,' said Max.

'I do hope so,' said Ruby. 'I'd better be going back to my seat now. Break a leg.'

The Southdown garage was at the bottom of Freshfield Road. They must have walked past it hundreds of times in the past few weeks. Through the high windows they could see the big green buses inside, off the road because of the snow. How many times had they seen those buses lumbering about Brighton? What had Max said about the waiter? *They're always there and yet you never see them.* Wasn't the same true of buses, the permanent backdrop to a city scene? Could one of these buses have held the dead bodies of Annie and Mark? Was Betty even now imprisoned here, amongst the double-deckers?

'The doors are locked,' said Bob, stating the obvious as ever.

'Then we'll have to break in.' Edgar started searching in the snow for a rock but it was Emma who found an old wheel hub leaning up against the wall. Edgar climbed onto the wall.

'Pass it up to me. I'll see if I can smash this window.'

'Let me do it,' said Bob.

'No.' Edgar knew that Bob was reminding him that he was younger and fitter but he wasn't going to let anyone else do this thing. He'd always known that he would have to be the one to find Betty. He just prayed that he'd find her alive.

Using all his strength, he threw the wheel hub against the glass. It shattered immediately and he could hear the crash inside as the metal hub hit more metal. If Betty was there, she would be terrified.

He hauled himself up onto the window ledge.

'Be careful, sir.' That was Emma.

'Let me do it.' Bob. Faint but persistent.

He was higher than he had thought, on a level with the top deck of the buses. 'Betty!' he called. 'Betty!' His voice echoed against the vaulted roof. Outside he could hear more voices. The squad car must have arrived. But whatever was hidden in this garage, he had to be the one to find it. He jumped down from the windowsill.

He fell awkwardly, twisting his ankle. He scrambled to his feet. 'Betty!' Silence, voices outside, then . . . a small scrabbling sound, like a mouse or a trapped animal. He limped towards it.

She was in the number 12 bus. He saw her sitting on the bench seat at the back, huddled in a blanket and sucking her thumb. When she saw him, she whipped out the thumb as if embarrassed to be caught doing something so childish. He climbed onto the running board. 'It's OK, Betty. I'm a policeman.'

She nodded. 'I've seen you before. Is the lady policeman here?'

'She's just outside.' He could hear bodies battering the doors. They would be inside in a minute.

'I'm cold,' said Betty, and he could see that she was shivering, despite the blanket.

'It's all right,' said Edgar. 'I've come to take you home.'

Maybe it was the magic word but Betty suddenly launched herself at him, almost knocking him backwards. He scooped her up and she clung to him, burying her face in his shoulder.

'Uncle Reg,' she whispered. 'He brought me here.'

'I know,' said Edgar. 'Everything's all right now. I'm going to take you back to your mum and dad.'

The doors caved in as he approached. Bob, Emma and the other officers crowded round. 'Is it her? Is she all right?' Edgar didn't answer any of them. With Betty in his arms, he started up Freshfield Road. Though small for her age, she was no lightweight but he didn't, for a minute, consider putting her down.

'Bob,' he called over his shoulder, 'Take Sergeant McGuire and go to the Websters.'

'Yes, sir.'

'Arrest Reg Webster and keep him there until I come.'

'Yes, sir.'

'Emma, you come with me.'

'Try and stop me,' said Emma.

The steep hill was nothing to him, even with his injured ankle and Betty clinging round his neck. The falling snow was soft beneath his feet. The light was on in the Francises' house. As Edgar was encumbered by Betty, Emma hammered on the door. Jim answered, with Sandra close behind.

'I've brought Betty home to you,' said Edgar.

It felt like the best moment of his life.

CHAPTER 29

Edgar left Emma with the Francises and walked seven doors down to the Websters' house. Reg Webster, handcuffed to PC McGuire, was sitting on the sofa. Edna Webster sat opposite, staring at her husband with a kind of silent horror.

'Get up,' said Edgar. 'Reg Webster, I'm arresting you for the murders of Annie Francis, Mark Webster and Daphne Young and for the abduction of Betty Francis. Do you have anything to say?'

He knew these words would have been spoken before, probably by Bob, but he wanted to say them again, to see the look in the man's eyes.

'You've got no proof,' said Reg, his eyes darting between the three policemen.

'Your fingerprints will be all over the sweets put into the children's grave,' said Edgar, 'and I'm pretty sure that we'll find traces of blood and hair on your bus.'

Reg Webster seemed to sag visibly. He was a small man

anyway but now he seemed to shrink into himself, to become almost animal-like. Edgar thought of Denton McGrew, halfway through transforming into the Dame. This was infinitely more disturbing to watch.

'And Betty confirms that you're the person who abducted her and imprisoned her in the garage,' said Edgar. 'Were you going to kill her too?'

Now the animal seemed to snarl. 'Probably.'

There was a scream from Edna Webster. 'Reg! Your own son!'

Reg turned on her. 'He wasn't my son.'

'How did you know?' asked Edgar.

'I'd always suspected,' said Reg. 'Mark was nothing like me, all bookish and la-di-da. But I didn't know until I saw them rehearsing their play. It was called *The Stolen Children* and it was all about a girl who finds out that she's got a secret brother. That Annie was too clever by half and she'd found out. I had to shut her up so I waited for them every evening. My bus went round the corner by the sweet shop. That Monday I saw them standing there arguing and I offered them a lift. The bus was empty, going back to the depot. They loved going on the bus.'

'Then you killed them,' said Bob.

'I didn't want them telling anybody,' said Reg, as if this was quite reasonable. 'I killed them and put them in the boot of the bus. I drove up to the Dyke the next evening and left the bodies there. I thought they'd be found in the morning but I hadn't reckoned on the snow. I threw the sweets in the grave to put the blame on the shopkeeper. I knew everyone would suspect him because Annie and Mark were last seen outside his shop. Anyway I never liked Gee. He short-changed me once. I had the sweets for the Southdown Christmas party. We've got a load of them, going back to before the war. Lovely do, it is. We have a Santa and everything. The kiddies love it.'

Max was right about the sweets being misdirection, thought Edgar. Reg sounded quite nostalgic about the kiddies' party, despite the fact that he was confessing to the murder of two children. Edna was sobbing hysterically.

'What about Daphne Young?' asked Edgar.

'Silly cow sent me a note,' said Reg. 'Said she'd found out about Mark's parentage. Parentage! Even when I went round there, she was all, "I'm not judging any of you, I just want to help." So I killed her.'

Daphne might have guessed about Mark being Annie's brother, thought Edgar, but she hadn't realised that Reg was the murderer. She probably despised him, little ill-educated Reg Webster. He wasn't a big, impressive man like Jim Francis. She would never have thought that he could be a danger to her.

'Why did you abduct Betty?' he asked.

'She knew too,' said Reg. 'Those Francis girls were nosy little bitches. That's why she insisted on putting that play on, her sister's play. Edna told me all about it.'

'Oh God, Reg.' The cry seemed to be torn out of Edna

Webster. 'Why didn't you kill me instead of Mark? I was the one who was unfaithful to you. It's all my fault.'

'I wouldn't kill you,' said Reg, sounding shocked. 'You're my wife.'

'Take him away,' said Edgar. McGuire dragged Reg towards the door. The policeman looked thoroughly shaken. Of course, he was a neighbour too, the first person to be called when the children had gone missing. Bob followed, also looking rather sick. Edgar told them to drive to the station and put Reg in the cells. 'I'll walk down in a few minutes.'

'What about your ankle?' asked Bob.

'I'll be all right.'

When they had gone, Edgar turned to Edna Webster. 'Can I get someone to sit with you?'

'A neighbour, you mean?' Edna laughed bitterly. 'Oh, they'll all want to sit with me after this. I'll probably be lynched tomorrow. You saw what they were like with Sam Gee. When they find out it was Reg all along . . .'

'I'll get some protection for you,' said Edgar. 'Maybe you could go away for a while. Have you got any family?'

'No.' Edna looked him in the eye. 'My family was Mark and he's dead.'

'Did Jim Francis know,' asked Edgar, 'that Mark was his child?'

'He probably suspected,' said Edna. 'We went together and, nine months later, a baby appears. But he never said anything. He knows when to keep his mouth shut.'

Like Mark, thought Edgar. Perhaps bookish, sensitive Mark was more like his father than he knew. At any rate there must be more to Jim Francis than met the eye.

Edna's account was brutally matter-of-fact. 'I wanted a baby. I was desperate and it was obvious that it wasn't going to happen for Reg and me. And there was Jim. Sandra had just got pregnant; Jim probably wasn't getting any sex at home. I asked him round one evening to help me put some shelves up and I seduced him.'

It was hard to imagine anything less seductive than Edna Webster, tear-stained and red-eyed, sitting on the sagging armchair in her hairnet. But Edgar supposed that she'd made more of an effort, that day thirteen years ago. And Jim was a good-looking man, a contrast to Reg Webster in every way. He wondered if Edna had been in love with Jim. Maybe that was why she hadn't liked Sandra.

It's like 'The Juniper Tree', he said to Emma as they walked back down the hill together. *A woman wished for a child as red as blood and as white as snow*. It was desperation for a child that was the motivating force behind half these stories. A man wants a son even if it's half hedgehog. But the bagpipe-playing hedgehog born into the wrong family hadn't been Annie, it had been Mark. And Mark hadn't been able to change his skin and turn into a handsome prince. He hadn't been able to lay a trail of stones that took him safely home. He had been killed by the wicked stepfather.

'It's not a happy ending,' he said to Emma, 'because we couldn't save Annie and Mark.'

'But we saved Betty,' said Emma, 'and maybe she'll do great things in the world.'

Yes, thought Edgar, wincing as he stumbled over the icy main road, maybe Betty would soar like a bird, rising above her traumatic start in life, returning only to shower blessings on her deserving family. He hoped so. He really did.

It was past midnight by the time he got back to his flat. Superintendent Hodges had ordered in crates of beer to celebrate Betty's return and Reg Webster's arrest. But Edgar hadn't felt like getting drunk. He was truly, deeply glad that Betty had been found, and relieved that Webster was behind bars, but there was still the memory of the other children, of the little bodies in the snow. *I killed them,* Webster had said, *and put them in the boot of the bus.* Just as if they had been rubbish to be thrown away. Well, Webster would probably hang now, but that thought couldn't bring Edgar any pleasure. Killing their murderer wouldn't bring Annie and Mark back.

He wanted to tell Emma and Bob how well they'd done, but when he looked over, they were in the centre of a crowd of young officers, laughing and toasting each other. Emma's hair was loose and she looked like an entirely different person. Edgar began to edge towards the exit.

'Are you leaving us?' It was Frank Hodges, standing by the door with a pint mug in his hand.

'I'm just feeling a bit tired,' said Edgar.

'I'm not surprised.' Hodges' little eyes were surprisingly kind. 'You did good work tonight, Stephens. How did you make the connection with Webster?'

'Just a lot of things falling into place,' said Edgar. He didn't feel up to explaining the train of thought that had started with Wishy Washy and ended up with the number 12 bus.

'You're limping,' said Hodges.

'Twisted my ankle climbing through a window.'

'Take my advice and leave that sort of thing to the younger officers. I'll have my driver take you home.'

Edgar tried to refuse but, in the end, the thought of a warm, comfortable car taking him smoothly back up the hill was too much to resist. The Jaguar skidded slightly at the bottom of Albion Hill but the driver skilfully steered onto the fresher snow where the grip was better. When Edgar thanked him, he simply touched his cap and began the process of turning the long car in the narrow street.

Edgar let himself into his flat. For the first time he thought about Lucy and the boys. He hoped that they'd got home safely. Gently he opened the bedroom door and could just make out three shapes on the bed.

'Is that you, Ed?' Lucy's sleepy voice.

'Yes. I'm sorry to wake you.'

'You didn't.'

Edgar tiptoed back into the sitting room. He hadn't wanted to disturb them to search for blankets; he'd just have to sleep under his coat. Maybe he would have a night-cap first. Taking the whisky bottle and a glass he sat down on the sofa. And stood up quickly.

'Edgar?' Another voice. A warm shape lying under a blanket. Black hair, white skin in the darkness. A hand on his arm.

'Ruby? What are you doing here?'

'I had a night off so I came to see *Aladdin*. I called for you at the station. Didn't that policewoman tell you?'

'No.'

'Well, I went to see Max backstage after the show and I met Lucy and the boys. Max brought us all back here in his Bentley. It was too late for my train so Lucy thought I should stay on the sofa. I hope you don't mind.'

'Of course not.'

'Max didn't seem keen for me to go to his digs. I bet he's got a woman there.'

That was a thought. He noted that Ruby was realistic about her father's private life.

'Did you find her?' asked Ruby. 'The little girl who was lost.'

'Yes,' said Edgar. 'Yes, we did.'

'You are clever.' She was sitting next to him now and he could smell her perfume, her clean hair, her minty breath. She was wearing what looked like one of his old shirts.

'I'll sleep on the floor,' he said.

But Ruby moved towards him and he found himself kissing her, pushing her back against the cushions, feeling her wonderfully soft body under the thin cotton. He heard her sharp intake of breath and started to draw back, but then it was Ruby pulling him onto her, undoing his shirt so that her skin touched his. 'We can't,' Edgar started to say, but somehow it was part of the night and the journey and the dark path through the forest. He kissed her more fiercely as, outside, the snow continued to fall.

CHAPTER 30

After everything that had happened, Edgar was surprised to find himself enjoying the pantomime. Perhaps it was because it was Christmas Eve, or because there was still snow outside, but there was an intense excitement amongst the audience as they waited for the curtain to go up. Edgar looked down the row at Betty, watching the stage with a composed, professional expression on her face, as if planning to compare Nigel Castle's writing with her own, and Richard, lost in wonder, eyes wide, mouth slightly open. He didn't quite know how he had ended up here with Bob, Emma and the two children. Emma had kept in touch with the family and she had been the one who suggested that the Francis children could do with a Christmas treat. Understandably, the parents didn't feel up to it ('I feel like I never want to see a play again,' said Sandra), so Emma had offered to take them. 'You're coming too,' she told Edgar and Bob. 'It'll be our Christmas outing.' 'She's getting very bossy,' Bob grumbled to Edgar, 'just because the super said she was a credit to women police officers everywhere.'

Bob didn't seem to be complaining tonight though. Edgar watched as he teased Betty about various film stars that he'd never heard of. 'I've seen that poster of Tex Ritter in your bedroom.' 'No,' Betty was saying seriously, 'I've only got a picture of Rin Tin Tin.' Emma was tousling Richard's hair and asking him what Father Christmas was bringing him tomorrow. 'Kevin says Father Christmas doesn't exist,' said Richard. 'Of course he exists,' said Bob, 'I've asked him to bring me a cowboy hat and a gun.' Edgar wasn't sure about the wisdom of encouraging children to believe in mythical figures (to say nothing about the gun) but there was no doubt that Bob and Emma were both genuinely fond of the twins. They all were. It was as if Betty and Richard had suddenly acquired a whole police station full of aunties and uncles. Superintendent Hodges had even bought the family a giant tub of toffees, probably purchased from Sam Gee and to be delivered by Father Christmas.

Edgar felt fond of Jim and Sandra too. The couple were never going to get over Annie's death but they were a strong family, close-knit and private. Edgar knew that they'd survive. Sandra had been incredibly forgiving about Jim's affair with Edna, if it could be classed as an affair. 'These things are different for men,' she said to Emma. Edgar asked Emma if she thought that Sandra had ever suspected that Mark was Jim's child. 'She says not,' said Emma. 'She said she never really noticed him, he was just one of Annie's friends. "I've only got time to think about my own children," she said.' Edgar thought that Sandra was still so grief-stricken about Annie that nothing else seemed to register, except the safety of her other children.

Jim, of course, had lost two children. He only mentioned this once, obliquely, to Edgar. 'I always suspected that the little lad might be mine but I thought, I've got four kids, Mark's all Edna and Reg have.' His fists had clenched and his face had taken on an alarmingly purple hue. 'If I'd known then . . .'

'None of us knew,' said Edgar, 'that's the point. These people walk amongst us until suddenly something happens and then the demons are unloosed.' He thought of Ezra Nightingale. What had driven him to his single murderous act? Again, they would never know but, thinking of Denton McGrew, the man who turned into a different creature every night, Edgar was sure that he, for one, would never forget Ezra's victim. Why else had he kept her picture all these years? Poor little Betsy, with her ringlets and dirndl skirt. Edgar knew that she'd stay in his mind as long as he remembered this case, which meant for ever. Roger and Diablo too, in their different ways, would never forget the events of that December, thirty-nine years ago.

Edna Webster had moved away, to stay with her sister in Newark. There would be plenty of publicity when the case came to court, of course, but for the moment the residents of Freshfield Road seemed to want to put tragedy behind them and look to the future. There was talk of a memorial to the children in the park, and Bristol Road Juniors would be presenting the Daphne Young Cup each year to the student who showed the most promise with their writing. Sam Gee was still talking about suing the police but Edgar was confident that the shopkeeper, too, would want to lie low for a while. Brian Baxter had closed the garage theatre. 'Too many memories,' he told Edgar when he called round to break the news of Reg Webster's arrest. 'I don't think I'll ever go to the theatre again.' Edgar hoped that wasn't true. He hoped that, in years to come, Brian Baxter would be taking Jimmy Francis and his contemporaries to the pantomime. After all, that was what uncles were for, whether honorary or not.

The lights dimmed, the orchestra started to play a tune that was vaguely oriental in aspiration. Betty turned to Edgar, her eyes shining. 'It's starting.'

The first number – manic dancers in silk tunics and tights singing about Peking – seemed to go on for ever. But then someone was shouting, 'Bow down for His Excellency the Emperor of Peking!' and Diablo bounded on stage. 'Hallo, boys and girls!' Edgar grinned. Max had told him about Diablo's loose interpretation of the part but it was nice to see the old boy enjoying himself so much. The audience loved it too, wolf-whistling when the Emperor introduced his daughter, 'The winner of Miss Peking 1951.' The Princess reminded Edgar of Ruby. She had the same self-contained grace on stage. Ruby. Whenever he thought of her, his heart beat so fast that he honestly thought he might be about to die. What a way to go. The night they had spent together had been one of the most wonderful experiences of his life. He had asked her to marry him the next morning. Even the fact that Ruby had just laughed and said, 'You don't have to marry me just because we slept together,' didn't depress him too much. 'I want to marry you,' said Edgar. 'I love you.' 'That's nice,' said Ruby. Then they'd had to stop talking because George and Edward had barrelled into the room demanding breakfast. Lucy had given Edgar and Ruby, sitting decorously side by side on the sofa, a very sharp look but she'd said nothing. She wasn't a bad sort really, Lucy.

On stage the Peking street scene had given way to Widow Twankey's kitchen. Twankey's antics with the ironing had the audience in hysterics. Richard was laughing so much that Edgar was afraid he'd be sick. His younger brother, Jonathan, had always been sick if he got too excited. It had happened when their Uncle Charlie had taken Edgar and Jonathan to the end-of-the-pier show in Hastings and they'd seen Max perform the Zig Zag Girl trick. Of course, at the time, Edgar hadn't known that Max would go on to become one of his closest friends, or that Jonathan would be dead before his nineteenth birthday.

Wishy Washy went into the washing machine and came

out as a cardboard cut-out. Richard was hiccoughing with laughter and Bob wasn't far behind. Even Betty was giggling delightedly. It must be rather a wonderful thing to be an actor, thought Edgar, to allow all those people in the audience to forget their troubles just for an hour or two. Maybe that's why they put up with it all – the grotty digs, the hard-faced landladies, the hours on the road – just for those moments of pure delight.

'Honestly, boys and girls, I despair of Wishy Washy. You'd never believe that he's Aladdin's brother. Well, between you and me, I did have a bit of hanky-panky with a handyman from Tonypandy. Ah yes, Handy Andy from Tonypandy. He's Wishy's father all right. Neither of them any good with tools. If only I had a real man.'

A flash of green light. A thrill of anticipation from the audience.

It was time for Max to make his entrance.

It was the best show yet. Max was glad of that. It was Christmas Eve and Edgar was in the audience with two children who had been through hell and back. If they couldn't put on a good show tonight, then what was the point of it all? But even standing in the wings, he knew that it was flying. Waves of laughter coming from the audience, all the actors playing up to it, old hams like Diablo and Denton laying on the double takes and double entendres, the dancers sharper and more focused, even Annette less wooden and more appealing. His own entrance was greeted with delighted boos and hisses, but also by some cheering. He quipped with Denton, the lines flying back and forth across the stage.

'Surely you wouldn't take my favourite son?'

'I'm offering him a treat, and don't call me Shirley. You'll have him back at midnight, my word as a gentleman.'

'Ooh, I've got into trouble that way before. I'm too trusting, that's my problem.'

'Believe me, madam, *that's* not your problem.'

Nigel Castle was watching from the wings but even he couldn't complain tonight. All his lines were getting laughs in the right places and, if Denton did make the joke about the Brighton Belle, he was surely entitled to a bit of licence. Even the trick went perfectly, Annette disappearing into the rock as smoothly as a seasoned magician's assistant. Ethel, Max's best-ever girl, couldn't have done it better.

By the time they got to the transformation scene and the reveal, the laughter and applause were almost constant. Aladdin and the Princess, resplendent in white wedding clothes, clasped each other in a bosom-to-bosom kiss. Widow Twankey and the Emperor made rather more of their facetious embrace.

'Now I've got a real man!'

'And I've got a real woman at last.'

In the original *Arabian Nights* version Abanazar is killed by Aladdin. Ezra Nightingale would undoubtedly have preferred this ending. But Nigel's script simply had the magician vanishing in a puff of green smoke, living on to do evil another day. This meant that Max didn't have to take part in the wedding scene. He could wait in the wings until the curtain call. When his moment came, he was almost knocked backwards by the roar of applause from the audience. He couldn't see Edgar or the children – he preferred to keep his audience faceless – but he hoped they had enjoyed themselves. The entire cast came back for five curtain calls, the audience whooping and stamping. The final number was ragged because people were laughing and embracing. Annette was necking with one of the chorus boys (doubtless to the confusion of some of the younger members of the audience) and the Princess was wearing Diablo's long white beard.

When the curtain finally fell, there was mass hugging and self-congratulation. 'The best pantomime ever!' 'Happy Christmas!' 'I love you all.' This last from a clearly inebriated Diablo. Max slipped away. He had promised Edgar that he'd see the children backstage.

All five of them were waiting by his dressing room: Edgar, two cute red-haired children, the blonde policewoman and the sulky sergeant. Except that none of them looked sulky tonight. Everyone was beaming.

'You were brilliant,' said Edgar.

'It was the best pantomime I've ever seen,' said the policewoman, who was looking extremely pretty in a rather good grey dress.

Max crouched down to the children. 'What did you think? Don't worry, I'm not wicked in real life.'

'You were good,' said the girl judiciously. 'How did you do the disappearing trick?'

'I liked the bit when everyone got custard in their face,' said the boy.

He invited them into his dressing room and performed a few card tricks for the children. He noticed that the girl, Betty, watched him extremely closely. She was a sharp one and no mistake. Eventually he produced an egg from the boy's ear and a bunch of flowers for Betty. Then he signed some photographs and wished them all goodnight.

'Can you take Betty and Richard home?' Edgar asked the younger officers. 'I'll wait for Max.'

'Of course.' But Max thought that the policewoman, Emma, looked disappointed.

'Happy Christmas,' she said.

'Happy Christmas,' said Edgar. 'Make sure you have a good rest.'

They walked back along the seafront. It hadn't snowed for a few days but there was still enough of it on the ground for tomorrow to qualify as a white Christmas. The night was fine and cold, white waves breaking on the black beach, the stars high and bright. As they walked, the lights went off on the pier and they were left with only the feeble glow of the Christmas lanterns strung between the lampposts.

'Thanks for seeing Betty and Richard,' said Edgar. 'It really was the icing on the cake for them.'

'How are they doing?' asked Max. 'It must all still be very raw.'

'It is,' said Edgar. 'Annie died less than a month ago. This Christmas will be very hard for the parents, but children are amazing, they're so resilient. And Betty and Richard have each other. I think they'll be all right.'

'How are you doing?' asked Max, as they crossed the deserted coast road. 'I always think that you forget that all this affects you too.'

'I'm all right,' said Edgar. 'In fact I'm better than I've been for a while.'

'Are you going to see your mother on Christmas Day?'

'Yes.' He had been trying not to think about it.

'That's good.'

Edgar knew that Max thought he should see more of his mother. Having lost his at such a young age, Max tended to be sentimental about mothers. In retaliation he asked if Max was seeing his father.

'Sadly no. It'll just be me and Mrs M and a turkey.'

'And the other pros.'

'Yes, Wee Bobbie and the rest. We'll be a merry little party.'

He didn't sound depressed though, thought Edgar. If anything, he sounded suspiciously high-spirited. In fact Max's Christmas sounded jollier than his. At least Lucy,

Rupert and the boys would be at his mother's house too. That would cheer things up a bit.

When they reached Upper Rock Gardens, Max said, 'Do you want to come in for a nightcap? It's nearly midnight. We can toast Christmas.'

'Thank you,' said Edgar. 'I'd like that.'

Max climbed the steps to the front door. Edgar stayed on the pavement, looking up at the stars, trying to see Diablo's Great Dolphin. He wondered what the old boy was doing tomorrow. He would bet money on him turning up here.

'What about Mrs M?' he asked. 'Won't she be waiting up for you?'

Max turned and Edgar saw his teeth gleam in a sudden grin.

'I'll have you know that this is a respectable boarding house.'

'But you're still sleeping with the landlady.'

Max came back down the steps. 'It's a funny thing. At first I thought it was just a one night stand, then I thought it was just for the season but the other day I realised that I'd miss her when the pantomime was over.'

'That's a big admission.'

'I suppose it is really.' Edgar had his own admission, of course, but it wasn't one that he could share with Max.

'When is the pantomime over?'

'New Year. I've got a short break, then I'm off on the circuit again.'

Edgar thought of his New Year, getting back to work, clearing up the loose ends on this case, trying to get Ruby to accept his proposal. He realised that he'd got quite a lot to look forward to.

'Come on then,' said Max. 'Let's find Mrs M's brandy.'

With one last look at the stars, Edgar followed his friend up the steps, humming a song from the show.

ACKNOWLEDGEMENTS

The people and the events described in this book are entirely imaginary. However, the locations are mostly real. The Pavilion, the Old Steine, Bartholomew Square, Queen's Park, Kemp Town and Freshfield Road are all real places in Brighton. Bristol Road Juniors is fictional but it owes a lot to my old primary school, St John the Baptist, which was in Kemp Town until 1989. The grammar schools are also fictionalised but there was a Brighton Grammar School in Hove. During the First World War it was a hospital for wounded soldiers; it's now a sixth form college. There is now, sadly, only one pier in Brighton (though you can still see the wonderful skeleton of the West Pier).

There were once shows at the ends of both piers, at the Theatre Royal and at the Hippodrome. The Hippodrome, built in 1897 and described by The Theatres Trust Guide as 'the best surviving circus/variety theatre in Britain', is under threat of destruction. For details of the campaign to save it, see the Facebook page 'Save the Brighton Hippodrome'.

I'm grateful to many people for their memories of Brighton in the 1950s, including Sheila de Rosa and Marjorie Scott-Robinson. For details of gay and lesbian Brighton in the 1950s, I'm very grateful to the website 'Brighton Our Story' (www.brightonourstory.co.uk).

Special thanks to two fantastic women – my editor, Jane Wood, and my agent, Rebecca Carter. Thanks to everyone at Quercus and Janklow & Nesbit for working so hard on my behalf. Thanks, as ever, to my husband, Andrew, and our children, Alex and Juliet, for their constant support.

This book is for my dear friend Carol Dodson – so many happy memories of growing up in Brighton.

Elly Griffiths, 2015